Coastal Justus

By
Ron Martinelli

First Edition

Published by Spring Creek Publishing, LLC

Boerne, Texas

This is a work of fiction, and all characters in this book are fictional. Some of the locations described are accurate, while others are fictional. The information on forensic investigations, criminal profiling, medical pathology, and Satanism is accurate to the best of the knowledge, understanding and experience of the author.

ISBN 979-8-89814-080-9

(Paperback Book & Digital)

Printed in the United States of America by

Spring Creek Publishing, Boerne, Texas

The Wade Justus Texas Ranger Book Series

Absolute Justus

Justus for All

Border Justus

Force of Justus

Runaway Justus

Golden Justus

Coastal Justus

Table of Contents

Acknowledgements

A driving force behind the success of the Wade Justus Texas Ranger mystery series is my wife, co-conspirator, and final editor, Linda, who helps me bring Dr. Dakota Shannon's soul and spirit alive.

Dennis Dolezal, a retired San Jose (CA) PD CSI Supervisor, lifelong friend, and police colleague, inspired this book during a vacation trip to Galveston several years ago. Thanks, Dennis. I hope I did you right with this one.

Retired Homicide Lt. Bob Prevot often collaborates with me on ideas and subplots for the Wade Justus mystery series. Thanks again, Bob, for your valuable advice.

Stan Kephart, friend, professional colleague, and devout Jew, provided excellent background information on the Jewish faith and religious rituals.

Budd Karunasekara, Marketing Director for Detego Global Digital Forensics, provided technical assistance for the forensic investigation in the story.

AI Illustrator Danial N., who uses the Fiverr platform, assisted me with developing the covers for this book.

Chapter 1
The Baptist Minister

It was a beautiful, cloudless April morning in Galveston, Texas. At 8:30 a.m., traffic in the city's Midtown District was light, with churchgoers arriving for early Sunday morning masses in several historic churches.

Standing at the bottom of the grey cement steps of the red brick building with white columns, the First Southern Baptist Church on 23rd Street, Reverend Jacob Jefferson—the church's beloved and respected minister—greeted congregants dressed in royal blue robes, a broad smile lighting up his face.

This was Reverend Jefferson's twenty-fifth year of service and his tenth year as the head minister at First Southern Baptist. Jacob's journey to this respected role was a testament to perseverance—an effort by a young Black man to overcome adversity and tragedy. Raised in a predominantly Black neighborhood in Houston, Jacob's parents were hardworking, low-educated blue-collar workers. His father worked as an auto mechanic; his mother was initially a hotel maid and later a seamstress. He had one younger brother, Jamal.

The Jeffersons lived in a two-bedroom townhouse surrounded by Section-8 high-rise complexes. The area, known as "H-Town," was controlled by one of Houston's oldest and most notorious gangs—the "H-Town Boyz." The gang managed the drug trade, mainly crack cocaine and marijuana, and operated a stolen car ring, dismantling vehicles in what is called a "surgical strip" operation out of a warehouse they rented in the district.

Jacob's devout Southern Baptist mother never missed a Sunday service. Although his father wasn't as religious, she insisted the entire family attend church every week. "The Lord forgives and protects those who believe," she often said. Jacob, Jamal, and their father respected her wishes out of love and respect.

The two brothers were strikingly different. While Jacob was studious and disciplined, Jamal was bold and adventurous, often uninterested in school.

Violence saturated the neighborhood. After sundown, residents became virtual prisoners in their homes, wary of stepping outside. Seniors ensured doors and barred windows were locked. Those who were not working shopped early before gang members and addicts awoke.

Car ownership was purely functional—there were no flashy vehicles. Owners used steering locks, cleared out valuables, and sometimes left windows down and trunks unlocked to prevent break-ins or theft.

Sleep was often elusive. At night, residents endured shouts, screams, screeching tires, forced entries by gangs or police, gunfire, and sirens. Mothers in ground-floor units converted reinforced metal bathtubs into temporary cribs for their infants. Children slept on floor mattresses away from windows to avoid stray bullets. That was everyday life in H-Town.

In Jacob's fifteenth year, tragedy hit hard. In the spring, his father, John, was shot and killed during a carjacking while stopped at an intersection. That winter, as grief still weighed on the family, Jamal was killed in a drive-by shooting. Police told Ethyl Jefferson that Jamal was mistaken for a member of the H-Town Boyz by a rival gang.

Ethyl had endured enough. She moved with Jacob to her hometown of Galveston along the southern Gulf of Texas. The change was positive. Galveston was smaller, quieter, and more peaceful. Ethyl enrolled Jacob in a local high school near her parents' Midtown home. They joined the congregation at First Southern Baptist Church and attended every Sunday. Jacob also participated in Southern Baptist summer camps.

Ethyl's fierce faith and determination to ensure Jacob received a strong education made an impact. School, church, and spiritual study resonated with him deeply.

At eighteen, Jacob graduated from high school with Honors and attended junior college, earning a scholarship to a private Southern Baptist religious studies program. After graduating, he volunteered for a two-year ministry in H-Town, working with at-risk youth.

When First Southern Baptist Church announced an opening for a junior pastor, Jacob eagerly applied and was accepted. That summer, he returned to Galveston a grown and spiritual man who was making an impact. His proud mother, Ethyl, family, and friends attended his first sermon. In his eighth year as minister, he lost his mother Ethyl to cardiac failure. Reverend Jacob Jefferson remained in the historic church, ministering faithfully to a growing flock.

At 8:50 a.m., Reverend Jefferson, known for his punctuality, checked his watch. Ten minutes remaining. He waved several latecomers inside and climbed the steps behind them beneath the towering white columns. He walked down the center aisle, smiling and waving to the congregation. He passed the raised podium at the dais and entered the vestibule to don his white and gold sacramental cloth. At exactly 9:00 a.m., Reverend Jefferson stepped up to the pulpit.

He raised his hands high and, with a radiant smile, exclaimed, “All glory to God the Father and our Lord, Jesus Christ. Can I have an amen, brothers, and sisters?”

The congregation stood, many with raised arms, and responded with a resounding “Amen!”

“Let us begin,” said Jacob, making the sign of the cross, which the congregants repeated.

“Thank you, God, and Jesus, for your blessings that bring us together again this Sunday morning. We recognize that we are all sinners, but we come before you in contrition to confess and seek forgiveness—so we may one day experience salvation, and sit at your right hand, Father. Can I have an amen?”

The congregation echoed, “Amen!”

Reverend Jefferson smiled and motioned for them to be seated.

Brothers and sisters, my heart and soul are proud to see you here this Sunday. The growth of this congregation is a testament to God's power and the resonance of His Word. And now, a reading from the Good Book,” he said, looking at the open Bible before him—a passage he’d chosen to support his sermon on faith during hardship.

"I say to you, 'Then Jesus was led by the Spirit into the wilderness to be tempted by the devil," Matthew 4:1.

"And in Revelation 12:9, it is written, "The Great dragon was hurled down – that ancient serpent called the devil, or Satan, who leads the whole world astray."

So, let me ask you to consider this: When we face adversity, does God give us strength—or does He present us with opportunities to be strong? Does God provide us with patience—or does He give us chances to demonstrate it? Does God save us from hardship—or does He guide us to seek salvation?

"Our strength comes not from riches gained from dishonesty or the false gods who come before you, tempting you to sin. Our inner strength comes only from The Father, and Our Lord Jesus Christ, his son. Move to the light, not towards the darkness, my brothers and sisters. Love, and forgive those who have trespassed against you, and I say to you that you, in turn, will be loved and forgiven your own trespasses. Be led not into temptation by Satan, but to the right hand of God Our Father, and his son Jesus Christ. Can I get an amen?"

The congregants echoed an enthusiastic "Amen!"

After Reverend Jefferson's powerful sermon, he asked the congregation to stand and show love by hugging the person next to them. As they did, he blessed them, with many making the sign of the cross. He wished them a wonderful week until they gather again next Sunday.

The crowd began to exit, spirits lifted by the presence of the Holy Spirit.

From a wing at the rear of the church, a lone white man—about forty, bearded, and sinewy—stood watching. He hadn't joined the congregants and looked distinctly out of place. His face bore not a joyous expression, but one of hateful contempt.

The man fixated his gaze on the Baptist preacher as Jacob walked down the center aisle to greet his congregation again. As the church emptied, the man turned and strolled down the street, vanishing from sight.

Reverend Jefferson held another morning service from 11:00 a.m. to noon before securing the church for the afternoon. As was his Sunday ritual, he spent the afternoon walking on the beach. The church was ten blocks north of the shoreline, and the sand and surf had always given him space for quiet prayer and reflection.

Today, as was his custom, Jacob had been praying for the members of his flock who had requested devotions for various illnesses, relatives in jail or prison, an upcoming birth, a recent death, or hope for future employment. Then he walked back to the church. He would prepare for the 7:00 p.m. evening service and reopen the doors for worshippers.

At 5:30 p.m., the man watching from the wings returned to First Southern Baptist Church. This time, he carried a black backpack. He tested the front and rear doors but found them locked. Circling to the shaded north side beneath the covered drive-through, he discovered partially opened windows—left ajar to vent out the afternoon heat from the stifling interior.

The thin-framed man pushed one of the windows fully open. It provided enough space for him to slip inside. He tossed his backpack first, then climbed in after it.

The intruder approached the raised dais and stood by the pulpit. Looking upward, he saw a ten-inch square wooden support beam running horizontally across the room, with a T-post holding it to the ceiling directly above the pulpit. This will work well, he thought.

He produced a one-inch braided hemp rope from the backpack, thirty feet long, to which one end was affixed a hangman's noose. He tossed the heavy noose end over the beam and drew the other end toward a vertical column to the left of the pulpit. After measuring to ensure an eight-foot clearance, he tied it off securely.

Next, the trespasser retrieved a long black hooded robe, a pair of black leather gloves, and a three-foot length of half-inch woven nylon anchor cord. In its center were two square knots spaced four inches apart. He placed the backpack on the floor in the left wing and waited.

Reverend Jefferson returned from his peaceful beach walk. "This morning's sermons were well received," he thought. "Let's go for the trifecta and deliver it again tonight." He entered the rectory, showered, changed into a comfortable shirt and slacks, and re-entered the church through the minister's private entrance, leaving it unlocked.

Reverend Jefferson's evening protocol was routine—ready the sanctuary, prep the pulpit, and mark the opening passage in the Bible. But when he reached the dais, he paused. A rope with a hangman's noose dangled ominously over the pulpit.

Jacob stepped closer to the rope and touched it. *What in the name of all that's holy is this? Some white supremacist madness?* The alarmed minister pondered.

Consumed by the disturbing sight, Reverend Jefferson didn't notice the man cloaked in black emerging from the shadows behind him. The pointed hood hid his face, and his gloved hands gripped the braided nylon rope.

The attack was swift and vicious. The attacker quickly thrust the short-braided rope over Jacob's neck, yanking it forcefully backward and downwards. The minister lost his balance as the ligature tightened around his throat, the knots pressing against his carotid arteries and jugular veins.

Jacob instinctively reached for the rope, leaning forward and trying to pull it away. But the attacker snuck up close behind him, using his body weight as leverage to strangle his victim. The pressure cut off oxygen to Jacob's brain, and within two minutes, Reverend Jefferson collapsed unconscious to the floor.

The hooded assassin untied the nylon rope and adjusted the hangman's noose around Jacob's neck. He loosened the tension of the long rope, fitted it snugly, and then re-tightened it. Using all his strength, he began hoisting the 160-pound pastor into the air, foot by foot, until Jacob hung motionless, with his feet three feet above the pulpit.

Reverend Jefferson's legs twitched violently in a death spasm, then fell silent.

Unfazed by the gruesome scene, the killer approached the Bible and turned to a pre-selected passage from John 8:44.

"You belong to your father, the Devil, and you want to carry out your father's desires. He was a murderer from the beginning... For he is a liar, and the Father of Lies."

Leaving the Bible open to the passage, he removed his robe and gloves, packed them with the short nylon rope into the backpack, and exited through the minister's private door.

No one noticed the hooded man with his head and face hidden in the dark hoodie as he walked calmly down the alley beside the church. Rev. Jefferson's assassin crossed Kempner Street, slipped through a narrow alley beneath the shadow of the old Congregation B'nai Israel Temple, and turned left onto Moody Street.

The killer entered the Galveston County Museum grounds and sat beneath the Dignified Resignation statue. He pulled a burner phone from his backpack and checked the time: 6:04 p.m.

He pulled a small digital recorder from his pocket—its message pre-recorded.

At exactly 6:06 p.m., the killer dialled 9-1-1.

"Galveston Police Emergency 9-1-1. State your emergency," said the complaint taker, pressing a key that opened a Computer-Aided Dispatch (CAD) log.

The killer pressed "Play."

A metallic, synthesized voice said, *"I am reporting suspicious circumstances—maybe a man hanging inside the First Southern Baptist Church on 23rd Street at Sealy Avenue."*

The operator updated the CAD to a "Suspicious Death Incident" template. Her screen displayed: *"Cell phone number unavailable for reporting person."*

"What's your name, location, and the cell number you're calling from?" she asked.

The killer replayed the message. The digital voice repeated word for word, *"I am reporting suspicious circumstances—maybe a man hanging at the First Southern Baptist Church on 23rd Street at Sealy Avenue,"* and then hung up.

Frustrated, the dispatcher saved the call, activated the red "Supervisor" alert above her kiosk, and sent the screen's data to the Call-for-Service dispatcher.

The dispatcher read the "Emergency Priority 1" flashing call on her screen and activated her CAD Incident Chronology, which would timestamp every action related to the call.

Keying her headset mic, she addressed the complaint taker, "Anything more on your possible man hanging inside the church call?"

"No—definitely suspicious RP," replied the complaint taker. "Didn't sound like a real person. It was like an AI-generated digital recording. The message repeated twice, no response to any questions, and the caller disconnected. I never heard a real person speak on the line."

A seasoned dispatcher, she felt a chill down her back. Adjusting her mic, she broadcast across the emergency channel:

"6-1-Mary-2, and Midtown units near First Southern Baptist Church—23rd Street, and Sealy. RP advises suspicious circumstances, possibly in progress, a male hanging inside the church. Fire, EMS, and a field supervisor are en route. You're authorized for a Code-3 response."

"6-1-Mary-2 copies. Responding from 9th and Seawall. Code-3."

"Other units to respond?" asked the dispatcher.

"6-1-Mary-4 responding from 18th, and K," came the second unit.

"Mary-6 responding from 31st, and Church," radioed a third.

"6-Mary-10—I copied the call on my MDT. En route from 67th and Stewart," reported the field supervisor.

Two Midtown patrol units arrived alongside Galveston Fire and EMS. Officers ran up the front steps and found the tall, bright white double doors locked. They split off to check other entrances. Mary-2 discovered the Minister's private rear entry ajar and radioed his position as he entered.

The rear vestibule appeared normal. But as the officer stepped into the sanctuary, he froze at the sight of Reverend Jacob Jefferson suspended three feet above the pulpit, and eight feet off the floor.

"Jesus Christ Almighty," the shocked Catholic officer gasped, grabbing onto a gold crucifix around his neck, and instinctively making the sign of the cross. The officer rushed toward the pulpit but couldn't reach the body.

Keying his shoulder mic, the officer exclaimed, "I've got one inside hanging. I need fire, and EMS in here, now!"

The officer identified the rope's tie-off point on a nearby support column and worked to loosen it. The sound of heavy axes chopping through the front doors was audible, and suddenly, firefighters burst through the front doors, followed by the police supervisor, more officers, and paramedics.

Straining to lower the body carefully, the officer shouted, *"Help me up here!"* His fellow officers joined in, gently lowering Reverend Jefferson to the floor together.

Paramedics quickly removed the noose and checked for vital signs. There were none.

Reverend Jacob Jefferson—the deeply respected and beloved spiritual foundation of First Southern Baptist Church—was pronounced deceased at the scene.

Chapter 2
Scene of the Crime

Detective Sergeant and Homicide Supervisor Gates Sullivan was at an early evening seafood boil with friends, reaching for more Cajun shrimp when the cellphone on her hip chirped. Gates wiped her messy hands and grabbed her phone. The display read “GPD Dispatch.”

Jeezus, not now. Come on, she thought to herself as she picked up, “Gates, what’s up, Control?” she asked.

“Sorry, Sergeant, but we have a homicide working in Midtown. Sgt. Diaz told us to call you. It’s bizarre. A preacher was found hanging inside his church, the First Southern Baptist Church, on the 800 block of 23rd. The sergeant wants an ETA,” said the dispatcher. Det. Sgt. Sullivan looked at her Smart Watch.

“Tell him thirty minutes, and text me his cell. Next, get CSI rolling, and call me back with an ETA. Text me with the address. Oh, pull, and save the 9-1-1 tapes. I’ll also want the CAD printout after everyone goes 10-8 from the scene. Understood? Any questions?” the homicide supervisor asked.

“No, ma'am,” the dispatcher replied and hung up. Gates then called Sgt. Diaz at the crime scene. They had been academy classmates. The sergeant immediately picked up.

“Diaz,” he said into the phone.

“Sergio, this is Gates. How’s it hanging over there?” the homicide supervisor said with some gallows humor.

"Well, not so good right now. This one's gonna make the news all over the country for sure," he replied.

"Have you ID'd the DB (dead body) yet?" the detective asked.

"Yes, the Reverend Jacob Jefferson, one of our officers here, knew him. He's the lead pastor, apparently a very popular and respected minister. This is gonna go over badly with his congregation," said Diaz.

Okay, we're doing this by the book. Everyone will be armchair quarterbacking what we do here. First, make sure the scene is completely taped off. It's better to have a larger crime scene and reduce it than to start with a small one and need to expand later. Next, if you haven't started a log, do that now. If fire and EMS are on scene, get their names, station numbers, and contact info. Gather preliminary statements from everyone going. I want all non-essential personnel out of the immediate scene.

"Don't anyone touch anything. I don't want anyone screwing with my crime scene. Before CSI arrives, I like photos and videos of everything, and I mean everything, right away. I know that CSI will record the scene, but I want prelim photos and videos now, just like you found it.

"One last thing, the media will be all over this. Keep them well outside the crime scene, and no one talks to them, and I mean no one. Your response is "This is an ongoing investigation. We have no comments." For now, do not release our vic's information. They'll find out soon enough. I'm now about twenty minutes out. See you soon," said Gates before hanging up.

It was a Sunday night, and Gates Sullivan was on weekend call duty. That meant she would be working alone until she could get some extra detectives to the scene. While driving, she checked her call list on her cellphone and called two more homicide detectives and one robbery detective to meet her there. Now, the entire GPD Homicide Unit with CSI was on the job. *One homicide response box checked,* she thought.

Gates pulled up in front of the First Southern Baptist Church in her dark grey Dodge Challenger. The religious edifice's rich and resilient legacy dates back to 1840.

Rev. James Huckins, a Baptist missionary, established the church with nine charter members in Thomas Borden's home. Baptisms, including that of Gail Borden Jr., the pioneer of condensed milk, took place on the beach shortly afterward. The first sanctuary was a log cabin built in 1847, reflecting the humble beginnings of the congregation.

In 1855, white businessmen purchased land for Black members to form their own congregation, leading to Avenue L Baptist Church, one of Texas's oldest African American Baptist churches.

The church's second building, erected in 1883, featured seven steeples—a bold architectural choice. The church and the original log cabin were tragically destroyed in Galveston's infamous 1900 hurricane, demolished by the falling debris. A new building with thick mortar walls, a dome, a steeple, and thirty-foot-tall white columns was completed in 1905 and has served the congregation ever since.

The church had long embraced a mission of authentic community and service, describing itself as "a church for real people" with a gospel-centered vision for Galveston.

Sergeant Diaz greeted Gates. Yellow tape reading, "*POLICE CRIME SCENE—DO NOT CROSS,*" had been placed around the main church's curtilage, and everything looked in order.

"Victim's inside near the pulpit. Other than taking him down, removing the rope and noose, and paramedics checking for vital signs, the body and scene haven't been disturbed. I made sure of that. We haven't called the Coroner yet. I knew you would want to do that," the patrol sergeant reported.

"Perfect, nice job. Let's go inside so I can look," replied Gates.

Detective Sergeant Gates had never been inside the church, although she was familiar with some of its historical importance to the City of Galveston. In fact, a Texas Historical Marker bore evidence of this just outside the front of the church. The two sergeants walked to the pulpit together.

"Poor guy. What a way to go. Can't even imagine how a guy gets killed like this. Maybe you and your team will be able to fill in the blanks," offered Diaz, pointing to the prone body of the minister.

Gates approached Rev. Jacob Jefferson's body, carefully watching where she stepped, bent down, and observed the ligature marks around his neck.

"Where's the rope and noose?" she asked.

"Other side of the pulpit," pointed the patrol sergeant.

“You get photos of these marks and the rope yet?” she asked.

“Yes, as you directed,” replied Diaz.

Gates put on a pair of blue latex surgical gloves, took out her 15 megapixel iPhone, and snapped several flash photos of the ligature marks on the body. She carefully pulled down his eyelids and lips, found evidence of petechial hemorrhage, and took several more photos of the medical condition. Then she examined the body’s wrists for any signs of binding but found none.

“Give me your flashlight,” she said to the sergeant. Once she had it, she illuminated the body’s head and hair, turning the head to examine all angles for any signs of injury. Again, she found nothing amiss.

Gates lifted the body’s right arm and performed a basic range of motion. Then she flexed the fingers, and took another look at the eyelids, and jaw to determine its state of rigor. She found the muscles to still be soft and pliable, absent rigor. This confirmed that the pastor’s time of death would have been within the past two hours. At around three hours after death, a body would typically be in the early stages of rigor mortis, often referred to as the *minimal* or *onset* phase.

“When did you get the call from dispatch?” she asked the sergeant.

“Dispatch time was at 1808 hours (6:08 pm), and the call came into dispatch at exactly 1806 hours,” Diaz replied.

“Yup, that works with what I’m seeing,” the homicide supervisor said.

"What's next?" asked the patrol sergeant.

"Well, while I'm examining the scene and waiting for the forensic team to arrive, I need you to assign a couple of your men to start a neighborhood canvass. Look for potential witnesses and any CCTV cameras like Ring or Blink. Old school detective work. Knock on doors, identify the cameras, if they find any, and get permission from the owners to view the feeds.

"Based on the RP's call into 9-1-1, I'm figuring that our Rev. Jefferson met his maker around 1800 hours. If they find any feeds, I'd want to go back at least an hour before that to see if we see anything like someone lurking around. Someone who seems out of place in the neighborhood– that is, if we're lucky that someone had a video camera going," explained Gates.

"Copy that. I'll get right on it," said Diaz, who left Gates to work and went outside to muster his men.

Det. Sgt. Gates Sullivan issued instructions that only her homicide team and CSI were allowed to approach the body or the rope with the hangman's noose. *The front doors were locked, so how did the killer gain entry into the church? Where's the POE (point of entry)?* she wondered.

She went to the back of the church and found the Minister's private door marked "Private Entry—Ministers Only," with a brass sign attached to the outside. There was no sign of forced entry. She tested the latch and found that the spring latch was locked. A key was needed to open it. She reached for her portable "hand pack" radio and keyed the mic.

"I need the officer who found the POE to report to me inside the church." She received an immediate response.

"6-1-Mary-2, that was me," the primary officer radioed back.

"Mary-2, this is David-12 inside. Meet me at the rear door," Gates directed. A uniformed officer approached the open rear minister's door within a minute.

"I'm Mary-2, Officer Dick Haus, the young officer announced as he approached Gates.

"I'm Homicide Det. Sgt. Gates Sullivan. I don't believe we've met", she said, smiling, and offering her hand.

"Well, actually, we met from afar. You taught the homicide and death investigations course at the academy. I was in your class," the impressed officer replied.

"Oh yeah, a couple of years ago, right?" Gates confirmed.

"Yes, ma'am, Sergeant. You taught a great class," said the officer.

"Well, thanks, Dick. Can I call you Dick?" Gates asked to build rapport with the young man.

"Of course, Dick will do fine, Sergeant," the officer replied.

"So, tell me, Dick, what was the condition of this door when you arrived?" Gates asked.

"I was searching the exterior for a POE, and when I came around to the back here, I found this door slightly ajar, so I radioed in the POE and entered," Officer Haus replied.

"Did you ever check the door lock to find out whether the door was locked at the time or had been pried?" the homicide supervisor inquired.

Officer Haus looked slightly embarrassed. “Ah... well, no, Sergeant. It was an urgent call, so I rushed inside as soon as I found the point of entry. I never checked it,” he responded.

“I see,” said Gates, playing with the locking latch. “Do me a favor, Dick. I’m going to shut this door to see if it automatically locks shut. The locking latch is spring-loaded to lock when the door is shut. I need to confirm that. I’m trying to establish the killer’s POE through elimination. When I shut the door, you try to open it from the outside, okay?” she directed as she shut the door and heard the spring latch click.

Next, she heard the officer trying the door, which was locked solidly. She opened the door to the officer waiting outside.

“Okay, before the murder, this door was locked and opened with a key by Rev. Jefferson. I’m sure we’ll find his keys with him when we inventory his clothing. That means that, assuming the killer had no key, there is likely another POE where he gained entry. I’ll take the right side of the church, and you take the left. Look at all of the windows for a possible POE,” Gates directed. The pair then split up.

Within two minutes, Gates found three half-open windows on the north side of the church, each measuring two feet by two feet. While she was inspecting them, Officer Haus joined her.

“I got nothing, Sergeant. Nothing open anywhere,” the officer announced.

“Well, as you can see, I’ve got three half-windows here, all partially open to let the church vent out warm air. This has to be how the killer got inside the church before the minister. Go outside these windows and look for any signs of entry," said Gates.

"Makes sense, will do," replied the officer just as CSI Supervisor Det. Leonardo "Lenny" Spazzito announced his arrival, followed by two GPD Homicide Unit detectives, Bill Hurd and Blake Chabot.

The short, chubby Italian CSI supervisor approached Gates with a smile. "Caught a night case, eh? I'll bet this screwed up your Sunday. Is that the faint aroma of Cajun spice I detect? No, don't tell me, let me guess," said the food aficionado, "seafood boil," right?" he inquired.

"Would you next like to take the category, 'What do people on the Gulf like to eat in R months of the year for $200," Gates replied, to the laughter of the two detectives and young Officer Haus.

"I never miss when the topic of food is raised," the overweight CSI supervisor smiled.

"There are police canines in this department that don't have your sense of smell, Lenny. Are you and your guys ready to work?" Gates replied.

"Yes, we are good to go," replied CSI Supervisor, Detective Spazzito, as he walked over to the prone body of Rev. Jefferson. Spazzito looked down at the deceased minister, carefully examining the ligature marks on his neck without touching the body. Then he saw the braided hemp rope with the hangman's noose and remarked, "Gives new meaning to the phrase 'At the end of one's rope,'" he quipped.

"Okay, Lenny. I would appreciate a more somber and professional mood. I'm told that the minister was a highly respected cleric. Do everything within your vast forensic experience to find a clue or two to help us solve this murder," said Gates.

"Sorry, boss. Of course we will," the chubby detective replied as he pulled out a 35 mm SLR digital camera and started snapping initial unmeasured photos of the body and the immediate scene, including the braided rope.

"Make sure you package that rope carefully. I'll want DNA swabs on the whole thing. I also want you to swab that column over there where the rope was tied off for DNA, and check it for prints," directed Gates.

While Det. Spazzito was busy swabbing and printing the column, Gates knelt beside Rev. Jefferson and checked his eyelids and jaw for any signs of stiffness. Then she picked up his right hand, bent the wrist and fingers, and examined these smaller muscles, testing their range of motion and rigor. She observed that the muscles were no longer soft or flexible, which indicated that rigor had just started to set in.

Gates knew from her death investigation training that after death, the body stops producing adenosine triphosphate, or ATP, a molecule essential in cellular energy metabolism that enables muscles to relax. Without ATP, actin and myosin filaments in the muscle fibers remain locked together, leading to stiffness. This stiffness spreads to larger muscles over the next several hours.

Gates checked her pocket notebook, where she had written in the complaint taker's CAD timestamp when communications had received the call. She then checked her smartwatch; it was just before 2100 hours. She accessed her temperature app. It showed seventy-five degrees Fahrenheit.

Gates pondered silently. *You'd expect partial stiffness at the three-hour mark, especially in the face and extremities, but not full-body rigidity yet.*

The suspicious, anonymous RP called in at 18:06 hours. Body cooling at one degree per hour at seventy degrees, and we're at seventy-five degrees now. Better roll the ME (Medical Examiner) so we can get a rectal or liver temperature, but I'm thinking that the time of death was right before 1800 hours.

Gates picked up her cellphone and called dispatch. "Roll the ME, and get me an ETA," she instructed the dispatcher. There was no *need to use the radio that the local press was always monitoring, she thought.*

"Stand by one, David-12," the dispatcher replied. After ninety seconds, the dispatcher spoke into the phone, "ME is en route from his home, should be with you in another fifteen," said the dispatcher.

"David-12 copies, thanks," said Gates.

One of Det. Spazzito's CSI techs at an open window called out across the room, "Sgt. Gates, I think I have something here that you might want to look at," the tech exclaimed. Gates left the minister's body and walked straight to the tech, who illuminated the aluminum bottom window sill and wooden frame.

"See the frame and wooden sill here?" he pointed. "See where the dust is displaced on both surfaces? I think this is your POE into the church," he remarked confidently. Gates carefully examined the surfaces and then walked to the other two adjacent louvered windows to check them. Both were dusty, and neither was disturbed. She returned to the window that the tech had identified.

Yes, definitely disturbed. He's right, this is the POE, she said to herself.

"Good work, officer. I agree. Take your time processing this window, frame, and sill. See what, if anything, you can recover here," she directed.

The ME and the van to transport Rev. Jefferson's body arrived on time. Gates met the ME, Dr. David Dyer, in the foyer.

"Doc, I want to make sure we lock down the time of death here instead of at your lab. We'll drape the body, but I want you to do a rectal or thoracic body core temperature right here," said the Detective Sergeant.

"Well, a bit unusual, but sure. Take me to the body," replied the ME.

Dr. Dyer knelt beside the deceased Rev. Jefferson and performed the same procedures to establish rigor as Gates had done. Then he examined the ligature marks around the minister's neck and throat and observed evidence of petechial hemorrhaging. He looked up at the detective sergeant.

"A hanging death is what the dispatcher told me. Looks like it, but that's just preliminary. Rigor has just begun to set in, so it's looking to be around three hours, maybe a bit less for TOD (time of death), but let's be sure," he said, opening his bag and removing a scalpel and a long thermometer.

Gates saw the scalpel and the thermometer. "You gonna do a liver temp?" she asked.

"Yes, since you want an accurate internal core body temperature, this time I'm doing a hepatic (liver)," replied Dr. Dryer. He opened the minister's shirt, palpated the abdomen, and used the scalpel to make a small incision in the abdominal wall directly into the liver.

"The liver is metabolically active and has a stable thermal mass, often considered more accurate than rectal temperature for estimating postmortem interval" (PMI).

Then the ME inserted the thermometer about ten centimeters into the liver and waited. While waiting for a reading, Dr. Dyer educated Gates on body temperatures after death.

"Gates, if you recall some pathology from your death investigations training, you might remember that in a seventy-five degree Fahrenheit environment, the average internal core temperature of a dead body decreases following what we call a cooling curve or Algor Mortis. The temperature doesn't drop at a fixed rate – but here's a general estimate based on forensic practice."

"After death, the body cools at a variable rate, but the classic estimate is 1.5°F per hour during the first twelve hours after death under average indoor conditions. However, this rate is affected by many factors." The physician removed the thermometer and read the temperature aloud.

"94.1◦F. Assuming a normal living core temperature is 98.6◦F or 37◦C, that works out to a time of death around 6:00 pm. How's that for medical science?" asked Dr. Dryer, smiling.

"Thanks for the education, Doc," Gates replied.

"Death investigations and pathology are a team sport. We both learn from every experience. By the way, I'm logging my official pronouncement of death now at 9:12 pm, but the time of death for my report will be recorded as 6:00 pm. When can I have the decedent?" the ME asked.

Gates called out to Det. Spazzito, "Lenny, Dr. Dyer wants to know when he can have the body. Do you and your team have everything you need forensically?" the detective sergeant asked.

"We're good, Gates. We have what we need. You're the lead, so you say when," the CSI supervisor replied.

"He's all yours, Doc. When will you schedule the autopsy? I'll be attending," said Gates.

"Be at the lab at 10:00 am. We will begin then," replied the Medical Examiner.

Gates released Rev. Jefferson's body to the ME. An hour later, after the CSI team had 3D-scanned the scene, Gates, the CSI squad, and all of the patrol officers cleared the area once the crime scene tape was taken down. Surprisingly, no media representatives showed up. Since it was a Sunday, they were probably all short-staffed.

Southern Baptist minister, the revered Rev. Jacob Jefferson, would be recorded as Galveston's fourth homicide of the year.

Chapter 3
I've got some good news.

It was 2:15 pm, and forensic pathologist Dr. Dakota Shannon had just finished an autopsy, removed her blue latex surgical gloves and scrubs when her cell phone chirped. She went to the counter where she had left her phone and looked at the display, which read, "Bexar County Commissioners Court."

Dakota applied for the Chief Medical Examiner position after hearing through the grapevine that the current ME announced his retirement. She performed well in her oral interview and was told she was a finalist for the job.

Now that call I'd better take, she thought, and picked up.

"Dr. Shannon, this is County Commissioner Pete Hodges. I was on your Zoom oral board two weeks ago," he said in a friendly voice.

"Commissioner Hodges, yes, I remember you. How are you?" Dakota asked.

"I'm doing fine, just fine. I'm calling to let you know that you scored Number One with the selection committee. I'm authorized and pleased to inform you that the job of Chief Medical Examiner of Bexar County is yours if you're still interested," the commissioner said. Dakota's heart skipped a beat, and she smiled.

"Well, Commissioner Hodges, that's great news. Yes, of course I'm still interested. Yes, I want the job. What is the process moving forward?" Dakota asked.

Just a few formalities. We need our County Counsel to draft a contract and submit it for your approval and signature. Once the contract is fully signed, we'll get you into the county's pay and benefits system. Our current Chief ME, Dr. Albert Forrest, whom you've met, will officially retire at the end of next month, so you will officially start thirty days after the paperwork is complete. Dr. Forrest has said he'll stay on for two more weeks after you start to help you get up to speed, ensuring a smooth transition. Can I tell the County Commissioners that we have a new Chief ME?" the commissioner asked.

"Yes, by all means," replied the happy Dr. Shannon.

"Great, you have time to give your people notice and maybe enjoy a nice vacation before you start in San Antonio. Enjoy your weekend, and congratulations," replied Commissioner Hodges before hanging up.

Ever since she and Wade returned from their adventure in Italy, she had been thinking about moving to Texas to start a life with Wade. It had been over five years since Wade's beloved wife Helen was killed in the line of duty, and she sensed that Wade was finally ready to move forward. She had cared for him after his shootout with the Tres Piases gang in Gila County, New Mexico, over a year earlier, and they had grown close while staying on his ranch in the Texas Hill Country. Neither of them was getting any younger. Wade Justus was a true man's man. He still wore his wedding band in honor of Helen, so she knew Wade was also a one-woman

man. This was their chance to build a life together. All Wade had to do was say 'yes.'

Dakota finished her pathology and toxicology reports and glanced at the clock on her office wall: 5:56 p.m. Everyone else had left an hour earlier. A leader stays last. I just have one more thing to do before I leave, she thought, closing the death investigation file and grabbing her cell phone.

It had been a long day watching yearlings, two-year-olds, and hopeful champion bucking bulls bursting out of the chutes in the small arena at Wade Justus' Spring Creek Ranch just outside Boerne in the famous Texas Hill Country. Wade and his favorite ranch hand, Fernando, had herded the young bulls back to pasture with plenty of fresh Spring grass. Then both men jumped into Wade's pickup truck with a hundred-pound sack of Halpain Protein Pellets and drove out into the pasture. Wade honked the horn, and the bulls ran from all over the pasture to follow his truck, while Fernando tossed handfuls of the large pellets from the bed of the truck. Wade's loyal, red-nosed Pitbull, Desi, was in the right front passenger seat with the window rolled down, howling at the approaching herd of seventy or more bulls, cows, and calves.

Now Wade was comfortably resting in his favorite rocking chair with an iced Garrison's Whiskey in his hand, Desi lying beside him. The retired Texas Ranger and bucking bull stock contractor was gazing out at the emerald, green pasture and heritage oaks that led down to the Guadalupe River, which separated the one-hundred-acre ranch from his neighbors to the west.

This is what it's all about: hard work followed by quiet serenity. God, I love this place. It's just a shame it's only me now. This was Helen's favorite time of day, Wade mused as he sipped the smooth, ice-cold Garrisons, unconsciously twisting his gold wedding band around his ring finger with his thumb. Wade's cell phone buzzed, and he removed it from the engraved leather phone holster on his left side. He looked at the display and saw, "Dakota."

"Hey, cowboy, what are you up to?" said Dakota on the other end of the line.

"Here's a hint, it's five o'clock somewhere," Wade replied.

"Well, then I know you must be on your porch with a cold beer," said Dakota.

"Close, but no cigar, Dr. Shannon. Actually, I had bigger ambitions this afternoon. I'd like you to know that right now, I'm sipping on a glass of Garrison's and enjoying the end of a hard workday. What brings you to call on a beautiful spring late afternoon?" Wade asked.

"Well, glad you asked. Depending upon how you look at it, I've got some good news to report," said Dakota.

"Depending on how I look at it? What a strange way to announce good news. I'll bite, what kind of good news?" Wade inquired.

"Well, the ME in Bexar County, Dr. Albert Forrest, is retiring, know him?" Dakota asked.

"Al Forrest, of course, I know him. Done many a death investigation with him back in my rangering days. He's retiring, eh? So how is that good news?" asked Wade.

"Well, Ranger Justus, you're talking to the new Chief ME of Bexar County," announced Dakota.

"What the H, you're kidding me, right?" replied the stunned Wade.

"Nope, I'm serious as a heart attack. I didn't tell you this before because you never know how the selection process works, but I had heard that he was retiring, and I applied for his job. Took the oral, passed the background check, and scored first on the list. A County Commissioner who headed up the selection committee just called me to offer me the job, and I accepted," explained Dakota.

"Wow... I mean, wow! That's great news. So you're moving from Nashville to here, horses and all? Selling your little ranch?" asked Wade.

"Well, depending on how things go, I'm actually going to lease out my place. Maybe sell it later if things work out in Texas," said Dakota with a hopeful tone.

"Well, you're the best there is, Dakota. Of course, things are going to work out. My God, you'll be right here in the Hill Country. That's exciting. No more long-distance romance. So, have you thought about where you'll live?" asked Wade.

"Well, I had been mulling a couple of options if I got the job, but ..." said Dakota when her office phone rang, abruptly interrupting their conversation.

"Wade, that's my emergency line. I've got to take it. I'll call you back," said Dakota before hanging up on Wade.

Since their time in Italy, Wade had considered taking his relationship with Dakota to the next level. Still, his love for Helen had prevented him from moving forward and making an offer. Wade finished his drink and looked down at Desi, who returned the gaze.

There's still plenty of sunlight left. Time to go down to the river and have a pow wow with Helen, thought Wade as he moved off the porch and headed for the barn to saddle his horse. Desi was perplexed. This was not her master's routine, but she dutifully followed in Wade's heels.

Wade saddled up and mounted his horse. "Let's go down to the river for a bit, young lady," Wade said as he rode out of the barn with Desi happily trotting behind. She knew the word "river." The river meant deer, rabbits, and all kinds of other animals to chase, and she was eager to go.

In the spring, the Guadalupe River flowed normally, at its clear and inviting level. When Wade and Desi arrived, it moved slowly, reflecting the green cypress and oaks along its banks. Helen had wanted to be cremated, and after the funeral, Wade and his son Hunter went to the river together to scatter Helen's ashes on the water. The two men had commissioned a beautiful headstone in her honor, and Wade often visits the modest memorial to share his thoughts.

Wade dismounted, knelt to place his hand on the headstone, and leaned against it, facing the river to talk with his wife. As always, he crossed himself, closed his eyes, and said a brief prayer as Desi lay beside him.

As sometimes happened, Helen appeared on the opposite bank, waving to him. "What brings you out without your fishing rod on this lovely early spring evening? How's life?" Helen asked. Wade smiled back.

"I'm surviving, trying to move forward with my life, sweetheart, but I need to decide, and I need some direction," Wade replied softly.

"Wade Justus needing direction, well, that's a first!" laughed Helen. "So what kind of direction did you come down to our river to discuss with me, my love?" Helen asked.

"Relationship direction," replied Wade, briefly.

"Oh... that kind of advice," Helen replied in a low, empathetic tone. I suppose we're talking about your lady doctor friend, right?" Helen inquired.

Wade looked from Helen's face down into the water's reflection and lowered his voice, almost out of embarrassment. The perceptive Helen immediately noticed the change in Wade's demeanor.

"Wade, when you were laid up in that hospital in El Paso and all shot up, I thought we had already moved past the subject of you moving on with your life. Did you forget what I told you that night?" asked his wife. Wade looked up from the water and into Helen's smiling face.

"No, I heard what you said that night, but I guess I just need some validation. It's coming on five years. It was four years after you left us, and you told me to move on, so I'm trying, but it sure hasn't been easy," replied Wade.

"So what is this important decision you have to make that you are seeking my advice?" asked Helen.

"Well, it's more than just advice; I'm seeking your blessing. Dakota has accepted a job as the Chief Medical Examiner in Bexar County. She's leaving Nashville and moving here. I was thinking of following your advice and asking her to move in with me at the ranch, but I wouldn't take that bold step without talking to you first," Wade explained.

Helen smiled and said, "Well, as a woman, I think that's a wonderful opportunity for you, and personally, I think you'd be crazy not to go for it. I've watched you two since El Paso, and I think you're a good fit. You ain't gettin' any younger, cowboy, and she's a nice catch. You both complement each other, like you and me when we were a pair," said Helen.

"Helen, with my hand up to God, I promise we will always be a pair. You've never left my thoughts, and you never will," said Wade earnestly.

"That's what I've always loved about you, Wade. Loyal as a man could ever be. So, let's just cut to the chase. You've got it if you've come down here to ask for my blessing. Just remember our agreement, in the end, I'll be waiting for you on the other side. Now make that doctor lady happy. We will always have our little talks, and I'll always be your wingman when your back is against the wall. I'll love you forever. Now scoot," said Helen, blowing Wade a kiss as her reflection in the water faded away.

Desi had been gazing intently across the river as if she could see Helen, then she looked up at Wade as he wiped tears from his eyes.

"Well, I guess that's that," Wade said with a sigh of relief. "Let's head back to the house, Desi," as he got up from the headstone, bent down, kissed its top, and mounted his horse. Wade and Desi strolled back to the barn through the lush, tall green grass as the sun was setting.

Wade was in the kitchen when his cell phone rang again. It was Dakota. Wade began the conversation right away.

"Hey there, did you put out the fire?" he asked Dakota.

"Sure did. Sorry for the interruption earlier. I wanted to make sure I called you back," said Dakota.

"Well, I'm glad you did. Listen, the sudden surprise of your good news kind of threw me off. I've been thinking that the best place for you to stay is here at the ranch. Our time together in Italy was incredible, and I've been meaning to ask if you'd like to take our relationship to the next level for some time. But I know you're a big deal in Nashville, and I didn't want to mess up your career. I'm a bit shy about stuff like that. The ranch is perfect for your horses, and it'd be fun to watch you practice for your military cavalry competition. So, what do you think about moving in?" asked Wade.

Dakota was quietly overjoyed. She would never have imposed and asked Wade if she could move in with him. *That's something a man should ask a woman,* she thought.

"Well, since you put it that way, how could I refuse? Yes, Wade, I'd love to move in with you and Desi. So here's the plan: I have thirty days to move out to Boerne and get my affairs in order. All of my furniture is in my place in Nashville. I'm packing my clothes, personal effects, and tack for my two horses and the beasts. It will all fit in the truck and my large horse trailer. It will take me about three days to drive out to Boerne, and then we'll have over three weeks together for me to move in before I start the new job," Dakota explained.

"That's a great plan, three whole weeks together before you begin work is a real bonus. I can hardly wait," said Wade happily.

"Wade, I'm so happy about coming to Boerne and being with you. Your ranch is a piece of Heaven. I gotta run, get out to a death scene, but I wanted to call you back first. Talk soon," said Dakota.

"You bet. I'll start to get things ready for your arrival. Talk soon," replied Wade before hanging up.

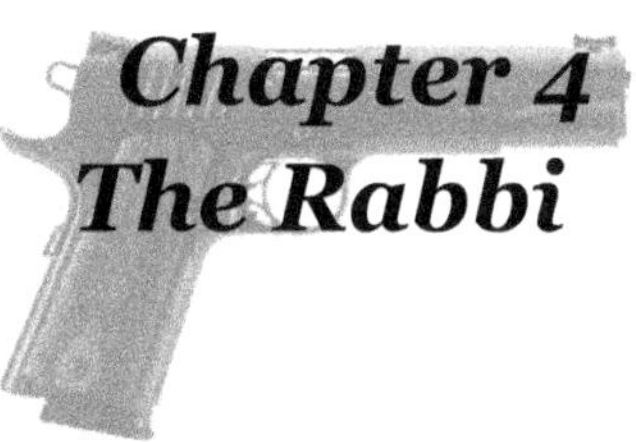

Chapter 4 The Rabbi

It had been a long and exhausting week meeting with members of the Congregation B'nai Israel. Now, Rabbi David Abramson, an Orthodox Jew, was getting his house in order for Shabbat on Friday morning.

It was late in the afternoon, and as was his ritual, David went to the credenza in his modest dining room, removed the tablecloth and two candles, then went to the cupboard where he took out a bottle of wine and a single set of his wife Hila's best dishes. On the kitchen's center island was a loaf of challah, the Jewish braided bread.

The Rabbi checked his watch for the official time of sunset. He would light the candles exactly eighteen minutes before sunset. Before his wife's tragic death at the hands of a Hamas terrorist suicide bomber who blew himself up inside a Jewish synagogue in Jerusalem, twenty years before, while the couple was living in Israel, Hila, the Rebbetzin, would have been the one to light the candles. The solemn widower now took his wife's place in conducting the ritual.

David covered his eyes, extending his hands toward the candle flame and then back to his eyes in a waving motion. He internalized the energy and spirit while reciting the Hebrew blessing transliteration, "Blessed are you, Adonai our God, King of the Universe, who commands us to kindle the light of Shabbat."

The rabbi then sang the Shalom Aleichem and Eshet Chayil before the Kiddush, or the blessing over the wine, and recited Lekha Dodi, a poem welcoming the Sabbath. During the Kiddush, the man lifts a cup of wine or grape juice while the couple says the blessing, *"Praised be Thou, oh Lord Our God, King of the Universe who created the fruit of the wine."*

How I miss my lovely Hila. We were so good together, like one voice reciting the Kiddush, David thought sadly as he completed the blessing while holding up the goblet of wine.

Before blessing the challah, David manipulated a two-handed pitcher filled with water and alternated his hands, pouring water over one hand and then the other while reciting the Hebrew prayer, *"Praised be Thou oh Lord Our God, King of the Universe, who has sanctified us by His commandments, and commanded us to wash our hands."*

David next uncovered the braided bread and recited the Hebrew prayer, *"Blessed are you, oh Lord Our God, Ruler of the Universe who brings forth the bread from the earth."*

Finally, Rabbi David Abramson concluded the religious ritual with the Birkat Hamazon, or "benching," thanking God for the food at the end of the Shabbat meal.

The sun had set, and during the twilight, David walked away from the modest, tan-colored Beit HaRav, or House of the Rabbi, heading west on Sealy Avenue. He then turned right and arrived at his Temple, the Old Congregational B'nai Israel, located at the northwest corner of 22nd Street and Sealy Avenue. It was a quiet evening with no passing cars or pedestrians.

The Old Congregational B'nai Israel Temple was a historic building in Galveston's Midtown District. Jewish worship in Galveston began informally in the early 1850s, often in private homes like that of Dr. Isadore Dyer. In 1852, the community established Texas's first Jewish cemetery. After the Civil War, in 1868, the congregation was officially organized by German-Jewish immigrants, making it Texas's oldest Reform congregation and the second Jewish congregation overall. Having an orthodox Jew as its Rabbi was unusual, but David was well respected for his tireless work in the Jewish community.

Generous local philanthropy helped fund the synagogue after it overcame a yellow fever epidemic. In March 1870, the Texas Masonic Grand and Master laid the synagogue's cornerstone; Rabbi Jacobs led the officiation from New Orleans. The original Norman-Gothic structure opened in 1870, designed by Galveston architect Fred Stewart.

By 1890, a larger Gothic Revival building, designed by renowned architect Nicholas J. Clayton, replaced the original Temple. This beautiful white structure has remained intact to the present day. From Gothic to Modern, the building reflected the evolving Jewish-American identity in Galveston. The Temple was conveniently located to the east, just across 22nd Street from Reverend Jacob Jefferson's First Southern Baptist Church.

Rabbi Abramson used his key to unlock one of the two modest front doors of the Temple and turned on the interior lights. He only planned a quick visit to pick up his Tanakh, which he had mistakenly left in his office at the back of the Temple.

Since the tragic yet unsolved murder of his dear friend and fellow cleric, Jacob Jefferson, David had made it a point to be especially vigilant. After turning on the lights, he immediately checked to ensure the door was locked and secured behind him. As he walked towards the back of the Temple, he scanned the interior for situational awareness. Satisfied he was alone, he quickly walked to his modest office, entered the dark room, and switched on a small wall sconce light.

David saw his Tanakh open on his desk and walked over to pick it up. *That's funny, I don't recall leaving my Tanakh open,* he mused. Suddenly, he was forcefully grabbed from behind as he reached over the desk. A strong leather-gloved hand covered his nose and mouth, pressing a rag firmly against them. At the same time, David's legs were kicked out from under him.

The Rabbi collapsed to his knees. Defensively, he immediately tried to raise his hands to pull the rag away from his mouth and nose, but he found himself in a bear hug, preventing his left hand and arm from moving. David's right hand desperately tore at his attacker's right hand, which pressed the rag even more violently against his nose and mouth. The hapless Rabbi briefly detected the sick scent of decaying fruit from the chloroform before passing out.

Rabbi David Abramson slowly awoke from unconsciousness to find himself lashed to his office chair, his chest and hands tightly bound with black duct tape, his feet secured with some ligature he couldn't see. The slight-statured man struggled to move, but the heavy oak chair refused to budge. He looked around the dimly lit room and saw no one. *Who would do such a thing?!* He thought frantically.

David cried out, *"If you want money, there is some in my wallet, and you are welcome. Just take it and leave. I won't call the police."* There was no response, only a deathly silence.

A moment later, the Rabbi heard a hissing sound. He began searching the room for its source. Looking at the bottom of his office door, he spotted four inches of what looked like one-half-inch diameter opaque flexible tubing. The hissing noise was coming from the end of that tubing. He soon detected a faint industrial or musty smell. *What is that odor?* he wondered. *It was some gas, but not propane... What is that smell?!* he thought to himself.

After a few minutes, David could parse out what the gas odor smelled most like; its scent was more like bitter almonds. He began to choke, gag, and finally, in panic, scream.

"Help! Is anyone out there? Help me, please!" the Rabbi screamed at the top of his lungs, but his pleas only hastened his inhalation of the toxic gas, which was rapidly filling his lungs. David felt an intense burning sensation in his nose, throat, and lungs. His voice was hoarse from yelling, but also from the gas, and he felt his chest tightening. The Rabbi was in the throes of respiratory distress as his lungs filled with fluid from pulmonary edema, the effects of bronchospasm significantly narrowing his breathing passages.

David was now experiencing agonal breathing, his mouth opening wide and shutting repeatedly, gasping for air like a fish out of water. His respirations grew fewer and shallower. The Rabbi was slowly spiraling into death as the room filled with Zyklon B gas, a cyanide-based pesticide infamously used by Nazi Germany in gas chambers during the Holocaust.

David's eyes involuntarily rolled back into his head, then... empty blackness.

Orthodox Jew Rabbi David Abramson sat motionless, restrained in his office chair, murdered on the Shabbat by an assassin he had never seen or met.

Rabbi Abramson's killer, dressed in a long black robe with a prominent pointed hood, waited calmly outside the door, glancing at his watch now and then. The hissing from the Zyklon B gas stopped as the canister emptied, and twenty minutes had elapsed. The killer never opened the office door to check on his victim. He knew precisely what the lethal gas would do to a person in an enclosed space. After all, six million dead Jews can't be wrong, he remarked with a smile.

The killer removed the canister and tubing from under the office door but left the towel he used to seal it in place. He then put the gas canister, tubing, and black duct tape into his black backpack. Then, he removed his black hooded robe, carefully folded it, and placed it in the pack. Now, he was only wearing a dark hoodie and jeans.

The killer pulled the hood over his head and exited through a rear window that he had pried open on the east side of the Temple. He slipped down a narrow walkway between the Temple and the neighboring Therapeutic Healthworks store. The assassin, carrying a backpack, jumped over a chain-link fence onto Sealy Street, quickly vanishing into the darkness.

Chapter 5
What, again? You're kidding me!

It was 10:12 a.m. on Monday, and Detective Sergeant Gates Sullivan was on her third cup of coffee while she and Detective Lenny Spazzito and his CSI team reviewed the evidence from the Rev. Jacob Jefferson homicide in the CID conference room. Detective Spazzito, the CSI supervisor, was summarizing the evidence and its processing.

"Microscopic and DNA swab analysis of the braided hemp rope found nothing. Same with the POE window, and we have determined the point of exit, the minister's private door into the church. Outside of the POE window was cement, so no shoe prints. In short, we found Butkus, the big donut," said the detective, holding up his right thumb and forefinger, making a zero.

"Thanks for another food reference, Lenny. You really need to seek help," replied Gates sarcastically before continuing.

"So in short, we've got a popular black minister with no enemies or complainants in his congregation who is violently murdered," replied Gates, who turned to her partner, Det. Bill Hurd.

"Bill, you've had a week to do a thorough background check on the Rev. Jefferson. Please tell me you found something... anything that advances this case toward a suspect or a person of interest," the homicide sergeant begged.

"Sorry to disappoint, Gates. Lenny, his people, and I did a search warrant on Jefferson's apartment at the church, including all digital devices. Lenny's people conducted a complete digital forensic sweep of his cell phone, iPad, and PC using our new Detego Global software. We scoured his emails and text messages and checked his browser to see his interests. We tracked his cell phone and obtained GPS positions for his movements going back seventy-two hours before the time of death. We also searched his vehicle. Like Lenny said, nothing unusual whatsoever. Just standard padre types of stuff.

This guy was, for all intents and purposes, a monk. No girlfriends, no secret affairs with women inside or outside his congregation, and no lewd or lascivious behavior. He was apparently, truly a man of the cloth. Hell, I found myself admiring the guy," explained Hurd with a smile.

Gates turned back to Lenny. "How's the neighborhood canvas going for wits, and CCTV video footage?"

"My people are still working on it. Springtime weekend with lots of people taking off for their weekend R&R. We left cards everywhere the uniforms identified as having CCTV surveillance cameras. Nothing so far, but we'll let you know the minute anything pops up," replied the CSI supervisor.

Gates' coffee was bitter, and her stomach was growling. She set her coffee down on the table, reached into her bag, took a couple of Tums, and addressed the small group of investigators.

"The Chief is feeling pressure from the black community and the local press. The last thing I want to do is tell him that there are some KKK members here who lynched a black

Baptist minister. Surprisingly, this murder isn't getting much attention from our woke legacy media across the country. But that could change at any moment. We need to get to the bottom of this. I don't want to be the one walking into the Chief's office to say we have a white supremacist problem in Galveston."

Gates' cell phone on the conference table started vibrating, its display flashing. She picked it up, saw "9-1-1 Emergency Communications," and answered.

"Homicide, Sergeant Gates," she said into the phone.

"Sergeant Gates, 5-Mary-10 in Midtown District is reporting a homicide at the Old Congregation B'nai Israel, 800 block of 22nd Street at Sealy," the Communications supervisor advised.

What again? Are you kidding me?! Gates' mind silently screamed out.

"Copy control. Can you tell me if this is a fresh or a cold homicide? Also, do you know how many down?" she asked the supervisor.

From what Mary-10 told me, it's probably cold. They didn't call for EMS or fire. From what I gathered, one male down, Mary-10 said it's the Temple's Rabbi," replied the dispatch supervisor. Gates' heart sank, and she immediately felt sick to her stomach, but she kept her poker face for the sake of the men in front of her listening and watching her reaction.

Got it, control. Text me with 5-Mary-10's cell number. Nothing over the radio, got it. Use cell phones from here on out. Put that order out over the MDTs for all units at the scene. No way I want the press hearing this, and inundating the scene," the homicide sergeant directed.

"10-4, copy, Sergeant. I'm texting you with Mary-10's cell now," the supervisor advised.

"Control, tell Mary-10 that homicide and CSI are all rolling to the scene from HQ. ETA within fifteen," said Gates, hanging up and looking at the curious group of investigators.

"People, we've got another clergy homicide in Midtown. This one's a Rabbi at the Old Congregation B'nai Israel over on 22nd at Sealy," Gates announced. The assembled detectives groaned.

"This is getting to be some serious shit, Gates," remarked Lenny.

"Come on, fellas, we're burning daylight. Saddle up. Hurt, and I will meet you there," said Gates as she grabbed her bag and headed out the door with Det. Hurd.

On the way to the scene, Gates called the number that the Communication supervisor had texted her. She recognized it immediately and dialed. The phone rang once, and Mary-10 answered.

"Sgt. Diaz," replied the Hispanic-accented voice.

"Buenos Diaz, Sergio, we have to stop meeting like this. People are going to ask questions," said Gates.

"Morning, Gates, but it's not good for one poor soul. We got another crazy killing down here, and this time it's another cleric; an orthodox Jew Rabbi named David Abramson," replied the patrol sergeant, somberly.

"What's the scene look like down there?" asked Gates while Det. Hurd listened to the speaker.

"Too hard to explain. Just get down here ASAP, and see for yourself," replied Diaz in a low voice.

Fair enough. You know the drill—same crime scene protocols as before. Lock everything down. No one touches the body or anything until we arrive. CSI is rolling with us. Take photos and videos before we get there. Tape off the entire temple. Keep a detailed crime scene log," directed Gates.

"Check, most of it is already done. We're just waiting for you. See you soon," said the patrol sergeant before hanging up.

Detectives Gates and Hurd arrived in Gates' unmarked car, pulling up in front of the Temple where Patrol Sergeant Diaz was waiting. The three shook hands.

Gates popped the trunk of the unmarked, and the detectives retrieved their crime scene bags. Both donned fresh latex surgical gloves from a box in Gates' bag.

"Okay, Sergio, take us to him," Gates directed. Diaz entered through the front right door with the two homicide detectives trailing behind. Diaz pointed to the far end of the Temple, "He's in a rear office. No one has touched anything. I photographed and videoed everything in the office, including the body. I was careful where I stepped," the sergeant said, moving forward.

"Good, give your device to CSI Supervisor Spazzito so he can download everything," said Gates as they arrived at the front door of the Rabbi's office and peered inside.

The RP is the Temple's clerk. She came in to open the Temple, preparing for the Rabbi. She thought it strange that he wasn't already here, and the front doors were still locked on a Monday at 9:30 am. She returned to the office and found him like this. We have her in one of our air-conditioned units with a female officer. She's pretty shaken up—who wouldn't be," Diaz explained.

Gates checked her watch; it was 10:45 am. She looked at Bill Hurd. "Bill, go out to the unit and get a recorded statement from the clerk. Nothing lengthy right now, just the basics with her contact information for your support. I'll be in here. Come back when you're done," said Gates.

"Sure, Gates. Sergeant Diaz, can you direct me to the unit where the RP is?" he asked. Diaz and Hurd left Gates to survey the immediate crime scene and body.

Before entering the office, Gates examined the door. The door and its lock appeared intact, with no signs of forced entry. She used her department-issued Smartphone to photograph both sides of the door, the door frame, and the locking mechanism. A white cloth towel was lying next to the door.

Strange place for a towel to be. I'll ask the clerk what the positions of the office door and towel were before she entered the office, and found the Rabbi, she thought as she photographed the towel.

Gates stood in the doorway, carefully scanning the inside of the small office. Aside from Rabbi Abramson being tied with black duct tape and half-inch zip-ties around his chest, wrists, and ankles to his office chair in the middle of the room, nothing else seemed out of place. Then she looked below his waist and noticed that his pants zipper was completely undone.

Whoa, what's that all about? she mused. Gates began photographing the body and the chair, then moved around the room in quadrants before videotaping everything from her position. CSI would be doing a much more thorough job. These were comparison photos and videos.

Before Gates formally entered the room, she carefully examined the floor for any evidence on its surface. Finding nothing, she entered and walked straight to the body. She observed that the victim's head was down, resting on his upper chest. She bent down to examine his face and noticed a dried bloody froth around his mouth and nostrils.

Gates used her pen to lift the collar of his shirt and found no signs of ligature marks. There was no petechial hemorrhaging in the eyes, eyelids, or lips. She checked the victim's head for signs of injury and scanned the entire body for blood or blood spatter but found nothing.

No signs of hanging, strangulation, or asphyxiation like with the minister. He also wasn't bludgeoned. It's strange that the killer used a combination of duct tape and zip ties to secure the Rabbi to the chair. Maybe we can get some prints off the duct tape, she thought to herself as she made notes and photographed the victim's face, neck, and head.

Gates carefully lifted the Rabbi's head from his chest and examined it to assess the body's state of rigor mortis. The body wasn't stiff, which indicated that it was in what is called "secondary flaccidity," where the body loses its stiffness and becomes soft again. Decomposition becomes more noticeable as enzymes and bacteria start breaking down the muscle proteins.

Gates understood that secondary flaccidity starts roughly thirty-six hours after death. Factors such as temperature, humidity, muscle mass, and cause of death can alter this timeline. Warmer settings accelerate the process, while cooler environments slow it down.

Gates looked at her watch at 10:55 am and started scanning the office walls for a thermostat. She found one on the wall next to the office door and checked the temperature, which was seventy-five degrees. She reached into her bag and took out her digital thermometer. She turned it on and waited for a reading, which also showed seventy-five degrees. Gates photographed both thermometers and made a voice-recorded note.

The ME will determine TOD (time of death), she mused and called Communications to notify the ME to respond to the scene just as Det. Hurd arrived at the doorway.

"What's the clerk RP have to say?" Gates asked her partner.

Our clerk's name is Hannah Cohen. She has been Rabbi Abramson's clerk for the past nine years. She spoke highly of her boss. Clearly, she's very upset about discovering him murdered, especially in this manner, so I kept it brief. We can always reinterview in a few days if necessary.

Hurd reported, "Hannah told me that, to her knowledge, the Rabbi had no enemies or recent confrontations with anyone. No money is kept in the office. Members of the Temple donate electronically or by check. The Rabbi changed the donations policy after the Temple was burglarized two years ago. There is not even a safe in the office. She handles the bookkeeping and told me there have been no unusual transactions. She has no idea why anyone would want to kill Rabbi Abramson, whom she describes as very respected in the Jewish community."

"Anything else?" Gates asked.

Yeah, now that you mention it, Hannah said that when she opened the office door, she was greeted by an unusual, musty smell. She didn't mention anything to the uniforms because she thought the odor might be related to the body. That's about it," replied Hurd.

Thanks, Bill. While I'm surveying in here, can you scope out the Temple for possible points of entry or exit? I've called for the ME, but don't have an ETA yet. Can you also ask Sgt. Diaz to have his officers do a neighborhood canvas for any CCTV? You know the drill," said Gates.

"Sure thing, I'll start right away," replied Hurd.

Medical Examiner Dr. David Dyer arrived thirty minutes later and was taken to the back office by Sgt. Diaz. The pathologist stood in the doorway, observing the body of Rabbi David Abramson secured to his office chair.

"Sweet Jesus, Mary, and Joseph. Not another one," muttered the Christian physician, crossing himself.

"Afraid so, doc. I'm gonna need some help with this one. Meet the former Rabbi David Abramson. I have no idea how he was murdered. So far, I haven't been able to find any clear signs of traumatic injury, just this dried, frothy blood coming from his nostrils and mouth," said Gates, pointing to the Rabbi's face.

"I also need your expertise in establishing a TOD. He appears to be in secondary flaccidity, so he has been deceased for at least thirty-six hours according to my training. Our RP, the Temple's clerk, found him at 9:30 am and called it in," explained the homicide detective.

"I see," replied the ME, putting on a pair of latex surgical gloves, entering the office, and approaching the body. "Have you taken the ambient temperature yet?" he asked.

"Yes, from both the thermostat on the wall, and independently with my digital thermometer. Both read seventy-five degrees," replied Gates.

Dr. Dyer looked at his watch, "11:40 am. Let's take a look," he said, lifting the Rabbi's head, and moving it up, down, and side to side to gauge a sense of rigor.

"Correct, detective. He's definitely in secondary flaccidity, so at least thirty-six hours deceased. When you're ready to remove him from the chair, I'd recommend checking his internal body core temperature," said the ME.

CSI Supervisor, Det. Lenny Spazzito, and his crew arrived in their crime scene van. Lenny appeared at the office doorway, saw the deceased Rabbi restrained in the chair, and exclaimed, "What the hell happened to him?" Gates looked over at the experienced, portly supervisor.

"That's exactly what we're trying to figure out. Obviously, he's been murdered. We just haven't figured out how yet. Lenny, I want you to personally supervise the evidence collection of the body, this chair, and the office. Don't leave a stone unturned. I want everything swept for prints and DNA.

Two clerics in two weeks, one block apart. What are the odds?" Gates asked.

"I don't like the look of this. A black guy lynched, and a Jew? The press is going to have a field day with this. Texas, the South, white supremacy..." Lenny's voice trailed off.

"What we might be looking at is the beginning of a serial killer targeting clerics. I don't know how the Rabbi was murdered, and maybe Doc Dyer here can tell us, but I already know what the Chief will say when I brief him this afternoon. There's got to be a pattern; an MO, and our team needs to figure it out before any more clerics are killed," said Gates.

"You got it, boss, and my people and I are on it. By the way, what's with his zipper; it's down," asked Lenny as he ushered in his CSI team. The detective walked over to the body and carefully examined the restraints without touching anything. Then he began directing the team's tasks.

"Yeah, I saw the zipper too. Have no idea why it's down, but when the body arrives at the MEs, I want one of your guys to be there with a black light and some DNA swabs for his pants, underwear, groin, and penis. The whole zipper being down is weird," said Gates. Lenny gathered his techs together for a brief.

"I want you guys to take photos and videos of everything before you even touch the body. This looks like waterproof duct tape, kind of like Gorilla Tape, securing his wrists. I want some close-up shots of the end of the tape; was it cut or pulled and torn by hand? Print and swab the chair and the duct tape. We might find some prints adhering to the adhesive side. Better yet, let's take the whole damn chair with us, but cover it first. After that, you can take your time with the office.

When you finish with the office, I want you guys to scour this temple inside, and out, and from top to bottom," the CSI supervisor ordered.

Dr. Dyer spoke up. "Detectives, if I may, the sooner we get the victim to my lab, the sooner I can start the pathology and toxicology tests," the ME said. Then he pointed to the decedent's face.

"This dried, frothy blood coming out of his nostrils and mouth is an indication that he was poisoned, but by what, I don't know yet. May I request that your CSI team process the body and the chair, and then release the body to me so we can begin the investigation?" Dr. Dryer asked.

"Sure thing, doc. Lenny, let's get your people working here first, then we can release the Rabbi to Doc Dryer and his team," said Gates.

"Sure thing, Gates. Give us thirty minutes, and we should be done with the body. Like I said, the chair's coming back to the office with us for complete processing," replied the CSI supervisor.

Gates turned to Dr. Dyer, "Doc, I want to make sure that we process the body and clothing for seminal or other fluids. One of Det. Spazzito's techs will meet you at your lab for that," said Gates.

"Sure thing, detective," replied the ME.

Det. Hurd appeared in the office doorway. "Gates, I found the POEs. Back of the Temple, a window next to an air conditioner was jimmied," he said.

"Good work. Show it to me," replied Gates as the two walked off together to examine the point of entry.

Bill Hurd pointed out the visible pry marks on the sill of a window next to an air conditioning unit at the back of the Temple. The two detectives stepped outside to examine what they now recognized as the POE. Gates looked down the narrow concrete walkway separating the Temple from the neighboring Therapeutic Healthworks business. She motioned toward the cyclone fence gate that opens directly onto the public sidewalk and Sealy Avenue.

"Well, there you go. In and out through the back window. This guy is a window entry guy," remarked Gates.

"No doubt. I'll tell Lenny's guys to ensure we process the window and take detailed photos of the pry marks. If we're lucky later, maybe we can match it with a pry tool," said Hurd.

Detectives Gates and Hurd remained at the crime scene for another hour before returning to the station.

The respected orthodox Jewish Rabbi David Abramson would be recorded as Galveston's fifth homicide of the year.

Chapter 6
Let's go to the coast!

Dr. Dakota Shannon loaded her Ford F-350 pickup with her belongings, towing her Sundowner Gooseneck horse trailer with her two prized military cavalry competition horses and all their tack. She crossed the Cumberland River on the Korean War Veterans Bridge, heading west on I-40, bidding Nashville a fond farewell. She turned on the radio, and a country western music station played George Strait's "Run." An appropriate song to start her journey, she mused.

Dakota spent most of her career at the Davidson County Medical Examiner's Office, advancing from ME Assistant to Assistant ME, and ultimately to Chief Medical Examiner. During that time, she personally performed hundreds of autopsies and built a reputation as an excellent pathologist and forensic medicolegal death investigator.

Dakota was a popular visiting instructor at national law enforcement conferences, teaching death investigations. Although she had made many friends along the way, her life felt unfulfilled when it came to love – until she met retired Texas Ranger Wade Justus. Wade captured her heart, and everything changed because of it.

This was a significant step for the brilliant, independent forensic pathologist. Her first encounter during the Sleeping Beauty serial murders investigation in Nashville had quietly drawn her to the handsome widower. Wade's wife of many years, Helen, who was also a law enforcement officer, had been brutally shot in an officer-involved shooting in New

Braunfels, TX, not far from their sprawling ranch in the famous Texas Hill Country. After nearly five years, Wade still wore his wedding band, a visible symbol of his devotion.

Moving in with Wade was a significant leap of faith for both of them. A lot depended on this decision, and it was elevating their relationship to a new level. They were both mature adults, not impulsive young kids. She cared deeply for Wade and believed he loved her too. She was confident they would handle this new chapter together as a team, each bringing their own strengths. Wade had told her that Texas would grow on her, and she hoped he was right.

It took Dakota three relaxed days to cover the 1,010 miles from Nashville to Boerne, traveling along I-40 to Little Rock, Arkansas. From Little Rock, she switched to I-30 until it connected with I-35 in Dallas–Fort Worth. Then, it was a direct route south to San Antonio, where she joined I-10, leading her straight to Boerne. Those three days gave Dakota time to unwind, relax, enjoy the scenery, and dream about a life with Wade.

Dakota arrived in Boerne in the late afternoon of her third day of travel. She pulled off the I-10 onto S. Main Street and soon found herself on the small town's famous Hill Country Mile. Dakota crossed over Cibolo Creek with its shady pedestrian walkway, looked north up S. Main with its classic Old Texas stone buildings, smiled, and remarked to herself, *This is my kinda place.* She called Wade from town.

"Hey, cowboy. Just giving you a heads up. I'm fifteen minutes out," she said.

"Desi, and I will be waiting for you. You know the way," Wade replied.

Dakota drove slowly up S. Main, turned right onto Blanco Road, and connected with the 474. After thirteen miles of beautiful scenery, she turned onto Lonesome Dove Road and soon reached the familiar gate with a sign that read, "Spring Creek Ranch." *Here's my new Home Sweet Home,* she mused happily. Having spent time at Wade's ranch during his recovery, she had memorized the gate code and buzzed herself in.

Dakota pulled past Wade's house, up in front of the barn, as Desi chased her, barking, and Wade was not far behind.

She stepped out of her truck and was greeted by Wade, who gave her a warm hug and kiss. "Glad you made it here safely. Let's get your horses into the barn; that's a long ride for them," he said.

Wade and Dakota led her horses out of the trailer and into the barn, where Wade had prepared two stalls with fresh hay for them to rest on. Then they walked back to the house together, hand in hand, with Desi walking alongside them.

The couple walked into the kitchen, and Wade asked, "Well, what will it be? Cold iced tea or something a bit stronger?"

"I'm thinking a nice cold beer would be good," said Dakota. Wade smiled, "Coming right up," reaching into the refrigerator and grabbing two beers. "Bottles or a glass?" he asked.

"The bottle will do just fine," replied Dakota, accepting the iced cold beer.

"Here's to us," said Wade, clinking his beer against Dakota's and leaning in to kiss her again. "Let's head out onto the porch. It's been such a beautiful day. You've had a long drive, and I thought we could relax before I make dinner. I'm going to grill some steaks with veggies if that's okay with you," he offered.

"Well, you sure know how to make a girl feel welcome," replied Dakota, smiling. Then she noticed that Wade was not wearing his wedding band, and her heart skipped a beat. *She thought happily that's a big change for this man, a sign of new commitment.*

Wade and Dakota spent the next couple of hours before dinner catching up. Wade was talking about the ranch and his bucking bulls. Dakota told him about her new job, and Wade told her about San Antonio, Bexar County.

"If you like, I can meet you downtown for lunch and show you around. I'll show you where San Antonio PD, and the Sheriff's Office are, along with the courthouses, a couple of good restaurants, places like that," he said.

"Yes, that would be wonderful, I'm going to be like a fish out of water for a while until I get settled," replied Dakota.

"Nothing to it. Downtown SA is not as big as Nashville. You'll get the hang of it soon enough, and it's pretty much a straight shot down I-10 to SA, and downtown," said Wade.

Wade cooked a wonderful dinner and changed the discussion to the Texas Gulf Coast. "Do you know anything about our Gulf Coast?" he asked.

"Actually, no, but I've heard some things about it. What's it like?" Dakota asked.

"Spring is a great time to visit the Gulf, especially during an 'R' month. We have some fantastic seafood down there; it's only about three hours south of here. We enjoy our blue crabs, delicious shrimp, and, of course, Gulf oysters. I love the coast this time of year—not too hot or humid, and far from the crazy summer tourist crowds. You can drive along miles of wide, sandy beaches. Desi loves going to the coast. I let her run free, and she never wants to leave.

"While you were on your way here, I had an idea. You've got almost four weeks before you start your new job. Why don't I show you the coast? My neighbors, the Dillons, have a camper. After we get you unpacked and settled in, I can ask to borrow the Dillons' camper, and you, me, and Desi could take off together to spend a week or so visiting the coast, sampling the beaches, and trying the seafood. I know a great camper park on the beach in Galveston, where we could stay for a few days. What do you think?" asked Wade.

Dakota was definitely interested in a romantic adventure with Wade. *An RV trip would be a great chance for the couple to spend time together, visit new places, enjoy seafood, and she loved the beach,* she thought.

"Wade, that's a great idea. Count me in!" she replied.

"Great, I'll call the Dillons tonight. Let's give you a couple of days to unpack and settle in, and then we can take off. Fernando can check on the ranch while we're gone. We'll get your horses used to the pasture, teach them to find their way back to the barn, and eat. Fernando will make sure they're bedded down each night. This will be a lot of fun," said Wade, beaming.

Three days after Dakota arrived, she packed up the RV and went on an adventure with Wade and Desi to the Texas Gulf Coast.

Chapter 7
A Person of Interest

It was 2:00 pm, and Detective Sergeant Gates Sullivan was alone in her office, deep in thought as she reviewed evidence in the murders of the Southern Baptist Minister and the Jewish Rabbi, when her phone rang. It was the CID secretary.

"Sergeant, I have an anonymous caller transferred from Communications. They say they have information about a possible person of interest in your cleric's murders. He says he'll only speak with the lead detective. Can I patch him through?" the secretary asked.

Gates and the Homicide Unit had been under significant pressure from the minority community and the news media. The authorities wanted the killer or killers caught. As she had predicted, the news media were following the murders closely. An abrasive local news reporter named Johnny Costa from Galveston's KWAV-TV 4, who was working overtime to make a name for himself, was openly speculating in a divisive narrative that "Southern White Supremacy had sprung new life in Galveston."

Two city council members who had read the stories had stuck their fingers in the air to see which way the political winds were blowing and told reporters, with similar unsubstantiated speculation, "These killings are a black mark on the fine City of Galveston." After that comment, the Chief called her and Lenny Spazzito into his office, shut the door, and said he wanted all hands on deck for this investigation.

"Sally, put him on," Gates said as she attached her digital recording device to her office phone.

"Homicide, Detective Sergeant Sullivan. How can I help you?" Gates said into the receiver. The caller spoke in a low, muffled voice to avoid being identified.

"It's how I can help you, detective. You record these calls, so I'll keep it brief. I've got a possible suspect for you in your white supremacist murders. A guy named Otto, Otto Pretorius. He's a fucking Afrikaner. Captain's a charter fishing boat here in Galveston," the caller said.

"Well, sir, right now we don't have any evidence that a white supremacist is involved in these murders. What's an "Afrikaner?" Gates asked.

"Look, you got a black minister and a Jewish rabbi, both dead within two weeks. Just who the hell do you think kills those kinds of people?" asked the caller sarcastically. "An Afrikaner is a guy from South Africa – you know, apartheid South Africa, the bastion of white supremacy?" the caller continued.

Gates had her notepad out and scribbled notes as the caller spoke. "Can you tell me why you believe that this Otto... Pretorius is a white supremacist?" she asked.

"Cause he's from South Africa. He's all tatted up like he's done prison time, and he's got a big tat of a white supremacist cross on the left side of his chest, that's how," the caller replied.

Gates kept taking notes as she talked with the caller. "Do you know this Otto personally? I mean, you've obviously seen his tattoos. Where can we find this Otto?" Gates asked.

"Look, lady, I'm not here to take you to school. You're the detective. I can tell you where to find him, but that's it. I also know you people trace these calls," replied the caller.

Gates didn't want to press the man too hard. She already disliked the tone of his voice. *Just a little more information,* she thought. "Well, okay, fair enough. Then tell me where we can find this Otto," Gates said.

"Sandpiper RV Park, just two miles north of the Pleasure Pier on the beach in Midtown. He's got a dark grey fishing boat he's working on. I think he also lives on the boat," replied the caller.

"Thanks. That's very helpful, Mr....?" said Gates before the line went dead.

Gates replaced the receiver and checked her digital recorder, hitting the playback button. She went back thirty seconds to make sure she had recorded the call.

Sandpiper RV Park, just east of the Pleasure Pier on the beach in Midtown. He's got a dark grey fishing boat he's working on. I think he also lives on the boat. "Thanks. That's very helpful, Mr....?" the recorder ended. Got it, said Gates to herself.

Gates swiveled her chair to face her desktop computer and accessed the Texas Department of Criminal Justice and Department of Motor Vehicles databases, typing "Otto Pretorius." It was such a unique name that she didn't even need a date of birth. In less than five minutes, Gates confirmed Pretorius's details, including a DOB, last known address, driver's license, and criminal history with photos. More importantly, she found out that Otto had served time in the Texas prison system and was currently on parole for drug trafficking.

Bingo! Winner, winner, chicken dinner, she remarked out loud, smiling.

Gates yelled over to Det. Bill Hurd across the room, “Bill, grab your stuff, we’re going to check out a lead on a possible person of interest in Midtown. An anonymous caller gave me some info on a possible person of interest in our clergy killings. Might be a good lead. The guy’s a parolee named Otto Pretorius. No crimes of violence, but a former drug trafficker. Definitely worth our time. Once we get into the area, we’ll call a couple of uniforms as backup.”

“Really? Where are we heading?” Hurd asked.

“Place called the Sandpiper RV Park on the beach, a couple of miles north of Pleasure Pier,” replied Gates.

“Let me get my vest, and I’ll ride with you,” said the detective.

“Copy. Meet you in the parking lot. My vest and gear are in my trunk," Gates said as the two homicide detectives left the office.

The Galveston Police Department at 601 54th St, Galveston, was about two and a half miles from the Pleasure Pier on Seawall Boulevard. The Sandpiper RV Park was another two miles north of the pier on Seawall Blvd. As the detectives navigated the busy Midtown streets, Gates called Communications to have two marked units meet them at the RV park entrance. The units were already waiting when Gates and her partner arrived.

Gates and Hurd exited their unmarked and met with the uniformed officers. Gates showed them a photo of Pretorius.

"This guy is a lead as a possible person of interest in our clergy killings. He's a parolee. We've got nothing on him, just a tip, but keep your heads on a swivel. He's supposed to be living on a dark gray charter boat in the RV park. It should be easy to spot. Det. Hurd and I will contact the park manager to see if we can get a space. You two keep a lookout. We'll be back in a minute, and we can go over together," said Gates.

The two detectives walked up the stairs of the main building to the manager's office and identified themselves. Gates showed the manager a photo of Pretorius.

"Seen this man before?" she asked the woman.

"Sure, that's Otto. He stays here on a boat that's on a trailer. Nice man. He's not in trouble, is he?" the manager asked.

"No ma'am. We just need to talk to him about a matter. Nothing to worry about. Know what space he's in?" replied Gates.

"Well, he's not in any space. He's around the south side of the building. Saw him working on his boat this morning," the manager replied.

"Thanks, ma'am. We won't be long," said Gates. The two detectives walked back down the stairs and met again with the uniformed officers.

One of you comes with us, and your partner can wait by the gate. We're going to walk around the south side of this building. The manager says Pretorius should be working on his boat around the corner," Gates explained.

Gates, Hurd, and the uniformed officer walked around the building. They immediately spotted Otto Pretorius up on a ladder at the stern of a forty-five-foot boat called the Grey Lady, working on one of three Mercury 250 HP engines.

Gates displayed her badge and called up to Pretorius.

"Otto Pretorius, Detectives Sullivan, and Hurd, Galveston PD. Can you come down so we can talk to you for a minute?" asked Gates.

Otto looked surprised to see the three officers. "Something wrong?" he asked, wiping a greasy hand on a rag.

"Just a few questions if you don't mind," replied Gates.

"Questions about what?" asked Otto.

"If you come down here, we'll explain why we're here," said Gates.

"Sure, give me a second," said Otto as he climbed the ladder and approached the officers. "What's this all about?" he asked.

"Nice boat, you own it?" asked Hurd, trying to build rapport.

"Wish I did. No, I only captain it. It's a charter fishing boat owned by a dot-com guy in Austin. Tax write-off, I'm sure. It's leased out by a charter fishing company here in town called Master Baiters. I captain it and also keep it maintained. Is this about the boat? I've got all the papers, registration, and license inside," said Otto.

"Very cool. I'll bet with those triple 250s, this boat hauls ass out on the Gulf," said Hurd, who loved to fish.

"You bet. Great for outrunning sudden storms that pop up. So this isn't about the boat, I take it. Am I in some trouble?" asked the curious and now concerned Otto.

"Can I ask you what you were doing this past Saturday?" asked Gates.

"Sure, I was running a charter on the Gulf, like most every Saturday and Sunday when the weather's good. Why do you ask?" asked Otto.

"And the Sunday before that?" pressed Gates.

"Same thing. The weather's been great, and the Barrel fish have been running, so the company books me with charters. I'm sure you guys already know I'm on parole. Am I being detained?" asked Otto.

"No, you're not being detained. We've just got some questions for you. Can you tell us when you finished your charters on those last two weekends?" asked Gates.

"Normal times. Charters leave the dock by 7:00 am, and I have them back by 4:00 pm," replied Otto.

"And do you remember where you were two weeks ago Sunday, and last Saturday after 4:00 pm?" pressed Gates.

Otto glanced around furtively, raised an eyebrow, and looked at the officers warily. "Look, you told me that I'm not being detained, and so far, I've been cooperative in answering your questions. But you still haven't told me why you're here. Two guys, a uniform, and maybe one or two more cops I haven't seen yet. I want to know what this is all about. I got rights," replied Otto.

"Fair question. How about we tell you what this is all about downtown at the station?" Gates suggested.

Otto laughed loudly. "Really, at the station? Do I look like a cherry to you? I've heard that line before, detective. I haven't done a damn thing wrong. I get reminded every day that I'm still on parole. I'm not going to screw up and lose a good job and my freedom. I'll go with you guys, but I want your word that I'm not getting busted. You give me your word first, and then I'll go with you," said Otto.

Gates smiled and lifted her right pinky finger. "Pinkey promise," she replied.

Otto chuckled. "Pinky promise? What is this, the Mickey Mouse Club? Okay, I'll go, but no detention, no cuffs, and I walk out of there anytime I want; promise?"

"Done deal. We'll give you a ride," replied Gates.

"Front seat next to you. No caged unit. Your partner can sit in the back here. Afterwards, you pay for the cab ride back," said Otto

"Deal. Come on, our car is over at the manager's building," said Gates, pointing the way. Otto followed the officers to the unmarked unit and got in the right front passenger seat next to Gates for the ride back to CID.

At CID, Gates and Hurd led Otto into Interview Room #2. Before the trio entered, Gates pressed the "AV Recording" button, and they all sat around a table.

"Coffee, a soda, water?" Hurd asked Otto, trying to maintain rapport.

"No thanks. I don't plan on being here long," replied Otto.

Gates brought a steno pad and a manila folder and laid them on the table. *I'm going to keep this low-key; just gather information for now. We know nothing about this guy, so we don't want to do anything to spook him, or we won't get him back in here without an arrest. If that happens, he's sure to lawyer up,* she thought. She began the interview.

"So, I've detected an accent. Where were you from originally? You got a German name?" she asked.

"South Africa. It's not a German name; it's Dutch. My people are Dutch, not German," replied Otto.

"A South African, Afrikaner?" Gates asked to confirm what her anonymous tipster had confided.

"Yeah, you know that term, eh?" replied Otto.

"Wild guess from something I saw on TV," Gates lied.

"Yeah, Afrikaner," said Otto.

"So, Otto, how long have you been in the States?" Gates asked.

"Almost twenty years. My folks brought us here for safety. We owned a farm next to my dad's brother's. They were murdered by black South Africans back then, when I was in high school. Been here ever since." Otto replied.

"Where are your folks now? You got any family here?" Hurd asked.

Just my parents. They live on a small spread up in Lampasas. My dad's retired from the Post Office. I've never been married, so no one else except them," Otto replied.

Gates opened the manila folder on the table. Otto saw his prison photo alongside his Texas Department of Corrections sheet. "Says here you did time seven years ago for drug trafficking. What was that all about?" she asked.

"Yeah, in my reckless and stupid days. Coke and marijuana. Rangers, and HAITA caught me over in Port A. I brought it by boat and got pinched. It was heavyweight, so I took a deal and copped a plea. I was sentenced to five out of the fifteen years. I did three years straight time, and CTS – credit for time served. Been out almost four years; got another year left on my tail," Otto explained.

"So full search, and seizure conditions for another year," said Gates, looking at Otto's record.

"Correct, I got to check in with my PO, test whenever, and cooperate with the po-po. That's what I'm doing now," said Otto.

"Says here that your parole officer is Manny Garcia. I know Manny. So if I call him, he's gonna give you a good report?" Gates said, looking Otto directly in the eye.

"Absolutely. I'm as good as gold. All my tests have been clean, and I haven't been hanging with felons. I'm sober; you can test me. I got a good job. Call my boss and ask—he'll vouch for me," said Otto confidently.

"Okay, maybe we'll do that. Good to know. I see you've got some tats. Mind if we ask you to take off your shirt so we can look and maybe snap a couple of photos of your tats?" asked Gates.

"If you really need to. Like I said, I got nothing to hide," said Otto, removing his shirt so he was bare-chested. Gates and Hurd immediately noticed the prominent bluish-black intricate tattoo of what appeared to be some kind of cross on Otto's left pectoral muscle near his heart. Hurd began photographing all of Otto's tattoos.

"That's an interesting tat, what does that one mean?" asked Gates, pointing to the unique tattoo. Otto deflected the question.

"Okay, so tell me why I'm really here. You guys aren't doing a census and aren't looking for a recommendation to get inked. Why am I really here? What are you looking at me for?" he asked.

Gates noted the deflection and redirected back to the tattoo. "That tattoo. What does it mean?" She pressed.

It's a Dutch medieval cross; it's Christian. I got it after my uncles were slaughtered to honor them. Like everyone in our family, they were Christians," said Otto.

Gates decided it was time to get to the point. She glanced at Hurd and then back to Otto. "Have you heard anything about what the local press is calling the "Clergy Killings?'"

“Sure. Who hasn’t? Galveston isn’t that big of a town. Some spooky shit. Rumor is it’s some Klan or white supremacist group involved. They lynched a black minister, and then a Jew Rabbi. Don’t know how they bumped him off,” said Otto.

“Right, some white supremacist group. Now you said that you’re originally from South Africa – an Afrikaner. Isn’t that where there’s been apartheid for generations? Didn’t you say your uncles were massacred by South African blacks back home?

“Whoa, wait a minute. Now I get it. I’m South African – an Afrikaner... murdered relatives. You’re interested in my tats... white supremacist, racist shit. A dead black guy, and a Jew... You guys think I’m involved in that shit... those murders?” replied Otto, incredulously. Hell, no! That ain’t me. I’m not a fricking Nazi or a KKK member. You guys got it all wrong,” protested the offended Otto, pulling back from the table with a look of disgust.

Gates knew she had to maintain control of this voluntary interview. She didn’t want to lose her potential person of interest now. The detective responded with a warm smile and a sympathetic gesture. *It was time to de-escalate,* she thought.

“Look, Otto, Det. Hurd, and I really didn’t mean to offend you. No one’s accusing you of being a white supremacist or a person of interest in these killings,” she lied. "We’re just following up on an anonymous tip. What would you do if you were in our place?"

“You’ve been very cooperative, and we’re not trying to hurt you with your PO or your boss. But we need to account for your time after work on that Sunday and last Saturday. Can you do that?” asked Gates.

Otto looked visibly worried. He looked down at the table and then back at the detectives. “Well, I was on the boat for a couple of hours cleaning up and getting the boat ready for the next day. It usually takes me that long, especially when I'm booked with multiple fishermen. That takes time to clean up the boat and get it ship shape for the next day," Otto explained.

"I'm sure it does. I'm a fisherman and take charters. It's hard work, so I get it," said Bill Hurd, trying to keep Otto calm.

"So, Otto, do you think anyone else saw you on the boat after work those days? Any other charter captains or deckhands who were also working next to you? You gotta help us out here," said Gates. Otto briefly lowered his head into his hands; he was thinking.

"Well, maybe. I could ask... I'm innocent, I'm telling you. I swear," said Otto in a pleading voice.

Gates smiled again at Otto to calm him down. "Well, that's a great idea, Otto. Det. Hurd, and I can definitely do that. You can also go back to the docks and see if anyone there can vouch for you," offered the detective.

"Yes, I can do that. You mean I'm free to go? You're not going to bust me?" asked Otto.

"Otto, I promised you that you are not being detained. Yes, you're free to go. We'll get you a free cab as we said. You have homework to do, and so do we. Here's my card with my cell number on it. We want you to stay in touch. If you have people who can account for your time after work during those two days, we need their contact information to interview them," explained Gates, handing Otto her card.

Gates escorted Otto from CID to the hallway and pointed toward the elevator. "Down one floor, turn right; that will take you straight past the front desk. My secretary will call you a cab, and they'll meet you right outside. Remember to keep in touch," said Gates.

Otto nodded, turned, and walked down the hallway to the elevator. Gates called out after Otto, “Hey, what’s your dock and slip number down at the marina?” she asked.

Otto turned around. “Dock D, Slip 38,” he replied, then turned back towards the elevator.

Gates made a mental note before walking back inside CID to her desk. Bill Hurd was waiting for her to debrief.

“Well, what do you think, Bill?” asked Gates.

“I didn’t get any bad feelings from his vibe. I kind of like the guy. He seemed genuine to me, even for a parolee. It looked like he was trying to stay out of trouble. How about you? What’s your take?” Hurd asked.

“I’ve got the same opinion. No unusual nervousness aside from what any parolee with just a year remaining on his sentence would feel. I didn’t detect any signs of evasiveness or deception. However, he’s genuinely concerned about establishing his alibi for those two nights. I suggest we go to the docks tomorrow and check for those CCTV cameras. Maybe we can talk to a few boat captains to verify his story,” said Gates.

Chapter 8
I need your help

The Dillon family gladly loaned Wade their thirty-one-foot Class-C motorhome for a couple of weeks. Wade drove the RV to his ranch, and he and Dakota packed it with clothes and provisions, making a bed for Desi between the two front seats. As they left Boerne at 6:00 am, Wade stopped at the Murphy's gas station at Walmart to fill up. They were heading to their first stop on the coast in Rockport. The first leg was two hundred miles, roughly five hours via I-37, then turning onto US-281 South, including rest stops for Desi.

The couple pulled into the Paradise Key Dockside Bar & Grill in Cove Harbor, North Rockport, just after 11:00 am.

"This is our first stop on the Texas Gulf Coast seafood tour. Some of the best there is," declared Wade, hopping out of the cab.

"Wonderful! But what about Desi?" asked Dakota.

"No problemo, it's dog-friendly. We're here for an early lunch. They open at eleven. I'll get us a table out on the deck," said Wade as he went around to the coach, met Desi at the door, and put her harness on. "Here we go, people!" he exclaimed.

The trio exited the parking lot and took a ramp up to the front doors of the bright, ocean-blue, and white-trimmed restaurant. Wade held the door open for Dakota and followed her with Desi on a leash.

“Great paint job, and interior, I almost feel like I'm in Key West, Florida,” said Dakota.

“I think that’s the idea. Table for two with a friendly dog on your deck if possible,” Wade said to the hostess. They were the first to arrive, so getting a good table on the back deck overlooking the water was easy. The college-aged hostess seated the trio.

“Your server will be with you in a minute,” she said with a smile.

In a couple of minutes, their server arrived with two menus. “First time here?” she asked.

“Not for me, but it is for my lady here. In fact, it’s her first time on the coast,” said Wade. The server said she would return with some water and take their drink orders. Wade and Dakota opened their menus and pointed out some of the best dishes.

“Do you like oysters? They’re fresh right here near Rockport. I’d also recommend the soft-shell blue crabs; they season and flash fry ‘em,” said Wade.

“Yes, I love oysters and blue crabs, but I’ve only had the ones on the East Coast, so order up, I’m ready!” exclaimed Dakota.

“That’s the Texas spirit I’m looking for!” laughed Wade. The server arrived, and Wade ordered iced teas, a dozen oysters, and two plates of Gulf blue crabs.

The couple’s orders came quickly, and they enjoyed a splendid lunch. Wade saved some of the blue crab for Desi.

“You’re feeding crab to Desi?” Dakota asked incredulously.

“The girl is nuts for crab. That’s her favorite snack,” replied Wade as he cleaned a crab leg and handed the meat to Desi. After lunch, the couple was ready to head to Galveston. Wade, Dakota, and Desi returned to the RV, prepared to go.

“Galveston is about two hundred thirty miles, or roughly three and a half hours, from here on I-35.” We’ll make a couple of quick potty stops for Desi along the way. I want to make sure we arrive before 6:00 pm to check in. I’ve already reserved our spot. At this time of year, sunset will be just before 8:00 pm, and you’ll want to see it. Today’s a beautiful day, and I’m confident tonight’s sunset won’t disappoint,” said Wade.

“Giddy-up, cowboy!” laughed Dakota, and the trio was off to Galveston.

Wade passed the Pleasure Pier, and two miles later, pulled off Seawall Boulevard toward the beach and through the Sandpiper RV Park gates. Wade exited the cab and walked up the stairs to the Manager’s Office to check in. Ten minutes later, they parked in their reserved site, facing the beach and ocean. Wade followed the printed directions for setting up and taking down the RV. He set the metal stabilizer feet, hooked up the water, electricity, and sewage lines, and then extended the entire left side of the RV. It was like a tiny home. They were set.

“Piece of cake. Home sweet home for the next few days,” remarked Wade proudly. Wade checked the storage compartments under the coach, retrieved two folding chairs, and set them up outside. He entered the coach, grabbed

Desi's snacks and bed, and tossed them outside beside the chairs. Dakota was inside the cab with Desi.

"Can you grab us a couple of beers? I've already got snacks for Desi. Let's sit outside until the sun sets. Then we can walk out to the beach and enjoy the view," suggested Wade.

Dakota and Desi stepped out of the coach and sat beside Wade. The couple cracked open their beers and touched the cans together in a toast.

"What should we toast to?" asked Dakota.

"Well, to our Galveston adventure together," replied Wade.

"To Galveston!" exclaimed Dakota as the couple sipped their beers. Once the sun was ready to set, the trio locked up the RV and walked out to the beach. No one was on the beach, so Wade unleashed Desi and let her happily run up and down the coast, barking at seagulls flying above. Wade and Dakota walked hand in hand to the water's edge. As the top of the bright orange ball melted into the water, Wade took Dakota in his arms and kissed her tenderly.

Well, what have we here, the normally stoic Wade Justus is a romantic after all, Dakota thought happily.

For Wade, the past five years without his dearest Helen had been tough. Helen appeared in his dreams and gave her approval for him to start a new relationship with Dakota, which was a relief. *I'm going to make this work,* Wade told himself as he looked into Dakota's eyes after she had kissed him back.

The next morning, Wade and Dakota were up with the sun. "Let's hit the beach for a jog. I've got to get some exercise in. How about one mile up, and one mile back?" Wade suggested.

Like Wade, Dakota was very fit and enjoyed a good workout. "Sure, this should be fun for Desi," she replied. The pair wore their workout clothes, harnessed Desi, and headed to the beach. Since it was so early, there was almost no one there, so Wade turned Desi loose so she could run and frolic alongside them as they jogged at the water's edge relaxedly.

Twenty minutes later, the trio returned to the RV from the beach. They were just about to enter their RV when Wade heard a voice call out behind them. "Ranger Justus, Wade Justus?" a male voice said. Wade immediately turned around to see who was calling out his name.

Walking up to Wade and Dakota was a man in his forties, roughly Wade's height but stockier and muscular. Wade took in the man's appearance, trying to recall where he had seen him before. *This guy looks familiar. Where do I know him from?* Wondered Wade. The man approached slowly and respectfully. Wade noticed the uncolored tattooed sleeves on the man's arms. Black and blue tattoos without color often signaled that the person had served time in prison. However, Wade didn't see any gang or prison-related tattoos on the man's arms or hands.

"Do I know you, sir?" asked Wade.

"You're Wade Justus, Texas Ranger Wade Justus, right?" asked the man.

“Well, I used to be, but not anymore. I’m retired now. Where do I know you from?" Wade asked cautiously as he put Desi into the RV so he wouldn’t get distracted.

“Well, what do you know? I thought so. Look, Ranger Justus, sorry if I surprised you and your lady. This is a bit embarrassing,” said the man, extending his hand outward to shake Wade’s hand. “You busted me nine years ago for muleing dope. You were on a drug task force—my name’s Otto, Otto Pretorius. You probably don’t remember that far back,” Otto explained.

Wade shook Otto’s hand and examined his face closely. “Well, I’ll be. You’re from South Africa, if I remember correctly, Otto. We don’t see many South Africans in Texas. That’s why I recognize you now. How’s life? What are you up to these days? Hope everything’s good,” Wade said.

“What an amazing coincidence, Ranger Justus. I was thinking about you last night... and to see you here in Galveston... that blows my mind,” replied Otto, smiling.

“Well, Otto, like I said, I’m retired from the Rangers. It’s just Wade, so please call me Wade,” said Wade, motioning to Dakota. "This is Dakota. We’re here for a little vacation for about a week or so. So, how have you been lately?” Wade asked, shifting the focus back to Otto.

“I'm Pleased to meet you, Dakota,” said Otto, offering Dakota his hand to shake. Dakota shook Otto’s hand and smiled.

“I don’t recall if you were at my sentencing hearing, but the judge gave me five years. With good time and credit for time served, I did three. I've been out for a couple of years and have just a little time left on my five-year parole term.

“I cleaned up my act in prison. I started taking online marine navigation classes, which eventually helped me become a boat captain. I got a deckhand position with a fishing charter company when I got out. They let me apprentice until I passed my captain’s license exam. I co-captained here in Galveston for a year and then captained my boat last year. It’s over there, around the side of the office building,” Otto pointed.

“Well, that's a great success story, Otto. I’m proud of you,” Wade replied. “So, you are captaining a fishing charter now?”

Yes, it’s good work. The boat owner lives in Austin and leases the boat to a local fishing charter company called Master Baiters.”

“Catchy name,” remarked Dakota.

“Well, the pay’s good, and I stay sober, I meet with my PO once a month, got no dings on my record, and at the end of my tail, I’ll be a truly free man,” said Otto.

“So, you said you were thinking of me last night. How did I come up after all these years?” asked the curious Wade.

Otto’s demeanor visibly shifted from pride and excitement to sullenness. “Not to be personal, but do you still frequent the Company F area?” Otto asked.

“Well, yes, that was my final assignment after I left the task force; Texas Hill Country, why?” asked Wade, now even more curious.

"I was just wondering if you guys have heard about these clergy killings we've been experiencing over the past couple of weeks here in Galveston," said Otto. Wade and Dakota exchanged a surprised look.

"No, nothing. What's that all about?" asked Wade.

"Well, two weeks ago on a Sunday, they killed a Black Southern Baptist minister. Then last Sunday, the cops found a Jewish rabbi murdered. The Black minister was hanged. The Jewish rabbi's death was also listed as a homicide. The local press rumble is that some white supremacist group or individual killed them," explained Otto.

"And you were thinking about me, why? I haven't been ranging for nearly five years now," said Wade.

"I'd been locked up, so I didn't know you retired from the Rangers. I thought you could help me because I could really use some serious help," said Otto.

"Otto, forgive me, but you're going in circles. Why would you need my help? You're not involved in any of this, are you?" pressed Wade.

Otto looked directly into Wade's eyes. "Hell no, I'm no Nazi, white supremacist. On my mother's life, I swear that I had nothing to do with any of this shit," replied Otto seriously.

"Okay, that's fine, but why were you thinking about me helping you. Help you with what?" said Wade.

"Well, some anonymous tipster dropped a dime on the cops and told them to look at me for those murders. A couple of detectives and a uniform came out here to visit me, and I ended up going downtown to the station with them for questioning. They asked me where I had been on the nights of the two murders, and they were also interested in my tats, especially this one," Otto said as he unbuttoned his shirt, baring his chest, and pointing to a large, intricate tattoo on his left pectoral muscle.

"They thought that maybe my tat was a white supremacist tattoo, but it's not. It's a Dutch medieval cross, it's Christian," explained Otto. Wade looked closely at the tattoo and recognized it as one he had seen other soldiers sporting in the Army.

"Yes, I know that's not a white supremacist tattoo," Wade said reassuringly. "So, how can I help you, Otto?"

"Well, first off, I thought you could talk to the detectives and tell them you know me, and that I'm not a white supremacist. Then, I thought maybe you could find a way for me to confirm my alibi on the nights of those murders. Each happened late afternoon or early evening when I was on my boat, cleaning it up after a day's fishing charter.

"I haven't had much luck finding captains or deckhands on the dock when I was there those days. I was hoping you might know how I can prove to this female detective that I was really on my boat that evening, like I told them," explained Otto. Otto pulled out his wallet, showed Wade a white business card, and handed it to him.

Wade took the card, read it, and looked at Otto in surprise. "Is this the lady detective who interviewed you?" he asked, showing Otto the card. The card read, *"Sergeant Gates Sullivan, Homicide Unit, Galveston Police Department."*

“Yeah, that’s her, Sgt. Sullivan, Gates Sullivan, and her partner is named Hirt or Hurd—something like that, a male partner. Know her?” asked Otto.

Wade looked at Otto, and then at Dakota, who had been quietly listening and taking everything in.

“Well, as a matter of fact, I do know Sgt. Sullivan. We go back a few years,” replied Wade.

“Ranger Justus... I mean, Wade, I know you’re on vacation,... and I don’t want to be a bother, but if you could talk to her... Tell her you busted me for dope years ago, and you’ve never known me to be a Nazi, KKK, or white supremacist. That would help. Maybe you can also figure out a way for me to prove my alibi, too,” pleaded Otto. Wade looked at Dakota and then at Otto.

“Well, of course, I can reach out to Det. Sullivan and tell her from my experience with you back in the day, you’re no white supremacist. However, figuring out how to help you confirm your alibi is a pretty tall and difficult order, Otto. Tell ya what, give me a day, and maybe I’ll come up with an idea. No promises, though,” Wade said as he took out his cell phone and took a photo of Sgt. Gates Sullivan’s business card before handing it back to Otto.

“I”ll call Sgt. Sullivan tomorrow. Where can I find you? I’ll also need your cell number,” said Wade.

“I live part-time on my boat here at the Sandpiper,” replied Otto. The men then exchanged cellphone numbers. Wade and Dakota went into the RV, and Dakota started cooking scrambled eggs and bacon while Wade took a shower. When

Wade finished and got dressed, Dakota had coffee and a hot breakfast on the table.

"Interesting fellow," remarked Dakota, referring to Otto Pretorius.

"Well, in my previous line of work, you meet all kinds. As I recall, our task force received information that a shipment of cocaine and marijuana was coming ashore at Port A. I was on the DPS fast boat that intercepted Otto's boat as it entered the marina. We had a DEA dope dog onboard who immediately alerted on the drugs, and the rest was history. Otto was just a deckhand at the time. He told us this was his first run. He knew there was dope on board and had been recruited to make the run for a sizable amount of money. He took a plea. As I recall, this was his first offense, so the judge went easy on him," explained Wade.

"Well, he seems to have cleaned up his life. You gotta respect that," said Dakota.

"Yeah, sure, it seems like it. He pulled himself together, found a trade with potential, studied, and applied himself, and according to him, he's been clean and checks in with his parole officer. I know a lot of guys his age who went right back to running dope or doing other illegal stuff. It's not an easy task when you're a convicted felon on parole. Looks like other people also saw promise in him," remarked Wade.

"Wade, I know we're on vacation, but do you think you *can* help him?" asked Dakota.

"Well, I've got Det. Gates Sullivan's number, so I'll definitely be calling her. Gates and I go way back. I was one of her academy instructors when she was a recruit. Years later, when she first made detective, she took a death investigations class I taught in San Antonio. I haven't seen her in years. As I recall, she's a pistol, so catching up will be nice. I will visit her personally at the PD and take you with me if you wanna go. But before we do that, I need time to figure out how to get Otto's alibi confirmed," said Wade.

"So, you believe him?" asked Dakota.

"Don't you?" asked Wade, smiling as he sipped his coffee.

Wade and Dakota enjoyed a nice day at the beach. They prepared the RV and headed to Gaido's on Seawall Blvd. Gaido's was well-known for its excellent seafood and was probably the oldest restaurant in Galveston. It sat just across the boulevard from the beach. The restaurant was easy to find because it had a giant blue crab mounted on its roof. Beneath the big crab, there was a sign that read, *"Our 115th year of service to you."* Gaido's was what older folks might call "Old School." The servers dressed in formal black outfits with white shirts and bow ties. The tables were covered with white linen tablecloths, and pictures of the restaurant's early days lined the walls.

Wade parked the RV in front of the restaurant, with the windows partially rolled down for Desi, who sat in the driver's seat watching them go inside. No one would mess with any vehicle that had a pit bull in the front seat.

"They have great chowder and are famous for their seafood tower. Let's splurge!" suggested Wade as they went inside.

Wade had been spending the day thinking about ways to help Otto verify his alibi, and Dakota had noted his periods of quiet reflection as they walked along the beach. She made it a point not to distract the new man in her life.

Sometimes, it's best just to let men think things out. I'm sure he'll come up with something. He'll tell me when he's ready, Dakota mused.

Wade and Dakota had enjoyed a bowl of the restaurant's excellent clam chowder and were working their way through the iced fresh seafood tower when Wade paused mid-bite.

"You know, I've been thinking... docks have expensive boats, and expensive boats have costly nautical equipment that thieves like to steal. Most of the marinas and docks I'm familiar with have CCTV systems and/or security guards. I wonder..." remarked Wade as he picked up his cellphone and dialed Otto.

Otto's cellphone rang, "Wade Justus" appeared on the display, and he immediately picked up.

"Wade?" he asked.

"Yeah, Otto, it's Wade. I've been thinking, where do you dock your boat when it's in the water?" he asked.

"Ah, the Galveston Yacht Marina over on North Holiday, Dock D, Slip 38, why?" asked Otto.

"Do you know if you have any surveillance cameras there or private security?" Wade asked. There was a moment of silence on the other end of the line, and then Otto responded excitedly.

Jesus, that's right! I have to pass through a locked gate to get into the marina where my slip is. I use a magnetic card, but there's also a keypad. There are security cameras everywhere. What an idiot, I was so stressed I didn't even think of that when they questioned me. Of course! The key card and cameras—security has to have me on those cameras!"

"If you used a magnetic key card to enter and exit, there will be a digital record of your in-and-out times, timestamped. Dakota and I are having lunch at Gaido's. Can you meet us at the marina in ninety minutes?" asked Wade.

"I'm at the Sandpiper, just working on one of the engines. It's not far from here. Meet you in ninety," replied Otto.

Dakota playfully stuffed a cold shrimp from the seafood tower into Wade's mouth. "There you go, I just knew you'd come up with something, Ranger Justus," she remarked, smiling.

"Well, even a broken clock strikes twelve twice a day," chuckled Wade. "Let's take our time finishing this tower. Remember, we're on vacation. We have an hour to spare. Everything's nearby here. It won't take long to drive over there," said Wade.

Wade and Dakota finished their meal and typed "Galveston Yacht Marina" into the Google Street View on his cell phone. The marina was less than four miles away at 715 N. Holiday Drive. They drove back down Seawall Blvd. toward the Sandpiper, then turned north on 4th Street, all the way to the Galveston Yacht Marina. Wade saw Otto waiting outside the front gate with a blue sign featuring a seahorse that read, "Welcome to Galveston Yacht Marina."

Otto got into his pickup truck, drove to the gate, and held his magnetic card against the reader. The gate opened, and Otto signaled them to follow him.

As Wade went through the front gate, he noticed a CCTV camera on a pole overlooking the entrance and pointed it out to Dakota. “See, just as I suspected,” he said.

The docks at the marina were numbered A—E. They passed a dark blue, white-trimmed building with a sign that read “Marina Office.”

“We’ll stop at the office with Otto on our way out. They should know him,” said Wade. They continued past the office and passed a blue storage shed near Dock-C with two CCTV cameras. Otto pulled into a parking spot next to another long blue brick building with a sign that read “Laundry Room” and got out of his truck.

The front gate to Dock-D was on the right side of the building. Wade parked the RV across the road, put Desi on a leash, and Wade and Dakota met Otto at the front gate. The gate had a digital keypad lock. Otto entered the code, the gate opened, and they went inside. Wade immediately saw that another CCTV camera was watching the front entrance from the metal roof of the covered dock and slips.

See what I mean? I'm pretty sure that when we go to the office, they'll have a display screen with all of these CCTV cameras so they can monitor who comes and goes and activities on the docks and property. Most of these systems today are digital, so there should be a record going back weeks, if not months.

"Okay, Otto, now take us down to Slip 38," Wade directed. When the trio reached the empty slip, Wade searched the dock for more cameras but found none. He glanced at Otto and Dakota.

"No other cameras, but from what I've already seen, we should be fine with the magnetic key card, the front gate camera, the ones on that storage shed outside Dock-C, and of course, the one here at the front gate of Dock-D. Let's head over to the office," said Wade.

Desi needed a walk, so the trio headed to the Marina Office. Wade briefed Otto on the key questions to ask about the front gate security system and the CCTV cameras.

Otto and Wade entered the office, leaving Dakota outside with Desi. Wade immediately noticed a flat-screen TV displaying several CCTV stations monitored with real-time timestamps. Kirk, the manager, greeted Otto by his first name and was friendly, indicating a close relationship. Wade allowed Otto to lead with questions about whether the front gate security system recorded entries and exits, if the CCTV system was digital, and if the manager could review videos by dates and times. Kirk was curious and seemed to know already that Otto was on parole.

"So, what's this all about, Otto? You're not in trouble with the law, are you?" he asked. Otto kept his response brief but somewhat vague.

"No trouble, Kirk. The cops asked me where I was on two different weekend nights over the past two weeks. I'm always working on my boat after a charter until seven or eight p.m. I need to give them some proof of that. It's really no big deal," he replied.

"No problem, son. Let's go into the back where the surveillance equipment is. The CCTV monitors are out here, but the digital recorders and another screen are back there," said the helpful manager who looked to be in his sixties.

"Thanks, Kirk. By the way, this is my friend Wade," said Otto, introducing Wade. Wade took the opportunity to smile and shake the manager's hand. The three men entered the back room where Kirk sat at a desk with a keyboard and monitor.

"Okay, what dates and times are you looking for, and we'll see if you're here. Your boat is slipped at Dock-D, right?" asked Kirk.

"Yeah, Slip 38. The first date was two Sundays ago, sometime after 7:00 pm. The second one would have been last Saturday, again after 6:00 pm," replied Otto.

Kirk looked at a calendar on the wall, saw the dates, pressed a few buttons, and brought up the CCTV camera over the front gate to Dock-D from two Sundays ago. "Let's see. Let's go to 6:00 p.m., and fast-forward until we see you," he said.

At 7:22 p.m., the CCTV footage for Dock-D showed Otto with a bag of tools opening the front gate to Dock-D and walking out into the parking lot. "There you are, son," said Kirk, using the computer mouse to rewind the video to 7:21 p.m. and play it forward in slow motion.

Wade spoke up. "Can I take a screenshot of Otto going through the gate with the timestamp?" he asked.

"Sure thing," replied Kirk as he froze the image at 7:22:13 pm. Wade took a photo and then switched his cell phone to video.

"Kirk, please move the video back ten seconds before Otto walks through the gate? I want to take a video of the time he exits the gate," said Wade.

Kirk reversed the video, and Wade stepped in front of the screen with his cellphone, videotaping Otto moving through the front gate. "Got it," Wade said after confirming he had both the still frame and video.

"Can we go to the next date?" asked Otto.

"Can do," replied Kirk as he punched the following Saturday. "About the same time, around 6:00 pm? He asked.

"Yes, if you can," replied Otto.

Kirk moved the video timestamp cursor to 5:55 p.m. and pressed play. Then he touched "fast forward," and the three men watched closely as time sped by. At 7:36 p.m., Otto suddenly appeared at the Dock-D front gate, carrying his tool bag and a white cooler, and walked through the gate into the parking lot.

"There you are," said Kirk as he moved the video back to 7:35:45 pm and pressed the slow-motion button. Otto appeared at the gate exactly at 7:36:22 pm.

"Kirk, can you bring it back again and freeze it at 7:36:22 pm so I can take a screenshot? Then we can do a video like before," asked Wade.

"Of course," replied Kirt, moving the surveillance video back to 7:36:22 pm and pausing it so Wade could take his screenshot of Otto going through the gate with the timestamp. Then Kirk moved the video back ten seconds so Wade could capture a video of Otto moving through the gate.

Wade double-checked his cellphone to make sure he had the still shot and the video of Otto talking through the gate with the timestamps. “Perfect, thanks,” Wade said.

Otto asked Kirk if he could show him the records of his front gate exits from the marina on those two dates.

That’s on a different system, but yes, I can do that. It’s much easier because you use your magnetic key instead of the keypad. Each keypad is registered to each tenant,” explained Kirk as he switched computer screens.

“Let me see your magnetic key,” said Kirk. Otto handed the manager his plastic magnetic key card. Kirk checked the serial number on the back of the card and entered the number into a template on the screen. Within a few seconds, an entire page of dates and timestamp data appeared on the screen.

“It’s easier if I just print out the entire month for you,” said Kirk as he entered the date parameters and pressed the print button. Two pages of date and timestamp data for the month came out of the printer.

“Can you make a second copy for me?” asked Wade.

“Sure thing,” replied Otto as he hit the print button again.

“Here you go, fellas,” said the manager, handing the printouts to Otto and Wade.

Otto and Wade examined the line of dates to the two specific ones. Each date and timestamp matched the videos of Otto leaving the dock. The front gate exit timestamps indicated that Otto had left the marine property within ten minutes after walking out of the Dock-D gate.

Wade had an afterthought. “Kirk, when we drove in, I noticed you have another CCTV camera on a pole monitoring the front gate. Can you pull up that CCTV footage and bring it back to match the dates and times of Otto leaving the marina we identified using the front gate security system?”

“Sure, good idea. Give me a minute,” said Kirk, switching to the CCTV surveillance system. “Here we are. This is that Sunday evening,” he said.

“Great, go back ten seconds and let me record it. Then stop it so I can get a still shot of Otto going through the gate,” said Wade. Kirk complied, and Wade captured his video and a still shot.

“Okay, let’s do next Saturday evening, and we’ll get out of your hair,” said Wade. Again, Wade's cellphone captured a video and a still shot of Otto leaving the marina property.

“Kirk, you don’t know how much you’ve helped me today. Thanks, buddy,” said Otto, vigorously shaking the manager’s hand. Kirk looked at Wade. “He’s a good kid. He's always helpful whenever I ask him to help me with something on the docks,” said Kirk.

“Yes, he is. Thanks for taking the time to help out. A pleasure to meet you, Kirk,” said Wade, shaking the manager's hand.

“Anytime, fellas. Anytime,” replied the manager as the pair left the office.

Dakota returned to the office with Desi when Wade and Otto walked outside.

“So, how did you guys do? I’m dying to know,” asked Dakota.

“We did great, the manager had videos of me coming out of the gate each evening like I told the cops,” said Otto.

The timestamps for each date from the front gate also matched Otto leaving the marina property. His alibi for both nights is confirmed. Time for me to call Detective Sergeant Gates Sullivan,” said Wade.

“Wade, I can’t thank you enough for your help. This evidence will definitely get me off the hook with the cops,” said the grateful Otto.

No problem, happy to help. But you know, the detectives would have eventually done the same thing. Like I said, I know Det. Sullivan. She’s a smart cookie. We just handled it a bit quicker," replied Wade.

“Well, just the same, I’m grateful for what you did,” said Otto, shaking Wade's hand firmly.

“Well, you get back to work. I’ll call Det. Sullivan, and give her my photos, videos, and this printout. I’m sure they will follow up with you, but this should take you off the persons of interest list, and you can get on with your life,” said Wade as he and Dakota bid Otto Pretorious goodbye.

Chapter 9
Could you lend us a hand?

After Wade and Dakota left the Galveston Yacht Marina, he wasted no time contacting Det. Sgt. Gates Sullivan.

As Wade drove, he handed Dakota his cell phone.

"Can you do me a favor and access my photos, find the picture of Det. Gates Sullivan's phone number is on her business card. Can you dial it for me? Then, get the address of the Galveston PD and put it into your navigator on your cellphone so we can drive over there," Wade asked. Dakota was eager to help. She dialed the detective's number and handed Wade his cellphone. It rang.

Gates and Bill Hurd huddled in the CID conference room when Gates' cellphone on the table buzzed. She looked at the display that read, "Wade Justus," smiled, and picked up.

"Detective Sergeant Gates Sullivan, homicide. When your day ends, ours begins. What's your pleasure?" she asked.

"Gates, this is a voice from your past. Guess who?" said Wade, playing along.

"Well, it can't be the Texas Rangers because they don't make house calls. "One riot, one ranger," is the motto as I recall. My display says, 'Wade Justus,' but that can't be because I heard he got wacked in a shootout in New Mexico. Who's this really?" chuckled Gates.

Yeah, I get that response a lot these days. Reports of my death have been greatly exaggerated. This is your old instructor, retired Texas Ranger, Wade Justus. I can see that you're still a pistol," Wade chuckled.

"So your death is merely a rumor? Hell, I sent flowers and a card," replied Gates.

"Well then, the rumor I started is working," laughed Wade. "How the hell are you, Gates?" Wade asked.

"Well, normally, I'd say I was doing fine, but not right now," she replied.

"Do tell. Something keeping you up at night?" probed Wade.

"Actually, more than one thing. In fact, right now, a couple of things: two murders. I'm surprised you haven't heard of them yet, even up in the Hill Country," said Gates.

"Well, to be honest, I've heard about the murders. From what I understand, a few members of your local clergy are involved. That's why I am calling. My girl and I are on vacation in your city, and I was wondering if we could stop by. I want to discuss something relevant to your investigation. I'm not far away. Do you have time?" Wade asked.

"For you, and anything you have on our cases, absolutely. Come on over. I'll tell the front desk to buzz you through. CID is on the second floor," said Gates.

"Great, see you in fifteen," said Wade before hanging up.

As promised, fifteen minutes after his call to Gates, Wade and Dakota pulled up into the front parking lot of the Galveston PD.

It wasn't hot, and a gentle Spring breeze was blowing, so Wade and Dakota left Desi in the RV with the windows down and plenty of water. Desi immediately took her guard position, sitting in the driver's seat and watching the pair enter the building.

The Major Case Unit conducted homicide investigations in the Criminal Investigations Division, known as "CID." Wade and Dakota approached the front desk. Wade displayed his Texas Ranger badge and ID to one of the desk officers. "Det. Sgt. Sullivan in the Major Cases Unit is expecting us," Wade said. The officer examined Wade's credentials.

"Yes, sir, Ranger Justus. Sgt. Sullivan called ahead and said you'd be stopping by," the officer replied, handing Wade and Dakota visitors' badges.

Wade and Dakota stepped through the open doorway to CID and found Gates and her partner, Det. Bill Hurd is waiting for them.

"Well, you're a sight for sore eyes," exclaimed Gates, giving Wade a firm, friendly handshake.

"Same here. It's been a while. Detective Sergeant Gates Sullivan, let me introduce my other half, Dr. Dakota Shannon, forensic pathologist. In fact, Dakota is the new Chief ME for Bexar County in San Antone," Wade said, proudly introducing Dakota.

"Just call me Gates, Dr. Shannon. This is my partner, Detective Bill Hurd," said Gates. The foursome shook hands all around.

"Please, Gates, and Bill, call me Dakota," said Dakota.

"Dakota, it is," replied Gates, pointing down the hallway. Let's go down to the conference room where we can talk privately," Gates suggested, leading the way.

The foursome sat around the conference table, which was spread with the case files of the slain Southern Baptist minister and Orthodox Jewish rabbi. Gates was eager to hear what Wade had to say.

"Wade, you said you had some information about our homicides?" she asked.

Wade pulled out two folded sheets of information from the Galveston Yacht Marina's front gate security system and set them on the table.

"By coincidence, Dakota and I booked an RV site at the Sandpiper RV Park off of Seawall Blvd. for a few days' vacation. That's what's brought us to Galveston."

The mere mention of the Sandpiper RV Park raised eyebrows of both detectives, who stole a glance at each other.

"A great time to visit the coast. Less crowded, great seafood, light coastal breezes, and almost no humidity," said Gates, smiling at Dakota. "Wade, you were saying," encouraged Gates.

"On our second day here, we happened to run into a guy named Otto Pretorius, whom I had arrested for accessory to drug trafficking a few years ago when I was on a HIDTA task force with the feds. He also stays there when he's working on his boat. He's now a fishing charter captain for a company at the Galveston Yacht Marina. When his boat is in the water, it's docked over there."

"Okay...., and?" replied Gates.

"Well, Otto told us about these clergy murders y'all been having here – a Black Southern Baptist minister, and an Orthodox Jewish Rabbi. In short, he told me that you had gone out to the Sandpiper on a tip and brought him here to question him as a person of interest," explained Wade.

"Well, Mr. Pretorius volunteered to come down and answer our questions. He's a parolee, so you know the routine. We're obligated to follow up on all leads," replied Gates a bit defensively.

"Look, Gates, I *do* know the drill, and I'm sure you figured out by now that it was my team's arrest that put him in prison," said Wade.

"Yes, we've now connected the dots. So tell me why he'd confide our interview with him to you, the guy that busted him?" asked Gates.

"Well, we didn't go into the details much, but I got the impression he thought I was fair with him, like a Texas Ranger. I'm sure he figured I had enough investigative experience to find a way to verify his alibi for the nights of both murders. He also asked me to tell you he's not a white supremacist. I assume that's what the local press has been focusing on," said Wade.

"Well, first off, in your experience with Pretorius, did you ever consider him a white supremacist? He is from South Africa, you know. Did he also tell you that his two uncles, who were farmers back there, were slaughtered by black revolutionaries, and that's why his family fled South Africa and came to the U.S.?" said Gates.

"In response to your question, no, I never believed Otto was a white supremacist. He's a Christian like his family, as I recall. That tattoo you guys were interested in, he said, is a medieval Dutch cross, a Christian symbol. I've seen several soldiers in the Army with similar tattoos. There's nothing white supremacist about it. No, Otto didn't mention the murders of his uncles, but that's a long shot as a motive for him to start killing religious clergy after all these years, suddenly," Wade replied.

"He was having a definite problem establishing an alibi of where he was, and what he was doing during the late afternoons and early evenings of each of the murders," replied Det Hurd.

"Have you guys had time yet to check out his alibi?" Wade asked.

"Not yet, but we will. He told us that he was working on and cleaning up his boat at the marina after the fishing charter clients left each night. He didn't leave the marina until after 7:00 pm each night," said Gates.

"Well, I think I can help you with that—confirming Otto's alibi for each of the homicides," said Wade, as he picked up the dates and timestamps from the Galveston Yacht Marina front gate security system.

"First, if I may, what were the ME's estimates for the minister and the rabbi's times of death?" asked Wade. Dakota and I promise to keep anything you tell us strictly between us. I'm confident I can help you at least clear Otto Pretorius as a person of interest," said Wade. Gates pulled out the autopsy reports for Rev. Jacob Jefferson and Rabbi David Abramson.

"The time of death for Rev. Jefferson was around 6:00 pm that Sunday. Rabbi Abramson's body was discovered on Monday morning. However, the ME estimated that he was killed at least thirty-six hours earlier, on that Saturday evening, shortly after 7:00 pm," replied Gates, showing the reports to Wade and Dakota.

"Got it. Then this will be important to your investigation," said Wade, passing over the printout for the month for the Galveston Yacht Marina's front gate magnetic key security system.

"Otto told me that y'all had him flustered during the interview, so he forgot to tell you about the marina's security systems. He's a tenant, so he has a magnetic key card that allows tenants to enter and exit the docks where their boats are docked. Otto's magnetic key card is specifically registered to him. His personal ID number is on the back of his card. Did he mention that his boat is docked over at Dock-D, Slip 38?" Wade asked.

"Yes, he did," replied Gates. Wade got up from his chair and stood beside Gates and Hurd, pointing down at the printout.

"Okay, here is the date for the Sunday when the minister was killed. You said the ME fixed the time of death to be around 6:00 pm? Well, you can see here that Otto's exit time from the marina was timestamped at 7:30:50 pm," said Wade, pointing to the next timestamp.

"Now, here's the date for the following Saturday when the Rabbi was murdered. You're saying that the estimated time of his death was around 7:00 pm. Now, if you look at the same date, you'll see that the front gate security system shows him leaving the marina at 7:44:12 pm," explained Wade.

"Interesting," replied Gates, rechecking the two dates and timestamps. Wade took his cellphone from his back pocket and accessed his photos and videos.

"Well, just to remove any doubt that Otto Pretorius could not be the killer, I also have videos and still shots of him leaving Dock-D, going through the front gate, and departing from the marina. All three videos and still shots match the timeline with the front gate printout you're holding," said Wade, showing Gates and Detective Hurd the three videos and still shots.

"Well, that's some fine detective work, Ranger Justus. You've made your point. We'll call Mr. Pretorius and tell him he's got nothing to worry about moving forward," replied Gates.

"I concur with Gates. Wade, thanks for saving us some important hours clearing Mr. Pretorius," said Bill Hurd.

"No problem, just happy to help out. Great seeing you again, Gates, and it was a pleasure meeting you, Bill. Well, vacation calls, we'll be on our way. Hope you catch this guy. He's a real piece of evil. Keep in touch," said Wade as he backed away from the table, preparing for him and Dakota to leave.

Gates stood up from the table to face Wade and Dakota.

“Wade, and Dakota, to be honest with you, Bill, and I have been banging our heads against the wall trying to stir something up to solve these brutal murders. The media and the mayor are breathing down our chief's neck, and as they say, ‘the shit rolls downhill. Bill and I are under a lot of pressure to pull a rabbit out of a hat, and so far, we've got no good leads, and the forensic evidence is, shall we say...lacking. What I mean is, we've got nada.”

Gates looked at Dakota, “So you're a forensic pathologist? What's the difference between an ME and a forensic pathologist?” she asked.

“Good question, Gates. Forensic pathologists and MEs are both M.D.s and death investigators, meaning we both determine causes and manners of death. I completed my residency and a pathology fellowship, specializing in toxicology, which gave me more detailed, specialized medical training in complex death cases. I'm also an expert witness, so I'm used to being questioned about cold cases. It really depends on the individual physician,” explained Dakota.

“So, you've worked a lot of death cases and homicides?” asked Det. Hurd.

“A few hundred, I'd say. That's how Wade and I met when I was the Chief ME in Nashville. We both worked a serial killer case, and managed to identify the killer,” replied Dakota.

“How was the case resolved, by arrest and conviction?” asked Gates. Wade and Dakota looked at each other briefly.

"He died—the Sleeping Beauty Murders. An interesting case to look up in your spare time, Gates," offered Wade with a wry smile.

Gates looked at her partner, who slightly nodded his head, and then back at Wade and Dakota.

"Look, I know you're on your vacation, and all, but if you've got some spare time and are interested, we could sure use some help, if you could lend us a hand. I'm not talking about a lot of help, maybe just a quick review of what we've got, and what our CSI techs have done so far," said Gates. Dakota looked at Wade, who returned her glance.

Gates knew that look. She sensed that the couple was interested. Old habits are hard to break, especially for Texas Rangers, even when you're retired. Fish on the line, *I've got to set the hook before they get away,* she thought.

"Tell ya what. You guys think it over tonight. Bill and I will meet you tomorrow at Miller's Seawall Grill for breakfast. Best chicken-fried steak in town. Our treat. I'll get permission from our chief, and we'll fill you in on the cases and where we are. Maybe you'll have a few ideas for us, what do you think?" pleaded Gates.

"We've got a dog," said Wade.

"I got you covered. I know the owners. I guarantee you that tomorrow, Miller's will be dog-friendly," she smiled. Dakota was interested and took the bait first.

"Geeze, Wade. It's free chow, dog-friendly, and we won't have to cook...." said Dakota.

"Well, it's your vacation, so your decision," replied Wade.

"No, it's *our* vacation, and I'm in if you're in," countered Dakota.

"If your chief permits you, just a few hours of joint consultation, but we come as a team. You get a retired Ranger, and a forensic pathologist, that's the deal," Wade said to Gates and Hurd.

Gates stepped forward and shook Wade's and Dakota's hands. "Deal, I'll call you after I talk with our chief."

"Deal," said Wade, returning the handshake and turning to Dakota. "Let's get some of that vacation in, partner. The dog's waiting," he exclaimed.

Wade and Dakota said goodbye to Detectives Sullivan and Hurd, walked out of the police department, and out to the RV where Desi was dutifully waiting for them.

"Good girl, now get in your bed," Wade told Desi as he patted her head, and they took their seats.

"I hope I didn't speak out of turn back there, accepting their request to do a little consulting on their cases," said Dakota.

"No, I'm good with it. As I said, it's your vacation and your decision. You were interested when Gates asked about the difference between an ME and a pathologist. I think she was hedging that perhaps you might see something their guy missed," Wade offered.

"I was just curious, that's all. Besides, we're getting a free meal from this," chuckled Dakota.

"Free meal, my ass. Didn't anyone ever tell you that there are no 'free meals' in life?" laughed Wade.

"Come on, cowboy, let's hit the beach with the pooch. After that, we relax, and after sunset, I'll be cooking dinner tonight," replied Dakota as the trio drove off.

Chapter 10
Crime Scenes

Wade, Dakota, and Desi were walking along the beach toward the Pleasure Pier when Wade's cellphone buzzed. It was Gates. Wade showed the display to Dakota and answered.

"Justus and Shannon Incorporated, homicide consultants. We're busy right now, so leave your message at the beep," he said into the phone.

"Very funny, ranger. Guess what, you're both in. The chief has permitted us to share the case details with you. He needs you guys to sign an NDA, a non-disclosure agreement, for liability reasons. I'll bring them when Bill and I see you tomorrow at Miller's. How does 8:30 am sound?" asked Gates.

"Wow, NDA's. Fancy-shmancy. I guess that we really will be consultants. We'll meet you there at 08:30. Remember, we'll be bringing the dog, and she'll want a snack," said Wade.

"Sure, I guess we can pop for the dog, too. See you there," Gates replied before hanging up.

Wade and Dakota walked into Miller's Seawall Grill the next day with Desi in tow. They saw Gates and Bill Hurd toward the back of the restaurant, where the owner had hidden them for privacy. Gates, who owned her own dog, brought a large bone for Desi to chew on while the four of them ate and discussed the two homicide cases over breakfast and coffee.

Gates expected that Dakota, as a forensic pathologist, would want to review the autopsy and toxicology reports, along with photos showing how the bodies were found and their presentation during autopsy.

Gates handed Dakota the paper autopsy and toxicology reports. "The digital photos and videos are in files here on my iPad. I knew you would like to see them," she offered.

After Gates and Hurd explained the basic details of each homicide, including how the calls came in, how the bodies appeared when found, the general crime scenes, and backgrounds on both victims, they were ready for questions from Wade and Dakota.

While Gates described how the bodies had been found and shared her personal observations of each body's appearance, she skipped between the photo files of Rev. Jefferson and Rabbi Abramson. She paid close attention to the evidence of traumatic injuries to the reverend, contrasting those with the lack of obvious trauma to the rabbi. Dakota mentally checked off items and began forming her questions.

"So, I'm seeing that Dr. Dyer listed the minister's cause of death as "anoxia by ligature strangulation." That's a lack of oxygen to the brain caused by hanging. I'm examining the abrasions and ligature marks on the neck, which appear to be about one inch in diameter. I see the photos of a rope near the body at the crime scene, but I don't have the evidence report. How thick was the rope with the hangman's noose you found there?" she asked Gates.

"As I recall, it was a hemp braided rope, about one inch thick," the detective replied. "There are a few photos of the rope in the file listed as 'Crime Scene.'"

"Ah-huh," said Dakota, enhancing the digital image of the minister on the autopsy table with his throat exposed. She noted two faint bilateral bruises near the right and left carotid arteries. She looked back at the autopsy report under "External Examination - *Evidence of Injuries" and saw that the ME had recorded "Evidence of abrasions and contusions on the neck consistent with a ligature approximately one inch in diameter," but found no mention of the bruising.* That's peculiar, but the ecchymosis is barely noticeable. Let's go internally, she thought.

Dakota next read the section under "Interior Examination - Neck," which read,

The tongue shows no hemorrhage. The hyoid bone, cartilaginous structures of the larynx, and trachea are usually formed without fracture. The airway is clear, lined by smooth, pink-tan mucosa, and contains no foreign material. The neck straps show evidence of minor hemorrhaging on both sides, near the right and left carotid arteries and jugular veins. The cervical spine remains structurally intact.

Dakota switched files on the iPad, went to the folder marked "Crime Scene Photos—Jefferson," and searched the medium-sized photo icons until she found the photos of the rope and hangman's noose beside the minister's body. She enhanced the image, carefully examining the noose and the length of the rope. Then she went back to Gates.

"Other than the hangman's noose, I can see no knots on this rope. Is that your recollection as well?" she asked.

"Yes, why?" asked the curious detective. Wade was engaged with Bill Hurd, but overheard Dakota's question, and turned his attention to her.

"What do you see, Dakota?" Wade asked as he and Bill Hurd drew closer to Dakota.

"Well, I'm just curious by nature," she said, switching electronic folders back to the autopsy photos of Rev. Jefferson, and pointing to the image of the minister's neck exposed externally, then enlarging it.

"See his neck in this photo? I can see two faint, bilateral, circular or oval-shaped contusions over his right and left carotid arteries that appear larger than one inch in diameter," said Dakota.

"Okay," replied Wade.

"Now look at this photo," said Dakota, selecting the photo of the minister's neck dissected and open, exposing the neck straps. Dakota laid the ME's autopsy report next to the image.

"Do you see these slight hemorrhages on both the right and left sides of his neck over his carotid arteries, here, and here? Now look at the autopsy report where Dr. Dyer notes the presence of these hemorrhages," said Dakota.

Gates, Wade, and Hurd looked closely at the photo.

"Well, sure, there are contusions and hemorrhages on his neck. The guy was hung," said Gates.

"Yes, no doubt the minister was hung. However, Gates, if you look again at the external contusions on his neck, they are bilateral and seem to be larger than one inch. You said that the rope was one inch in diameter. If that's true, why would these contusions be bigger than one inch?" asked Dakota.

Wade and the detectives fell silent for a few seconds, deep in thought. "Well, the rope certainly moved up his neck as the killer lifted him off the ground. Couldn't that account for those larger marks?" asked Hurd.

"Perhaps, Bill, but if that were the case, the ligature mark would be uniform and not depressed in those two areas. That's where the bilateral contusions and hemorrhages to the neck straps come from: two separate and distinct depressions.

"Since the rope and noose have no other knots, what made those depressions?" Dakota asked the now perplexed group.

"Just food for thought for the time being, but we're going to need to clear that up," said Dakota, now switching gears and moving on to the files for Rabbi David Abramson.

Dakota pulled out the autopsy report and photos of the Rabbi at the crime scene and on the autopsy table.

"Dr. Dryer has identified the cause of death as poison ingestion. Dakota pulled out the toxicology report, which read, "Traces of thiocyanate were found in the blood, indicating cyanide poisoning."

Dakota spread out the crime scene and autopsy photos, then looked at the detectives. "You see that dried, frothy blood coming from his nostrils and mouth?" she asked. "That's an indication of poison ingestion." "Do you have the statement from the first person who found Rabbi Abramson in his office?"

Bill Hurd rifled through the file and found the interview with the Rabbi's clerk, Hannah. "Here you go," said the detective, handing the supplemental report to Dakota, who scanned it.

"Here, look at this. Hannah states that she opened the door to Rabbi Abramson's office and was immediately greeted with a strong musty smell. Gates, when you and Bill entered the office, did you notice any musty odor?" Dakota asked.

"Not really, but then we weren't there until at least an hour after the homicide was called in," replied Gates.

"No doubt, when Hannah opened the door, the air inside rushed out. The room had time to regain its normal scent by the time you arrived. Did either of you notice anything odd about the exterior or interior of the office that day when you examined the crime scene?" Dakota asked as she placed the crime scene photos before the two detectives.

While Gates and Hurd reviewed the crime scene photos, Dakota returned to reading Hannah's statement.

"Wait, here's something curious. Hannah said that when she went to open the door, there was a white towel on the floor in front of the office door. She moved it well before she opened the door. Find the photos of the office doorway," said Dakota.

Gates picked up the photo of the doorway and handed it to Dakota. "Wait, I saw that white towel off to the open side of the door. Yes, that's the one," she said, pointing to the photo. The foursome studied the photo.

"Does anyone have a copy of the evidence list? I'm looking for that white towel," said Dakota.

Bill Hurd searched through the file until he found the evidence and the property list, which was several pages long. He skimmed his finger down the list until he found the towel.

"Got it, page three, item twenty-two—one medium-sized white cotton cloth towel. Yes, we have it," Hurd replied.

"Good, because you're going to have it tested," said Dakota.

"Tested for what?" asked Gates.

"Hydrogen cyanide, and the Rabbi's clothes tested as well for the same thing," replied Dakota.

"But the toxicology report has already shown us that the Rabbi was poisoned by cyanide. What will more testing accomplish?" asked Gates. Wade sensed Gates's apparent anxiety and wondered where it was coming from.

Wade is right—this girl is a handful. It's almost like she thinks she competes with me. It's best to be patient and teach. But Det. Gates also needs to understand that she's at Level-3 knowledge—she doesn't even realize what she doesn't know, thought Dakota with a pensive smile.

"Well, that's a good question, Gates. How much do you know about European World War II history, specifically what was referred to as Hitler's Final Solution, which was the Holocaust of the Jews?" asked Gates.

"Just that Hitler and the Nazi's hated the Jews and killed several million of them in the death camps," replied Gates.

"Yes, and do you know how the Nazis exterminated those approximately six million Jews?" Dakota asked.

"Yeah, he shot some but gassed most of them," said Gates.

"Correct again. Do you know what type of poison the Nazis used on the Jews in the death camps to kill them?" asked Dakota.

"Not really," replied the detective.

They used a specific type of cyanide gas called Zyklon-B. It was developed in Germany during the 1920s as a pesticide and fumigant for killing lice, bugs, and rodents.

Our medical death investigations and pathology classes show that Zyklon-B, or hydrogen cyanide gas, can be detected on fabric for an extended period. When fabrics are stored correctly, we can test for and find traces of Zyklon-B decades later. This is because the gas can form stable bonds with iron in the fabric, which remain detectable long after the gas has evaporated.

"Seriously, that's amazing. Thanks for the history and medical lessons," Gates replied with a clearly impressed expression.

I'm winning her over, mused Dakota, smiling genuinely at Gates. "Of course, I'm just here to help. It's a team sport," replied Dakota.

That's my gal. Listen, and learn, Gates, thought Wade, noting that the female detective was slowly realizing that she was clearly out of her league with Dr. Dakota Shannon.

"Well, let's say we test the Rabbi's clothing and that white towel, and find out they contain traces of this Zyklon-B hydrogen cyanide gas. Along with a lynched black minister, doesn't that kind of confirm that we are dealing with a Nazi, white supremacist?" asked Hurd.

Before Dakota could answer Det. Hurd's question, Wade interrupted. "Maybe yes, and maybe no. It might point in that direction, but I'd be careful about putting all your eggs in one basket," he warned.

"If you two were running this case, what would be your next step?" Gates asked Wade and Dakota. Dakota spoke first.

"I'd go back to the bodies. You've actually got several crime scenes here. The bodies are separate crime scenes that need to be properly reconciled," said the forensic pathologist.

"Gates, you remember the definition of a crime scene from my class?" asked Wade.

"Sure, any place where evidence can be recovered," replied Gates.

"Exactly. Dakota is trying to tell you that these bodies are repositories of forensic and factual evidence. We need to dig deeper," said Wade.

"We need to head over to the ME's office and re-examine the bodies for evidence that may have been missed the first time," said Dakota.

"And I think we need to go back to the Temple and the Rabbi's apartment to see if we missed anything," Wade said. "How much do you two know about the Jewish faith?"

"Nothing, I'm Christian," replied Gates.

"Me neither, I'm a Catholic," replied Det. Hurd.

Well, that makes three of us; I'm Catholic too. However, I know someone who is an expert in the Jewish faith. His name is Dr. Lyeb Tzabar. He's a professor of religious studies here at the Texas A & M Extension campus. He teaches Hebrew studies in the Department of Global Studies and Cultures, if I remember correctly. Would you mind if I try to call him? I think we'll need his expertise," said Wade.

"Sure, but I'll have to clear any consulting he does with my chief," replied Gates.

"Fair enough," said Wade, looking at Dakota. "How about we conserve some of our consulting time? Dakota, I don't think we need to be together for the next two things that need to be done."

"I suggest that we divide our forces. Bill can take Dakota to the Medical Examiner. Gates and I can head over to the Rabbi's apartment and the Temple to revisit those scenes, but I gotta make a call first," said Wade, picking up his phone and searching his contacts list. He found the name Lyeb Tzabar and pressed the dial button. After a few rings, Wade's call was answered.

"Dr. Lyeb Tzabar," the recipient answered.

"Shalom, Professor. A voice from your past, Wade Justus," Wade replied.

"Shalom, Wade. How are things with the Texas Rangers?" asked the professor.

Well, I'm retired from the Rangers, but I could use your help with something new here in Galveston," Wade replied.

"You're here in Galveston?" Professor Tzabar asked.

"Yes, I'm on vacation for a few days, but I got pulled into a couple of homicide investigations that I am consulting with the Galveston PD on," replied Wade.

"Not those horrible murders of the Baptist minister and Rabbi Abramson. I've been following the news reports. I am a member of Rabbi Abramson's congregation. Of course, Wade. What can I do to help out?" asked Tzabar.

"Well, professor, first, we must agree that everything we discuss, and share will be strictly confidential. The homicide detectives I'm working with would also need special permission from their Chief of Police to clear you as an unpaid consultant if we decide to move forward," explained Wade.

"Certainly, I would never charge for my work. Rabbi Abramson was a friend. His death has sent shock waves through our small community. He was an orthodox Jew, a true practitioner of the Hebrew faith. How can I be of service?" asked Tzabar.

"I was thinking, Professor, that the two homicide detectives and I, who are working on the Rabbi's death investigation, are all Gentiles. The police have searched the Temple where the Rabbi was murdered, as well as his apartment on the Temple grounds. I'm thinking that, as Gentiles, they might have missed something that someone with your knowledge and background would notice.

"If they can get you onboard, we'd like you to join us in researching the Temple and Rabbi Abramson's apartment," Wade explained.

"And when would these searches take place?" asked the professor.

"As soon as the detectives can get their chief to approve you as a consultant. Today would be great if you could manage it," said Wade.

"I don't have a class until later this afternoon, so I can be ready this morning whenever you are. I can meet you at the temple; just let me know when. I'll be coming from campus on Pelican Island," replied Professor Tzabar.

"Great, let me call you back once the detectives get permission, and I'll call you shortly," said Wade, hanging up.

"So, fill us in a little about this professor from Texas A & M," said Gates.

"Sure, I met Professor Lyeb Tzabar about eight years ago when I was assigned to investigate some hate crimes at a couple of Jewish temples in San Antonio. He had been recommended by one of the rabbis there whose temple had been repeatedly vandalized. In working with Tzabar, I learned that we weren't dealing with white supremacists as the local news media had portrayed. The culprits were actually pro-Palestinian, Hamas sympathizers.

Dr. Tzabar knows his stuff, and he's a tough cookie. He's a native-born Israeli and a former IDF commando with Sayeret Matkal, the Israeli Defense Force's most elite counterterrorism unit. Sayeret Matkal is often compared to our U.S. Delta Force or the Brits' SAS. I wouldn't want to tangle with Lyeb. He used to teach hand-to-hand combat. He was actually part of the famous Entebbe raid in Uganda, Africa, back in 1976, where Israeli commandos freed over one hundred Jewish hostages at an airport under the control of then-dictator Idi Amin. He must be close to eighty now.

The professor left Israel after his wife was killed in their kibbutz by a suicide bomber. He studied to become a rabbi, left the IDF, and immigrated to the U.S... He's been teaching religious studies for years. After his retirement, the university offered him a Professor Emeritus position," explained Wade.

"Such personal tragedy," remarked Dakota.

"I think his faith has carried him through a lot. You can imagine the violence he's gone through," replied Wade.

"Well, he sounds like the right guy for the job. I'll get right on the horn to the Chief," said Gates, dialing the chief's office. Following a fifteen-minute briefing to the chief, the team had their Hebrew expert approved.

Dakota looked at Bill Hurd. "It looks like Wade and Gates have got Professor Tzabar engaged. Call the ME and see if we can go over there so I can look at the two bodies for more evidence."

Detective Hurd called Dr. Dyer, the Medical Examiner, and asked if he and their consultant, Dr. Dakota Shannon, could come by so she could examine the two bodies. Dr. Dyer recognized Dakota's name immediately and said he'd be ready whenever they arrived. Hurd told Dr. Dyer they would be there within the next forty minutes.

Wade called Dr. Tzabar back and asked, "You're in, professor. How long will it take you to get to the Temple?"

"I'm less than five miles away. How about I see you in thirty minutes?" replied Tzabar.

Great, we'll meet you at the Temple's front door," Wade replied before hanging up.

"Looks like our morning, and perhaps some of our afternoon, is set. Let's divide up and get going," said Gates.

Dakota and Det. Hurd left for the ME's office in his unmarked vehicle, and Wade drove the RV to the Temple so Desi wouldn't be left alone. Gates called and spoke with the Temple's clerk, Hannah, to arrange access and visitations.

The new Galveston County Medical Examiner's Office was located at 1205 Oak Street in La Marque, about sixteen miles and thirty minutes from Seawall Blvd. Hurd drove along I-45, exiting at FM-1764. The pair pulled into the parking lot and parked in front of the tan brick building with its impressive stainless steel-paneled roof façade. A bronze State of Texas seal with the words, "Galveston County Medical Examiner's Office," decorated a wall in front of the building.

Det. Hurd and Dakota walked up the steps, through the tinted glass, into the stainless steel entryway, and into a foyer. The clerk at the front door recognized Hurd. Once Dakota showed the clerk her ID and signed the visitor's log, they were waved through. They walked down the hallway to the double doors labeled "Pathology." ME Dr. Dyer was waiting for them.

The main autopsy room measured about fifty by forty feet. The walls were bright white tiles, complemented by a light grey sealed cement floor. Twenty square, bright white LED lights illuminated the room well, spaced between stainless steel exhaust and AC/heater vents. The right and left side walls featured continuous banks of stainless steel counters and sinks. Six stainless steel autopsy tables with drains on top of white motorized support modules were positioned next to each sink.

Next to the counters, weighing platforms for human organs hanging from the ceiling were in front of each table. Above each table, also suspended from the ceiling, were movable close-up lights and microphones, enabling the medical examiners to record their pathological findings and write them into reports.

Det. Hurd took the lead, introducing Dakota. "Dr. David Dyer, let me introduce you to our homicide consultant and forensic pathologist, Dr. Dakota Shannon, formerly the Chief ME for Davidson County, Nashville, Tennessee. Dr. Shannon was recently appointed as the Chief ME in Bexar County."

Dr. Dyer stepped forward with a smile and extended his hand to Dakota. "A real honor to meet you, Dr. Shannon. I'm an admirer of your work. In fact, I just finished reading your published articles on *"The Myths of Positional Asphyxia from Prone Restraint,"* and *"The Importance of Toxicological Secondary Scanning Using the Gas Chromatograph Mass Spectrometer to Reconcile Exotic Cannabinoids in Death Cases,"* in the American Journal of Forensic Medicine, and Pathology. Interesting findings and opinions that I completely agree with," said Dr. Dyer, shaking Dakota's hand.

"My word, meeting someone who reads my articles is gratifying. Please call me Dakota," replied Dakota, returning Dr. Dyer's handshake.

"Certainly, if you will call me David," replied the ME. "I've got Rev. Jefferson and Rabbi Abramson ready for you on tables two and three. Who would you like to start with?" the physician asked.

"I've had a chance to briefly review your autopsy and toxicology reports on both victims, along with the crime scene and autopsy photos. Since the reverend was the first victim, let's start with him," replied Dakota. The trio walked to table two, and Dakota noticed the suspended microphone above the table.

"David, could we record our session so that we won't be distracted by notetaking?" Dakota asked.

"Certainly," replied Dr. Dyer, activating the mic. For convenience, Rev. Jefferson's body had been removed from its zippered body bag and lay naked on the autopsy table beneath a white sheet. The ME lifted the sheet from the body as Dakota stepped forward and pulled down the flexible light. Dakota brought Det—Hurd forward, carrying copies of the autopsy reports with photos.

"Bill, can you pull the exterior and interior examination photos of the reverend's neck so I can point something out to David?" Dakota asked. Hurd produced the photos and held them up so Dakota and Dr. Dyer could view them. Dakota pointed to the images as she addressed the ME.

"One of the things that stood out to me in these exterior and interior examination photos was the presence of what appeared to be bilateral contusions near the right and left carotid arteries on the outside. They seem to be well over one inch in diameter. You can also see the amount of external pressure or force applied against the neck, which explains the hemorrhaging observed bilaterally over the neck straps. Do you see it?" Dakota asked Dr. Dyer.

"Yes, it definitely appears so," replied the ME.

"Did you have a chance to review the crime scene photos of the body and the rope used to hang the victim?" asked Dakota.

"Actually, no. The attending detectives informed me that the first responding officers found Rev. Jefferson suspended off the floor—hanging from a rope. I asked Dets. Sullivan and Hurd heard what kind of rope it was and were told it was hemp. I don't recall if the diameter of the rope was mentioned or if I asked about it at the time. It appeared to be a classic hanging; ligature strangulation causing hypoxia—the lack of oxygenated blood to the brain, as I wrote in my report," the ME replied.

"Well, I'm thinking of something additional here," said Dakota.

"Like what? I'm no ME, so can you explain where you're going here if it's pertinent to our case?" asked Det. Hurd.

"Do you mind, David? This is your house," said Dakota, seeking permission.

"By all means, Dakota. I'm intrigued, as well as our detective friend here," replied Dr. Dyer. Dakota pointed to the victim's neck and throat.

"Okay, Bill. In a ligature hanging or strangulation, the ligature presses on the trachea and larynx, here, narrowing or completely blocking the airway. This prevents oxygen from reaching the lungs, stopping gas exchange. Within seconds, blood oxygen levels start to fall.

"But now, look at the ecchymosis or contusions right over the areas of the carotid arteries in exterior examination photos, the day after our victim was found deceased. Compression of the carotid arteries, which, as you know, bring oxygenated blood to the brain, and the jugular veins, which drain blood from the brain, disrupts circulation.

"Not to get too technical, but arterial compression blocks oxygen from reaching the brain tissue. Venus compression causes blood to back up. This raises intracranial pressure, which makes oxygen deprivation worse. Follow me so far?" Dakota asked.

"Yes, I'm with you," replied Hurd.

"Great. As Dr. Dyer knows, pressure on the carotid sinus in the artery walls can trigger the vagus nerve, slowing the heart rate or even causing cardiac arrest," explained Dakota.

"So what are you trying to say?" asked the detective.

"I don't think that Reverend Jefferson was murdered by ligature hanging. I think he was already dead. Yes, there is no doubt that he was, in fact, strangled to death by a ligature. But from my military physician experience, and my association with Special Forces operators, I think the actual murder weapon was a knotted garrote. I think the hanging was staged for effect," explained Dakota.

Dr. Dyer was smiling. "Well, that would certainly match the bilateral contusions over his carotid arteries and the corresponding bilateral hemorrhages on his neck straps. Nicely played, Dakota," offered the ME.

"So, to clarify for my report, you believe that our killer strangled the minister to death with some military garrote, then hung the noose around his neck and suspended him above his podium so we would think he was lynched, correct?" asked Hurd for clarification.

Nothing's one hundred percent, but that is my forensic medical opinion. It reconciles the injuries to the reverend's neck and throat. We also know it's not a drop hanging, or Dr. Dyer would have seen fractures to the hyoid bone. There is no such fracture," said Dakota.

"True enough," remarked the ME.

Bill Hurd was diligently taking notes in his notepad. "Doc, can you ensure I get a copy of the recorded transcript with Dr. Shannon's observations and medical opinion here? I don't want to miss anything," requested the detective.

Dakota turned to Dr. Dyer. "David, that's pretty much all I have for the reverend. Can we proceed to Rabbi Abramson?"

"Sure thing, right over here," replied the ME, stepping over to Table 3 and uncovering the Rabbi.

Dakota turned to Det. Hurd. "Bill, can you pass me Dr. Dyer's toxicology report?" she asked. The detective pulled the document out of the file and handed it to Dakota.

"So, David, I see that you've got the COD – Cause of Death as cyanide poisoning," she said.

"Yes, we found some minor traces of thiocyanate in the victim's blood, but this was challenging because we estimated the Rabbi's death had happened about thirty-six hours before the clerk found him dead in his office. I didn't get to perform his autopsy for another twenty-four hours after that. However, I ensured that we properly preserved his blood, lung tissue, gastric contents, and some organs in case a more detailed analysis was needed," replied the ME.

"Wonderful, because that's exactly what I like you to do," said Dakota.

"What are you thinking, doctor?" asked the inquisitive ME.

"Well, David, the Rabbi's clerk, I believe that her name is Hannah, told the first responding officers that when she opened the door to the Rabbi's office, there was a white towel in front of the door. She found that odd. When she opened the door, she immediately detected a strong musty odor, which she felt was odd; the Rabbi's room was well ventilated and had never smelled musty before.

"Next, we've both noted the presence of dried frothy blood coming from his nose and mouth," said Dakota, holding the crime scene and autopsy photos in front of Dr. Dyer. Both are clues of cyanide gas poisoning," said Dakota.

"Yes, of course, and my preliminary tox did show the presence of cyanide," replied the ME.

"I know, David, but in this case, since our victim is an Orthodox Jewish rabbi, I want this white towel, the rabbi's clothes, and everything you've preserved tested for the presence of a specific type of hydrogen cyanide – Zyklon-B. If you can access a gas chromatograph mass spectrometer, the GMS will detect its presence," explained Dakota.

"If we already know our victim was poisoned by cyanide, why would a final determination of Zyklon-B be important?" Dr. Dyer asked.

Because I believe Rabbi Abramson wasn't just poisoned with cyanide, I think he was gassed. The white towel in front of the office door, the clerk smelling a strong musty odor, Abramson being secured to his office door, and the fact that he was a Jew all point to this. Zyklon-B was the type of hydrogen cyanide gas the Nazis used to murder over six million Jews during World War II systematically. It was central to Hitler's plan to exterminate the Jews and other undesirables in what he called his "Final Solution," explained Dakota.

"Well, I can see you know your European history, Dakota," replied the ME.

"David, think this through for a moment. We have a black Baptist minister supposedly lynched and an Orthodox Jewish Rabbi gassed. Don't the clues point us toward a white supremacist as our suspect?" offered Dakota.

"Well, yes. I see your point," replied the ME.

"And that's what troubles me. It's too in your face and too easy for me. That's why I'm not so sure," said Dakota.

"But why not? A lot of killers aren't rocket scientists. It could certainly be some whack job Nazi, a KKK wannabe, or a white supremacist," replied Det. Hurd.

I'm not dismissing the idea. This is more Wade's area, not mine, so I'll let him handle it. I'm just sharing my own humble theory. I wouldn't be surprised if someone's intentionally trying to throw you guys off course," said Dakota.

"Observations, and opinion noted, Dr. Shannon," said Hurd, furiously writing in his notepad.

"Well, David, I think my work is done here. Can you let the homicide detectives and me know when you get the GMS test results back?" asked Dakota as she handed Dr. Dyer her cell number.

"I'll pull out all the stops with the state lab. I know these are high-profile cases. I watch the news," replied the ME.

"Much obliged, doc," said Bill Hurd, shaking the ME's hand.

"Same here, David. Thanks for the opportunity," Dakota replied, shaking Dr. Dyer's hand.

"It was really nice seeing you at work, Dakota. Like I said, I'm a big fan. I'll call you as soon as I know anything," said Dr. Dyer.

Detective Hurd and Dakota left the Medical Examiner's Office and returned to the detective's unmarked car.

"Can you give a gal a lift back to town?" Dakota asked.

"Sure thing. I wonder how Gates and Wade are doing with their Hebrew expert at the Temple. How about we call them? If they're still there, we can meet up with them over there," Hurd said as he grabbed his cellphone and called Gates Sullivan.

Gates told Hurd that they had finished searching the temple and the rabbi's office, found nothing of note, and were heading to the rabbi's apartment.

"We're twenty minutes out. We'll meet you there," said Hurd.

Bill Hurd and Dakota pulled up in front of the Old Congregational B'nai Israel at the northwest corner of 22nd Street and Sealy Avenue. In the historic Midtown neighborhood, Dakota saw several churches of different denominations. She looked across the street at another church.

"There sure are a lot of churches in this neighborhood," remarked Dakota.

"This is the city's historic church district. You'll find several churches of different denominations within just a few blocks," replied Hurd.

Dakota pointed across the street. "What's that one over there?" she asked.

"That's the First Southern Baptist Church. Our first victim, Rev. Jacob Jefferson, was the pastor," replied the detective.

"That's a bit coincidental. Eerie, don't you think?" remarked Dakota.

"I really hadn't thought of it," said Hurd as he and Dakota exited the car.

"The Rabbi's apartment is around back. He lived alone," Hurd said.

Detective Hurd and Dakota found Wade, Gates Sullivan, and Professor Tzabar standing outside the Rabbi's apartment. A yellow notice reading, "CRIME SCENE," was taped on the front door, and crime scene tape sealed the door to keep unauthorized people out.

Wade introduced Dakota and Bill Hurd to Professor Tzabar. "Please call me Lyeb. The professor's title is just for students. We are all professionals here. Did Wade mention that I was in the service back in Israel?" Lyeb asked.

"As a matter of fact, I did mention it," replied Wade.

"Then you'll appreciate that, as a Jew who has fought against terrorism, I'm fully committed to helping you in any way I can. What happened to my dear friend Rabbi Abramson is the work of a Godless animal. What kind of animal predator can I help you resolve?" offered Lyeb.

"Again, Lyeb, your offer to work with us is greatly appreciated. Shall we?" said Gates, using a pocket knife to cut through the crime scene seals on the door and unlocking it.

The foursome entered the Rabbi's spotless apartment. Gates, who was holding what homicide detectives refer to as the "Murder Book," or case file, allowed Lyeb to walk freely around the premises. Lyeb walked into the small dining room and stopped to examine the dining room table, which displayed two partially burned candles, a two-handed pitcher of water with a matching bowl, a bottle of wine, and a loaf of now stale bread.

Lyeb pointed to the items on the table. "Ah, Rabbi Abramson had prepared for Shabbat Friday. I'm just checking, but I'm assuming you are Gentiles, correct?" he asked. The three nodded affirmatively.

"So let the lesson in Hebrew 101 begin," Lyeb said, smiling.

"As Jews, our weekly day of rest and sanctification is Saturday, which we call Shabbat. The Friday evening before Kavod Shabbat, or simply "Shabbat," marks the start. Just before sundown, Jews prepare by participating in this religious ritual. Friday begins with cleaning the house and setting out flowers to beautify it. Knowing that Rabbi Abramson was a widower, I'm not surprised we see no flowers in the apartment.

"The word 'Shabbat' comes from Hebrew and means 'cease' or 'rest.' The ritual commemorates both creation and the Jews' exodus from Egypt.

"See these two partially burned candles? The ritual begins with lighting the candles. Songs are usually sung before lighting them. Traditionally, eighteen minutes before sunset, the house woman will light the candles that symbolize the commands to remember and observe Shabbat. In this case, these candles would have been lit by Rabbi Abramson. With eyes covered, a short blessing is recited," he explained, then pointed to the bottle of wine and the loaf of bread.

"At the dinner table, two key blessings are recited. First is the "Kiddush," which is said over the wine. This blessing sanctifies the day, and the wine is sipped as it is recited. The water pitcher and bowl are used for the "Netilat Yada'yim," or washing hands. The hands are washed before saying the second blessing, called the "Hamotzi." The loaf of braided bread, known as the "challah," is covered during the first blessing to keep everything in order. The Hamotzi is said over the challah, which recalls Temple sacrifices," explained Lyeb.

"Very interesting, Lyeb. Our people found no forced entry into the Rabbi's apartment, and nothing appears to have been stolen in a robbery or burglary. So, does anything look out of place as far as you can tell?" asked Gates.

Lyeb examined the dining area again, paying close attention to every detail. "Can I see the photos taken of this room?" he asked. Gates placed the Murder Book on the table and flipped through the photos. She found the images and showed the pages to Lyeb, who carefully compared them to the scene.

"May I see the photos of his office, including how his clerk discovered him?" he asked. Gates flipped through a few more pages and showed the photos he requested. The Hebrew expert was lost in thought for a few minutes before speaking.

"After seeing David's apartment and already visiting the Temple and his office, I realized I might have missed something at the Temple. Before I answer your question, I'd like to see David's office again. Would that be okay?" asked Lyeb.

"Of course. If we are finished here, we'll head right over," replied Gates. Lyeb said he was done with the apartment, and the four of them headed back to the Temple.

Once inside the Temple, Lyeb went straight to Rabbi Abramson's office and looked down at his desk. He asked Gates for the Murder Book again so he could re-examine the crime scene photos, including those of the Rabbi restrained in his chair. Lyeb pointed to the Tanakh on the desk.

"Do you know whether anyone from your team touched the Rabbi's Tanakh?" he asked the homicide detectives.

"I don't believe so, but I can check with our CSI supervisor, Det. Spazzito," Gates replied.

"Yes, please do, and I'll explain where I'm going with this," Lyeb replied. Gates immediately contacted the CSI supervisor to confirm that no photos were being taken of the items on the Rabbi's desk, and none of his technicians had touched the Tanakh.

"Splendid," replied Lyeb, studying the open pages in the Tanakh and quietly pondering how he would explain his theory to the investigators. After a few moments, he spoke.

"This large book is what we Jews refer to as a Tanakh. For you Christians, it would be the Jewish Bible. The Tanakh includes the Torah (Law), Nevi'im (Prophets), and Ketuvim (Writings). It is a sacred text in Judaism. It includes the Instruction from God. Do you follow me so far?" the Hebrew scholar asked.

"Yes, somewhat like our Bible," said Wade.

"Exactly. So, unlike the Christian religion, where priests and ministers deliver their sermons on Sunday, in Judaism, the main weekly sermon, called a "derasha," is usually given by the Rabbi during Shabbat services on Saturday morning, after the Torah reading, and before the Musaf prayer.

"Son, in my opinion, the most logical time and place for Rabbi Abramson to have prepared his sermon by finding an appropriate passage in the Tanakh would have been at his apartment, not in his office. Before he came here, we knew he had already completed the ritual Shabbat Friday, so why would his Tanakh be here?" Lyeb asked the trio.

"I don't know, Lyeb," replied Gates.

"Me neither," said Det. Hurd.

Wade was quick on the uptake. “Are you thinking that Rabbi Abramson forgot his Tanakh and came over here to retrieve it when he was attacked?” offered Wade.

“That’s certainly a possibility, but there is something far more ominous I’m going to suggest to you all,” said Lyeb.

“Like what?” asked Gates.

Lyeb examined the murder book, opening it to a photo of the Rabbi restrained in his chair. “Do you see that his pants are belted, but his zipper is pulled down? Isn’t that the one thing that doesn’t fit for any man of the cloth, especially an Orthodox Jewish Rabbi?” he asked. The foursome was silent as they looked at the photo.

Lyeb next pointed to a passage in one of the open pages of the Tanakh. “I’ll admit that this is a bit deep, and I may be reaching here, but hear me out. This passage comes from Genesis or Bereishis, 34 1-31, and discusses Dinah, the daughter of Jacob, and Leah. Dinah, the daughter of Jacob, and Leah was an outgoing young woman who went out to “look over the daughters of the land,” and was seen by Shechem, son of a Canaanite Prince Hamor. In doing so, Dinah’s actions conflicted with the Jewish code of modesty.

“Shechem was an Amorite, an Aramaic word for “serpent,” which explains his treacherous behavior as the son of a Hivite prince named Hamor. When he saw Dinah, Shechem forced himself on her, and she resisted; however, no one came to her aid because Shechem’s father Hamor was a prince," explained Lyeb.

“Sorry, professor, but you’ve lost me,” said Hurd.

"I'm not tracking either, Lyeb. Can you break this down for us Gentiles?" asked Gates.

"Certainly. I apologize; the Hebrew professor in me is sneaking out. What I'm suggesting here is that this passage refers to a violent crime committed against a daughter of Israel by a member of royalty. If you change the word "royalty" to "clergy," there may be some similarity here between your perpetrator feeling violated by trusted people, i.e., priests, just as Dinah, who naively believed she was a guest in a foreign land, and the daughter of a holy man, Jacob, and could not become a victim," explained Lyeb.

Wade noticed that the lights were beginning to flicker on in the detectives' minds, and his own mind was racing as he pieced together what the expert in Jewish religion and culture was suggesting.

"Lyeb, are you suggesting that our perp isn't a white supremacist and that this might be some kind of revenge killing?" the retired Texas Ranger asked.

"Look, everyone, as I see it, my job here is to interpret this crime scene to see if it has anything to do with an Orthodox Jewish Rabbi being murdered. I've read the newspapers and watched the news reports on TV. I think that the murders of the black Baptist minister and my friend Rabbi David Abramson, and the manner in which both were slain, are canards. The clues are too in-your-face and easy to follow," he said when Det. Hurd interrupted him.

"A canard? What's that?" the detective asked.

"A false or misleading story, Bill; a hoax," replied Lyeb.

"Copy, sorry for interrupting. Please continue," said Hurd. Everyone was listening intently as Lyeb went on.

"Notice that David's zipper is down, but there's no other sign he's been sexually violated or physically harmed. However, he was murdered. The same goes for the black minister, correct?" asked Lyeb.

"Correct, go on, Lyeb," said the enthralled Gates.

"On the way here, you told me you had interviewed a person of interest—someone from whom you received an anonymous tip, who believed the man was possibly a white supremacist. I think that's exactly the misdirection—the canard—that the real killer wanted you to fall for," Lyeb explained.

"So what do you think the right direction is? What's the profile we should be considering?" asked Gates.

"The Rabbi's zipper down, the open passage in Genesis referring to the rape of Dinah. I think your killer is a person who has a history of being sexually abused by a priest or other member of the clergy. By the way, I will tell you that when Dinah's father Jacob discovered that she had been raped, he went out and put Hamor and all of his family to the sword," said Lyeb.

"Jesus. Are you telling us that we might see more members of our clergy here being murdered?" exclaimed the incredulous Hurd.

"Look, everyone, this is only my speculative theory based on a couple of pieces of the evidence puzzle with many pieces. Someone else equally learned might see things completely different than me," replied Lyeb, trying to assuage the impressionable detective.

"Well, it's definitely something we all need to think about. Your theory has merit. That's why I asked you to help us out," said Wade.

Gates chimed in. "I agree. We can't afford to be led astray if you're right. Your advice and consultation are much appreciated, Lyeb. But your analysis brings us back to the drawing board."

Wade's experience compelled him to speak with restraint and encouragement. "Gates, and Bill. I don't see this as a setback. I see Lyeb's work here as a real chance to learn more about who we are dealing with as suspects. He's definitely opened our eyes to other possibilities. As always, we follow the evidence, no matter where it leads us, right?"

"Agreed," replied Gates and Hurd in unison.

Chapter 11
Reliving the Past

Bradford D'Ablo Natas woke up startled from another one of the seemingly endless nightmares that had haunted him since childhood. His trembling hand reached for the tumbler of ice water on his bed. Even though it was a cool spring evening in Galveston, he was sweating heavily, and his breathing was over twenty per minute. He looked up at the ceiling, where his clock displayed the time; it read 02:22 a.m.

Bradford wiped the tears from his eyes caused by tonight's emotionally traumatic experience as he consciously slowed his breathing, which in turn lowered his racing heart. Tonight's nightmare had lasted longer than most, perhaps triggered by his horrible activities over the past two weeks.

In his dream, Bradford was a ten-year-old fifth grader and a new altar boy attending Saint Margaret of Perpetual Faith Catholic Church in San Francisco. St. Margaret's had an attached parochial school operated by the Jesuits for grades K through 8. The parish also had a rectory for the priests and brothers and a convent for the Jesuit Sisters of Perpetual Faith, who taught at the school.

The Jesuits were what Catholics called a "more conservative" order of priests in Catholicism. As any Catholic who attended a Jesuit parochial school as a child knew, the nuns were strict disciplinarians who were quick to use the ruler at the first sign of disobedience or any lack of focus on studies.

Bradford's parents were hardworking, devoted Roman Catholics from the working class who sacrificed to ensure their only son could attend St. Margaret's. Bradford's father drove a trolley for SF Muni, and his mother worked as an assistant librarian at nearby St. Ignatius "SI" High School. The combination of weekly donations and the mother's connections at SI had helped secure Bradford's acceptance into St. Margaret's. His proud parents saw Bradford's "elevation" to altar boy as a crucial step in their plan to get their son into the transitional Catholic high school at SI.

Father Charles Fogarty had taken a personal interest in Bradford during daily catechism classes and weekly confessions. The young priest's encouragement and mentoring had worked, and Bradford was offered the position of an altar boy.

Initially, Bradford was happy and proud to advance through tough competition to become a new altar boy. He studied hard to recite most of the Mass in Latin and to help the parish priests perform various religious rituals in the Catholic church. He also appreciated that Father Fogarty was spending extra time with him after school in the church and increasingly in the rectory, helping him understand and assist priests with the religious rituals.

However, after several months, Bradford began to feel uneasy with Father Fogarty's physical contact. The touching of his hair and skin, along with arm and leg massages, gradually turned into unwelcome back rubs. Small gifts and special privileges followed these initial touches. "Let these presents be our little secret," said the priest. Bradford agreed, keeping their secret because he did not want to upset his parents by telling them what was happening with Father

Fogarty. After all, being an altar boy in their parish was a special privilege.

Father Fogarty approached him after school, the day after Bradford turned twelve, with a smile and a warm handshake. "I heard it was your birthday yesterday. Follow me to my office in the church. I have something very special for you," said the priest.

Once inside Father Fogarty's private office, he closed and locked the door. Then he congratulated Bradford and gave him a gold-colored Timex wristwatch with a brown leather band. "You are growing older, and older boys get special presents," said the priest, smiling. Bradford was impressed and very happy with the gift. It was definitely something his parents wouldn't have thought to give him for his birthday. But Bradford soon learned that there was a price to pay for such a gift.

"Come over here, sit with me on the couch, and tell me about your birthday," said the priest. Bradford told Father Fogarty about his day, the new basketball he had received from his father, and the birthday cake baked by his mother.

The priest moved closer to the boy. "Now that you are older, you can keep more important secrets. At the end of this school year, you will graduate from St. Margaret and head to high school. Your folks tell me they hope you can attend St. Ignatius High. Is that something you would like to do?"

"Well, I have some influence there. The Principal, Father Volante, is a friend of mine. I'm confident I can arrange for you to be accepted into SI. Is that something you would like me to do for you?" Father Fogarty asked Bradford.

"Yes, Father, very much. My folks are trying hard to get me into SI but are worried about so much competition..." Bradford's voice trailed off as the priest slowly placed his hand between the boy's legs and began to rub his inner thigh.

"Well then, there is something we can do for each other that no one needs to know about. I can get you into St. Ignatius, and you can do something for me," Father Fogarty whispered as he slowly unbuttoned and unzipped Bradford's trousers and placed his warm hand into the boy's white jockey briefs, and onto his penis. Bradford shuttered and froze in hypervigilance, not knowing what to do.

"I like you a lot, Bradford, and I think you like me too," said the priest as he began to caress the young boy's small penis, which became erect. "For now, you don't need to do anything to me, but there is something I want to do with you. Unbuckle your trousers and let me see what you have down there," said the priest. Bradford remained frozen, scared out of his mind. Father Fogarty knew he had complete control over the young boy who hadn't screamed or pulled away.

Bradford is the perfect boy to be groomed. He wants to go to St. Ignatius so severely that he'll never resist or tell his parents. He's the ideal partner for what I need, thought Father Fogarty.

"I promise that I won't hurt you, son. In fact, this is all part of growing up. You'll soon see," said the priest as he unbuckled Bradford's trousers and pulled the boy's pants and briefs down to his knees. Father Fogarty began caressing and stroking the boy's penis until it became erect again. Bradford stiffened up and closed his eyes, trying to make this bad dream go away, but the priest's molestation continued. Father Fogarty leaned over to Bradford's crotch, placed the boy's penis into his mouth, and tongued it as the hapless boy gasped in fright.

Father Fogarty's sexual assaults of Bradford continued into his first two years of high school. Bradford silently endured the assaults until his sophomore year at St. Ignatius, when the priest introduced him to SI teacher Brother Boyd Chester. That year, the priest and the brother took turns sexually assaulting the teen.

Then one day, San Francisco Police Inspectors John McKenna and Robert Mells stopped Bradford outside the high school while he was waiting for a Muni bus to take him back to his neighborhood. The detectives were very discreet. They told him that they were building cases against Father Fogerty and Brother Chester on multiple counts of long-term child molestation and sexual assaults of other Catholic boys in the parish. They asked for his cooperation before speaking to his parents about their knowledge of the cleric's horrific activities.

"Is anyone else cooperating?" asked the embarrassed and frightened teen.

"Not yet. We had hoped you would be the first," the lead detective replied.

"I don't want you talking to my folks. It would kill them," replied Bradford.

"So you admit that you have been one of Father Fogerty and Brother Chester's victims," asked the detective.

"My life and my relationship with my parents would be ruined if I cooperated with you. So no, I won't cooperate," replied Bradford.

"How will you find justice? How will you find peace?" asked the partner detective. The boy was nearly brought to tears and thought for a few minutes before responding.

I'll have to walk a dangerous, thin line with these detectives. My own form of justice would come later, thought Bradford.

"I won't cooperate with you, but I will help you if you agree not to involve my parents," said Bradford.

"How can you...how can *we* do that? The juvenile laws clearly state that we must tell your parents if we interview you," said the lead detective.

Bradford's terrible experiences had matured him beyond his years. He had already researched the juvenile and sexual assault laws and court rulings in California. He knew exactly how to handle this. He had done so thousands of times during sleepless nights.

"Well, the trick is that you will not 'interview' me. I will tell you what they have been doing to me, and how to get these evil men. It may not be your way of legal justice, but it will save kids from here who have been molested and raped, and I get to live my life without fear. That's the deal, take it or leave it," replied Bradford with finality.

The two detectives looked at each other. They saw the serious expression on the boy's face and knew that at least with him, this was the best offer they would get.

"Can we give you a ride somewhere?" the lead detective asked.

“Yes, let’s get out of here. Meet me at the end of the street and pick me up. There’s a park near my house where we can talk, and then I can walk home from there,” replied Bradford.

Over the course of an hour at the park, while the detectives took written notes, Bradford filled them in on the entire disturbing story of his forced sexual relationships with Father Fogarty and Brother Chester, from his days at St. Margaret’s to the present at St. Ignatius High School. The detectives’ faces remained grim throughout Bradford’s nauseating descriptions.

Bradford explained to the detectives how the priest initially groomed him as a naive, scared ten-year-old boy during his sophomore year at SI. He also shared details about the pair's methods of operation and what evidence might be found in Father Fogarty’s private office at St. Margaret Church.

“Will you at least allow us to make a recommendation on a sexual abuse counselor, perhaps a psychologist to help you through this?” offered the lead detective.

“What would be the point? I know the juvenile laws; there is mandated reporting to the police. That’s who you are, so that we would have come full circle. Again, sooner or later, my parents would find out. Thanks, but no thanks, detectives,” replied the cynical teen.

“Then what can we do for you?” asked the partner.

“You can do your jobs. Find other victims who are willing to cooperate. I wish I could help you with that, but I don’t know anyone they molested and raped but me. Just get hold of me when it’s all done, tell me what happened, and promise you will get them out of San Francisco. San Quentin Prison would be best," replied Bradford as he stared down the detectives with piercing dark eyes.

"We'll do our very best. No matter what, I can promise that you and the other kids will never be bothered by Father Fogarty and Brother Chester again," said the lead detective.

"That would be a start. Thanks," said Bradford, shaking the detectives and walking home.

Three weeks later, Father Fogarty and Brother Chester suddenly left St. Ignatius Loyola parish and the City of San Francisco. No one seemed to know where they disappeared to. Bradford checked the daily newspapers and listened carefully to his parents' conversations when Father Fogarty's name was mentioned. The clerics' disappearance was a mystery.

Chapter 12
Rebirth Into Darkness

Bradford graduated from St. Ignatius of Loyola High School. However, to his parents' disappointment, he chose not to attend one of the many Catholic colleges and universities nationwide, even though his grades were good.

Even more surprising to his parents, Bradford stopped attending mass and completely distanced himself from the Catholic church. His parents believed this was a phase many young people experience and never discussed the subject with him.

Bradford became more elusive and withdrawn from his Catholic parents. He worked at various odd jobs across the city. According to his parents, he had no male or female friends. By the time Bradford turned twenty, he had moved out of his parents' house and lived independently.

By chance, in the late 1990s, Bradford met Anton Szandor LaVey, a former lion tamer and police photographer who identified himself as the "High Priest of the Church of Satan" in the city. LaVey invited the isolated and impressionable Bradford to a Black Mass at LaVey's Victorian "Black House" on California Street, which served as the headquarters of the Church of Satan.

Bradford was sold after attending the Black Mass and listening to LaVey preach against the hypocrisy of the Catholic Church and its priests. The shaved-head, articulate, and animated LaVey was happy to take Bradford under his wing as a new apprentice. Within two years of loyal apprenticeship, LaVey anointed Bradford as a priest in the Church of Satan. That year, Bradford officially changed his name from Bradford Ciarelli to Bradford D'Ablo Natas, "D'Ablo," a play on the word "devil," and "Natas" for Satan spelled backwards.

When LaVey died, and the Black House was sold and torn down, Bradford started his own Church of Satan in the city with his own small congregation of Satanic followers.

Bradford's strong belief in the power of Satan somewhat eased the heavy emotional and sexual trauma he endured as a youth at the hands of Father Fogarty and Brother Chester. However, he occasionally checked the newspapers for any news about what had happened to the two clerics. Years later, a story appeared in the San Francisco Chronicle about a significant class action lawsuit against the San Francisco Catholic Diocese filed by male child victims of sexual assault.

Bradford could look up the histories of Father Fogarty and Brother Boyd Chester using the Internet and public records websites. Seven years earlier, Bradford had discovered that both clerics had been quickly transferred out of the SF Diocese. He had followed Brother Chester to a small Catholic church, Nuestra Señora del Desierto, "Our Lady of the Desert," in Pueblo, New Mexico. Pueblo was a small, poor border town in the south populated by legal and illegal aliens. Father Fogarty proved to be more challenging to find. It would take several more years to locate him.

Bradford rented a car and drove out to Pueblo. He shadowed Brother Chester for several days to learn his routine. One afternoon, Chester appeared in plain clothes from the church's small rectory. Bradford followed him to a nearby playground, watching him interact with small Hispanic children. *The leopard doesn't change its spots. Yet more future victims to be groomed,* Bradford thought angrily.

That Saturday evening, Bradford followed Brother Chester to the church where the parish priest took confessions. After the priest and the parishioners left, the priest told Brother Chester to lock up the church. Bradford had brought a walking stick and a backpack containing his "kit," the items he needed to carry out his own form of justice on the cleric.

Just before the priest finished confessions, Bradford concealed himself in the church restroom and waited for his chance to find Brother Chester alone.

When the moment arrived, a gloved Bradford, dressed entirely in black and wearing a devil's mask with horns, sneaked up behind Brother Chester and pressed a chloroform-soaked washrag against his mouth and nose. The cleric tried to resist the attack, but Bradford kicked Brother Chester's legs out from under him, brought him to the floor, and held him tightly until Chester lost consciousness.

Bradford reached into his backpack and pulled a thirty-foot, one-inch braided hemp rope. He rolled Chester onto his stomach, then quickly tied one end of the rope around his ankles. Bradford stretched Chester's arms and tied them behind his back to his wooden walking stick. Afterwards, he threw the rope over a thick wooden support beam and hoisted the cleric up so he was six feet off the floor before the altar.

Bradford was far from finished with Brother Chester. He pulled a sharp four-inch Buck knife from his pocket and carved a pentagram into Chester's forehead while the Brother hung upside down. The pain from the deep cuts woke Chester up. His eyes, now wide with surprise and pure terror, looked at Bradford, who was dressed as the devil, and he screamed out.

Bradford laughed, reached into his backpack, grabbed a mason jar of gasoline, and then returned to the suspended Catholic Brother.

“Go ahead and scream all you want. No one will hear you. The church is two blocks from any residence, and all nearby businesses are closed for the weekend. Don’t you remember me, Brother Chester?” Bradford smirked.

"Who... My God, who *are* you? If it’s money you want, Father Samuel is the only one who has control of the safe and its combination. I have nothing, and our modest church has nothing of value,” said Brother Chester.

“Money is the last thing I want from you, Brother Chester, formerly of Our Lady of Perpetual Faith. I’ll tell you what I want, Chester... I am Satan, and I want your evil soul,” replied Bradford, laughing out loud.

Brother Chester looked completely perplexed. Bradford grabbed the cleric's hair and slapped him hard across the face. Then he pulled the suspended Brother’s head toward his, just inches away.

“Look at me, you evil fuck! You really don’t remember, do you? I’m one of the many little boys and young teens you and Father Fogarty raped day after day after day. We were your sex toys...objects really to be used for your sexual pleasure, and then discarded...thrown out with the trash,” said Bradford with anger in his voice.

I'm Bradford Ciarelli. I used to be an altar boy and later a student at SI. Look at me!" exclaimed Bradford as he slapped the Brother again and tore off his devil mask.

Bradford could see the light in Brother Chester's mind as he finally recognized his former victim.

"Please... please, Bradford. That was a long time ago... I was a sick man. It was Fogarty... Father Fogarty, who led me astray. I never wanted to hurt any of you. Please don't hurt me... please!" exclaimed Chester, who was now frightened.

Bradford would hear none of it. He had watched Chester interact with the small migrant boys in the park. "There is only one way that you can make penance for your sins. The fires of Hell must absolve you. But first, I want something from you," exclaimed the Satanist as he approached Chester with the mason jar of gasoline.

Bradford slowly removed the lid from the jar of yellow liquid and laid the jar down on the floor in front of the cleric. Then he opened the blade of the Buck knife and held it in his right hand as he cut open the crotch of Brother Chester's trousers. Bradford cut through the cleric's underwear and removed his penis with his left hand. He stretched out the penis and then severed it with the razor-sharp blade in his right hand.

Brother Chester screamed like a wounded banshee. Blood squirted out, and down the Brother's black dress shirt, onto his face, and into his eyes, and mouth. The cleric groaned loudly. Bradford snapped the blade of the knife shut, put it away with his right hand, and grabbed Chester by the hair, shoving the man's severed penis in front of his eyes.

"Why... why...?" muttered the Brother, now weak from blood loss.

"Confess your sins now before you experience absolution by the fires of perdition, and you meet Satan!" exclaimed Bradford as he picked up the mason jar and poured its contents onto Brother Chester's crotch, down his shirt, and onto his head and face.

"My God...forgive me...please...I'm sorry. I'm sorry for what I did to you. Don't do this," pleaded the Brother.

"You took my childhood from me. You took my innocence from me. You took my life from me. Now it's your turn!" shouted Bradford as he set his tormentor ablaze. Bradford then stepped back to watch Brother Chester, now being simultaneously crucified and burned, slowly hanging from the rope. Chester screamed in agony for several seconds until the petrochemical flames consumed his face.

As the pedophile cleric burned brightly like a torch, Bradford casually picked up the mason jar, its lid, and his devil's mask and carefully stowed them in his backpack. Then the Satanic priest nonchalantly walked out of the church and into the deserted streets of Pueblo, disappearing into the darkness.

Two years before the Galveston clergy murders, Bradford D'Ablo Natas finally tracked down Father Charles Fogarty. Bradford learned that the pedophile priest had been transferred from the Archdiocese of San Francisco to the Metropolitan Archdiocese of Galveston's Parish of the Holy Family. The wicked priest had apparently found refuge at Our Lady of the Blessed Ascension Catholic Church on Church Street in the Midtown District.

Bradford went to Galveston and quickly found the church, a cathedral and a baptismal school. Our Lady of the Blessed Ascension Catholic Church covered a one-square-block area in the Midtown District, with an attached rectory and a nearby parochial school.

Bradford rented an eBike from downtown, which he used to tour the district. The Satanic priest soon discovered that there were several churches of various denominations in Midtown, which he learned was the Historic District of Galveston. He found two Jewish synagogues, an evangelical ministry, a Buddhist temple, and an Islamic mosque within a ten-square-block area of Midtown. On Bradford's first visit to Galveston, he began to plan his diabolical scheme of deadly revenge against the Catholic priest who had stolen his youth and innocence nearly thirty years earlier.

Our Lady of the Blessed Ascension was one of Galveston's historic churches. It was a large building made of tan stone blocks with two tall steeples. The front and side windows of the cathedral were stained glass. A spacious courtyard led from the street directly to two huge wooden doors. The rectory, also constructed of tan stone, was attached to the back of the church and extended along Church St. on its north side. In front of the rectory, there was a row of tall palm trees. On the south side of the church complex was its two-story red brick parochial school bordering Winnie St., the Galveston County Museum, and a park.

Bradford's strong desire for revenge against Father Fogarty was paramount in his life plan. The Satanic priest decided that he liked Galveston and would move there to set up a new Church of Satan and eventually spectacularly slay the priest.

After confirming that Father Fogerty was indeed working as a priest at the Catholic church and living at the rectory, Bradford made good use of his five-day visit by finding both a duplex apartment in Midtown and a dilapidated corrugated metal building near the Port of Galveston, not far away, where he planned to build and open his new Church of Satan.

Chapter 13
The Son of Satan Arrives

Two years later, Bradford D'Ablo Natas had closed his Church of Satan in San Francisco and moved to Galveston. He took up residence in a red brick, two-story duplex apartment on the 1700 block of 17th Street near Market Avenue. Bradford drove past the duplex and saw its twin black gargoyle statues sitting atop twin red brick columns on the second-floor outside porch, just outside his bedroom on the top floor. The duplex was only six blocks northeast of Our Lady of the Blessed Ascension Catholic Church.

Satan has chosen this new home for me. This is how it was meant to be, he mused when he paid the owner a deposit and three months' rent in advance.

Bradford also selected a small, dilapidated abandoned corrugated metal warehouse on Harborside Drive at 15th Street in the port district, only five blocks northeast of his apartment. The building was the perfect location for his new Church of Satan. Since it had been unused for years, the surprised owner easily offered Bradford a generous discount on the rent.

Bradford aimed to stay off the radar. He didn't get a Texas driver's license or ID card, and he had no bank account or credit lines. He simply paid for everything in cash, which his landlords accepted without question. Bradford's only form of ID was a Social Security card in his old name, Bradford Ciarelli. He was almost impossible to trace. B. KAMISS

Within a week of arriving in Galveston, Bradford found work managing a carousel at the Pleasure Pier, which was owned by the "Gulf Entertainment" limited liability company. Bradford purchased an eBike, which provided him with cheap and easy transportation throughout the downtown and Midtown districts. Bradford settled into a routine of working at the Pleasure Pier during the day and, on some evenings, cleaning up the abandoned warehouse, which would soon become his new Church of Satan, keeping tabs on Father Fogarty.

Within six months, Bradford had cleaned the warehouse, built an altar, and bought folding chairs and tables from an auction. He used his PC and a printer to make flyers advertising his new church and distributed them around town at local vape shops, marijuana dispensaries, and underground music bars. A few months later, Bradford D'Ablo Natas had gathered a small congregation of fifteen loyal followers. Services at the New Church of Satan were secretly held each Friday night at midnight.

Chapter 14
Wade's Killer Profile

It had been two days since Wade and Dakota consulted with Det. Sgt. Gates Sullivan and her partner, Det. Bill Hurd. The couple had been enjoying a real vacation, taking in the beautiful spring weather on the beach and indulging in the seafood at the city's unique restaurants. Wade, Dakota, and Desi were on a morning walk along the beach near the Pleasure Pier when Wade's cellphone buzzed. The display showed "Galveston Police Department," and Wade answered. It was Bill Hurd.

"Morning, Wade, I hope I didn't catch you at a bad time, but Gates asked me to update you on our current status," said the detective. Wade pressed the speakerphone button so Dakota could listen in.

"Nope, Dakota, and I are enjoying the beach," Wade replied.

"Glad Dakota is with you because we got a call from ME, Dr. Dyer, this morning. He got some new toxicology results from Rabbi Abramson's autopsy. It's pretty interesting, and we think it adds more to our killer's MO," offered Hurd.

"I've got Dakota on speaker. Go ahead, Bill," replied Wade.

"Great. Dr. Dyer tried Dakota's suggestion about using that GC-MS contraption, and guess what he found—traces of chloroform on the Rabbi's clothing; the collar of his shirt, actually," said the detective. "What do you think about that?" he asked.

Dakota spoke up. "Bill, do you recall how CSI had packaged Rabbi Abramson's clothing?" she asked.

"Hold on, it's in Dr. Dyer's report. Let me find it," replied Hurd. A minute later, the detective found the answer to Dakota's question and read it aloud. "Says here, "I tested the decedent's clothing, which was presented for testing, packaged in air-locked plastic bags. Gas chromatograph-mass spectrometry revealed traces of chloroform residue on the collar of a dress shirt." Does that help, doc?" asked the detective.

"Yes, it does. If the rabbi's clothing were not damp, there would be no need to package them in paper bags and place them in the air-drying closet. It would be better to package them in plastic bags, remove the air, vacuum-seal them, and store them in a dark, cool, temperature-controlled evidence locker. This ideal preservation method could produce positive results for detecting evaporative chemicals like chloroform with sensitive analytical techniques like GC-MS weeks or months later," explained Dakota.

"Thanks for the explanation, doc," replied Hurd.

Wade said, "So this discovery of the presence of chloroform definitely gives us new information about our killer and offers a plausible explanation for how he managed to get the drop on poor Rabbi Abramson."

"I'm thinking a rear attack using a cloth or rag soaked in chloroform. The attacker sneaks up from behind, presses the soaked rag over the Rabbi's nose and mouth, and then waits a few seconds. Our victim, caught off guard, would inhale the vapors while struggling for air. This would speed up the effects of the chloroform. Rabbi Abramson would have been unconscious in seconds," Wade explained.

"Yeah, kind of what we're also thinking," replied Hurd.

"There might be more to our killer's method of attack as well. Reflecting on what I saw during the autopsy and photos of Reverend Jefferson, I believe our guy also snuck up behind the minister with his garrote and strangled him," Dakota suggested.

"If both of these initial attacks on our victims were carried out through stealth and surprise, I would speculate that parts of a criminal psychological profile of our killer are that he's intelligent, he's definitely an organized offender, and he may be smaller in stature but very strong. I have a few ideas about our killer. Can you and Gates meet Dakota and me this afternoon so I can share some of my thoughts?" asked Wade.

"Absolutely. How about lunch at Bubba Gump's around noon at the Pleasure Pier? It's an easy walk for you guys," said the detective.

"Sure thing. We'll see you there at noon," replied Wade.

Wade and Dakota finished their walk with Desi and returned to the RV. An hour and a half later, they found a booth for four inside Bubba Gump's restaurant on the lively Pleasure Pier. Gates Sullivan and Bill Hurd arrived shortly after and took a seat.

"So Bill tells me you have a couple of ideas concerning our clergy killer," began Gates.

"Yes, I've been reflecting on this whole situation. I'm increasingly agreeing with Professor Tzabar that we might not be dealing with a white supremacist targeting minorities and Jews. I've made some mental notes piecing together the criminal psychological profile of our killer," said Wade.

"Like what? We're all ears. So far, none of our leads have panned out," replied Gates.

Well, Gates, I have to disagree. You have some leads if you consider that a psych profile can offer useful clues. Dr. Tzabar mentioned that our killer might be intentionally trying to distract the police by making it look obvious; the killer hangs a black man and gasses a Jew. I agree with Lyeb. I think it's misdirection," said Wade.

"Misdirection, how? Why would the killer want to mislead us?" asked Hurd. Wade looked at Hurd and Gates thoughtfully, trying to piece together their puzzle in a way that made sense.

"First, we're dealing with a very intelligent suspect. He's an organized offender. There's been nothing random or chaotic about how he commits the murders. Both crime scenes were clean, with no evidence that his victims fought back.

"He finds discreet points of entry, uses stealth, and employs very unique and historically frightening methods to kill his victims. He lynches a black minister in a Confederate state and uses Zyklon-B, hydrogen cyanide gas, to exterminate an Orthodox Jewish Rabbi—akin to Hitler's Final Solution. He knows that the murders will attract attention on the nightly news.

"Next, there is evidence of proprietary interest in each crime scene," Wade explained before being interrupted by Det. Hurd.

"Proprietary what?" asked Hurd.

"Fair question, Bill. "Proprietary interest" refers to a suspect taking something from a crime scene, leaving something at a scene, or the way they manipulate a crime scene.

"In our crime scenes, the bodies of both Rev. Jefferson and Rabbi Abramson were displayed for shock value. Hanging the Baptist minister from a rafter in his church in front of the podium and gassing a Rabbi by securing him to a chair in his office and filling the room with toxic gas are definitely evidence of proprietary interest," explained Wade.

"Oh, I get it. That makes total sense, thanks," replied Hurd.

"As I said, I think our killer may not necessarily be a person of large stature, as evidenced by his using that column as leverage to hoist up the minister and restraining the rabbi to his office chair after he had knocked him out with chloroform. Again, stealthy points of entry into the church and temple, stealthy approaches, and incapacitation of both victims. Both murder scenes showed evidence of organization with no physical evidence left behind for normally trained detectives or CSI techs to find," said Wade.

"Thank God Dakota has been here to help, as has your friend Professor Tzabar, who has expertise in the Jewish faith. Certainly, you've discovered things we never would have found," replied Gates.

"Like I said, this guy is smart. No way he's a run-of-the-mill bigot or white supremacist. I think there's something deeper with this guy," said Wade.

"Deeper? Like how... what?" asked Hurd.

First, having an organized crime scene and believing they are not leaving any evidence behind shows proprietary interest. Remember how he manipulates his crime scenes, especially with Rabbi Abramson; he pulled his trousers' zipper down? I'm thinking that this might indicate some repressed sexual trauma. That could be an essential aspect to consider.

"But there was nothing like that with the minister," Gates quickly added.

"You're right, Gates, but remember something about psychological profiling. Profilers are less than twenty percent accurate in their assessments. I'm not saying everything fits perfectly; it's called a puzzle. But let me add something here. If you completely remove the idea that we're dealing with a white supremacist, some sick Nazi or KKK'er, what do these two homicide victims have in common?" asked Wade.

"They're both members of the clergy, and both of them were murdered in their places of worship," replied Gates.

"Exactly. So if our killer deliberately targets members of the clergy and poses one of them with their zipper down, doesn't this unique detail possibly tell us something about our suspect that we should at least consider?" asked Wade.

"You think this guy has some negative history with clergy, like maybe he was molested?" asked Gates.

"Who knows, Gates. You know what we say in police work, 'cops hate coincidences.' Two members of the clergy in Galveston were murdered within two weeks. That's no coincidence; it's intentional and, worse yet, planned. I think we're dealing with a goal-oriented killer—a guy who deliberately targets clerics. He's smart, methodical, and planned," said Wade.

"How so?" asked Hurd.

"Look at the methods and deadly tools used in the murders. The Baptist minister used a knotted garrote and thirty feet of braided hemp rope. He murdered the Rabbi by first knocking him out with chloroform, tying him to a chair, and then gassing him with Zyklon-B, hydrogen cyanide. No one walks around with thirty feet of rope or a gas canister on the street. This suggests that this guy carries a kit with his murder tools. It also indicates he is an organized killer. These details help complete our profile puzzle.

"Good points, Wade. This is very helpful," said Gates.

"Gates and Bill, this guy worries me. I think he likes killing holy men, and even more concerning is that he enjoys showing off his killings to shock us. That's why he displays them on purpose; it's intentional. You will do everything possible to catch him before he kills again. If he kills one more clergy member, we'll know our suspect is a serial killer of clergy. He'll keep killing until we stop him. Please keep us updated. That's the direction we must take, so keep us informed. Now let's eat,"

Chapter 15
They Messed with the Wrong Guy

The spring weather in Galveston suddenly changed a few hours after Wade and Dakota returned from their lunch at Bubba Gump's on the Pleasure Pier. The south winds picked up, and dark storm clouds gathered off the coast. By sunset, they had moved inland and brought a heavy rainstorm.

The couple sat comfortably around the dinner table, enjoying a beer and watching Galveston's local KWAV TV-4. Wade's red-nosed pit bull, Desi, relaxed on the opposite couch, looking for her chance to beg a leftover snack. Wade and Dakota's ears perked up when they heard the news reporter.

"This is Johnny Costa reporting. In tonight's news, a new wrinkle in Galveston's Clergy Killer homicide investigation. Galveston Police have brought in an expert identified as Dr. Lyeb Tzabar, a professor at Texas A&M's Galveston campus, and a renowned expert in Hebrew studies, to review evidence in the murder of popular Jewish Rabbi David Abramson of Congregation B'nai Israel Temple in the city's historic Midtown District.

"According to confidential police sources close to the investigation, Professor Tzabar has opined to homicide investigators that the killer may not be a member of any white supremacist organization, and that the suspect who police believe also murdered revered Rev. Jacob Jefferson the week before may be trying to misdirect police.

"KWAV-TV 4 News has reached out to homicide detectives involved in the case who have refused to comment, citing the ongoing investigation. And now to tonight's weather...."

Wade hit the mute button on the remote. "Damn, the proverbial poop is going to hit the blower now. I'd sure like to know who gave this information to the press," Wade said to Dakota.

"Certainly not good. Do you think Gates or Bill Hurd knows anything about this?" asked Dakota.

"Well, I'm going to find out," said Wade, picking up his cellphone to call Gates, but as he did so, his cellphone buzzed. It was Gates. Wade picked up.

"Did you see tonight's news about your case? What the hell!" exclaimed Wade.

"You're telling me. We definitely got sucker punched. Thirty minutes ago, I just got off the phone with that insufferable KWAV-TV reporter Johnny Costa. I have no idea where the scuttlebutt came from, but I can assure you it wasn't from our team or anyone in CSI," replied Gates.

"Well, the cat's out of the bag. My next call is to Lyeb to warn him that he's been linked to this case. I might sound a little paranoid, but whoever talked to the press may have just put a target on his back. Keep us posted," said Wade, hanging up.

"I hope we didn't get your friend Dr. Tzabar into trouble," said Dakota.

“Me too,” replied Wade, dialing Lyeb Tzabar’s cell. Lyeb didn’t answer his phone, and his voicemail was full. Wade turned to Dakota.

“Damn, Lyeb isn’t answering, and his voicemail box is full. He’s probably teaching an evening class or something. I’ll call him again in a couple of hours,” replied Wade.

Professor Tzabar finished teaching his bi-weekly 7:00 pm to 9:30 pm Introduction to Hebrew Studies course at Kirkham Hall and walked down the hall to his office, followed by a few of his students who had questions about an assignment. Thirty minutes later, Dr. Tzabar left the building and walked west into a nearly deserted parking lot, except for his vehicle, which was parked next to a dark-colored, old 1980s Ford Econoline utility van.

Tzabar took his car keys out of his pocket and pressed the remote key fob to unlock his doors. The vehicle beeped, unlocking the doors and turning off his alarm system. The professor was about to get into his car when he noticed movement in his peripheral vision to his far left. He turned to his left just in time to see a male figure, wearing a hooded sweatshirt and black pants, with a black face mask, charging at him with a fixed-blade knife in a right-handed thrust.

Tzabar’s Israeli Sayeret Matkal commando training immediately kicked in. He turned his body to the right while simultaneously blocking the assailant’s right hand with his left. The former hand-to-hand combat instructor grabbed his attacker’s right wrist and forced it back toward the man, breaking his wrist and causing him to drop the knife, which Tzabar then caught. Tzabar’s move had caused his attacker to fall to his knees, where he now delivered two quick knee strikes to his head, knocking him out.

A second blacked-out assailant attacked from Tzabar's right rear. The professor spun to his right, meeting his attacker's overhead stab with a double-forearm block and stopping the knife thrust in mid-air. Tzabar then spun the suspect around off-balance to the left as he sliced through the man's throat with his right hand, which held the knife from his first attacker. The deep cut severed both right and left carotid arteries and jugular veins, which spurted outwards. The assailant dropped his knife and thrust both of his hands up to his throat in a useless effort to staunch the flow of blood. Then he collapsed to his knees before faceplanting into the asphalt.

As Lyeb Tzabar moved toward his disabled attacker in the semi-lit parking lot to check his condition, the first attacker, who had recovered, got up, ran to the van, and sped off. The surprised, now slightly out of breath, professor of Hebrew studies managed to stay calm enough to perform a secondary scan for additional threats but found none. He was left alone in the parking lot with a dead body. At that moment, his cellphone rang.

"Lyeb, it's Wade Justus. I've been trying to call you to inform you about a possible threat," said Wade before Tzabar interrupted him.

"You're too late, my friend. They already tried but failed. You're going to need to call 9-1-1. I'm in the west parking lot across from Kirkham Hall on the Texas A&M University Pelican Island campus. Two people with knives just attacked me. There is one down," Tzabar replied.

"One down?! Are you alright, Lyeb?" Wade exclaimed.

“Yes, Wade. Fortunately, I’m fine, but unfortunately, I had to defend myself. One of my attackers is dead at my hand. Please call the police. I’ll contact campus security," explained Tzabar.

“You said ‘they.’ How many attacked you?” asked Wade.

There were two. I believe they initially disappeared from my sight, probably from a dark brown older model van parked next to my car. The second attacker, whom I temporarily disabled, managed to get up and drive away.

“Geeze, how would they know where you would be, and what your car looked like?” asked Wade.

“Well, you tell me. You said you were calling me about a threat. I’m certain that these guys had something to do with that. It wouldn’t be hard to tell which car was mine. I worked late and met with students afterward. My car was the only one left in the parking lot when I went outside,” said Tzabar.

“We’ve got to get the cops to you, pronto. I’m having Dakota call 9-1-1. Don’t touch anything before the cops get there. Are you armed? You said that one of your attackers was deceased,” said Wade as Dakota dialed 9-1-1 to report the assault.

“I’m not carrying a gun. I killed him with a knife. I still have it,” replied Tzabar.

“Jesus Christ, Lyeb. You killed him with your knife?” asked Wade.

“Well, not exactly. I actually killed him with his partner’s knife after I knocked him out,” replied Tzabar.

Wade was incredulous. “Well, they sure messed with the wrong guy, didn’t they,” he exclaimed. “Hold on a minute,” said Wade, telling Dakota to inform the dispatcher that she was calling on behalf of the victim, Professor Lyeb Tzabar, and to contact Gates and Bill Hurd to have them respond. Dakota also advised the dispatcher to contact the Texas A&M campus police, who would likely arrive first.

“Lyeb, the Galveston PD, and Texas A&M cops are coming. The campus cops will probably arrive first. Tell them not to touch the body and to secure the crime scene when they get there. Are you sure the guy is dead?

“Dead as Adolf Hitler. I slit his throat during the fight,” replied Tzabar in a low tone.

“You slit his fucking throat? What the hell! That’s how you killed him?” replied Wade.

“Unfortunately, that’s how it happened because of how he attacked me. Like I said, both of these guys were armed with knives. As I said, I was forced to defend myself. The only thing I had with me at the time was the first attacker’s knife, so I used that,” replied Tzabar.

“Well, for an old guy, you are one badass Jew,” replied Wade.

“I prefer the term ‘senior citizen university professor.’ I thought my commando days were over years ago, back in Israel. I’m a man of peace now,” said Tzabar quietly. Wade and Dakota could hear the sounds of multiple sirens approaching.

“The police are coming. Looks like there are several of them, from what I can see,” said Tzabar.

"Well, we forgot to give them a description of you. Set the knife and your cellphone down, walk away from them, get on your knees, and raise your hands high. They will approach you with their guns drawn. Whatever you do, don't flick. Just follow their commands, and you'll be fine. Don't hang up. Just leave the phone on and tell the cops who you are. Then tell them to pick up the phone and talk with me. Tell them who I am. Okay, now do it, and we'll talk as soon as Dakota and I get there," said Wade.

The sirens grew much closer. Tzabar set the knife and cellphone on the pavement, then stepped back, dropping to his knees and raising his hands high as instructed. Wade and Dakota exchanged glances, waiting for an officer to answer the phone.

"Don't you move! What's this about?" Wade heard an officer exclaim.

"I'm Professor Lyeb Tzabar. I work here. I was attacked by two men with knives and had to defend myself. I'm unarmed. One of my attackers is over there; he's quite dead. Texas Ranger Wade Justus is on the line on my cellphone over there. He's waiting to speak with you. He suggested that you not touch the body," Tzabar told the unknown officer.

Wade and Dakota saw the officer telling Tzabar, *"Stand up. Put your hands behind your back so we can search you."* Then, they heard the distinct sound of handcuffs being applied.

After some moments, the cellphone was picked up, and a voice spoke. "This is Officer Brent Paulson. Who am I speaking to?" the officer asked.

"Officer Paulson, this is retired Texas Ranger Wade Justus. I am a consultant for the Galveston PD homicide unit, working with Det. Sgt. Gates Sullivan and Bill Hurd on the clergy homicides. I believe that the detectives are en route to you. The man you have detained is Professor Lyeb Tzabar, who is also working for GPD as a consultant on the same cases. He is an innocent victim of this assault," Wade explained.

"And I should believe you because...?" asked the skeptical officer.

"Just get on the radio and ask for Detectives Sullivan and Hurd. Tell them you are on the phone with me and have Dr. Tzabar detained. Then follow their directions closely," replied.

"Wait one, sir," replied the officer, who immediately called dispatch. Two minutes later, with a change in tone, he was back on the line with Wade.

"Sorry for the delay, Ranger Justus. Sgt. Sullivan has verified what you told me. I'm releasing Dr. Tzabar from custody and securing the scene," replied the officer.

"Thanks, Officer Paulson. Remember not to go near or touch the body, and keep fire and EMS out of the scene. The guy is dead, so there is no need to have anyone contaminate the crime scene," said Wade.

"Copy that, sir. Sgt. Sullivan gave me the same instructions. I'm going to hang up now, sir," replied the officer, ending the call.

Wade called Gates and asked if CSI Supervisor Lenny Spazzito responded. If he did, have him drop by the Sandpiper RV Park to pick him and Dakota up.

Wade and Dakota arrived with Detective Spazzito thirty minutes later at the Pelican Island's Texas A&M parking lot. Spazzito found Gates Sullivan and Bill Hurd standing next to the black-clad body of the would-be attacker that Lyeb Tzabar had killed. The professor was seated in Gates's unmarked detective car.

Wade and Dakota split up; Wade went to Lyeb, and Dakota walked over to the detectives. Wade walked over to Gates' car and opened the door. Tzabar stepped out so the men could converse.

“I'm sorry I wasn't able to warn you earlier. I called you, but you didn't answer, and your phone went directly to full voicemail,” said Wade.

“Warn me about what, this?” asked Tzabar.

“Yes, at least the potential of a threat, and for you to be on your guard,” replied Wade.

“That some goons would try to kill me? Well, they definitely tried. I'll give them that. What tipped you off?" Tzabar asked.

“Tonight, there was a news story on the Houston TV News channel reporting that you have been consulting with the GPD homicide on the clergy murders. An anonymous source told a reporter that it was your opinion that a white supremacist may not be the killer of our minister and Rabbi. Undoubtedly, our killer isn't working alone,” said Wade.

"Well, after this, apparently not. This definitely suggests he might have had help. We can't rule that out. But why the hell try to kill me? I'm not a cop, I'm just a professor; a consultant at best," replied Tzabar.

"I think your opinion frightened whoever is responsible. You may have disrupted their efforts at misdirection. At the same time, perhaps by killing you, a Jewish professor, they believe that might strengthen their story that a white supremacist is targeting everyone," Wade explained.

"And also reduce police concerns that the killer or killers are solely targeting clergy members," offered Tzabar.

"Exactly," replied Wade. "So, tell me what happened out here," said Wade.

"Actually, not much happened until the attack. I taught my Intro to Hebrew Studies evening class as usual. Afterwards, two students came to my office with questions about an assignment. That took about thirty minutes. Just after 10:00 pm, I locked my office and headed out to the parking lot to leave in my car. As I recall, the lot was empty except for my car and an older brown van. I didn't pay much attention to it at the time.

"I was just about to get into my car when I noticed movement to my left out of the corner of my eye. I turned in time to see this guy, completely covered in black from head to toe—wearing a hoodie, face mask, and pants—coming at me with a knife in his right hand. I was partly stuck in the doorway with the door open to my right. I sidestepped to my left toward him, bladed my stance, and blocked the knife thrust with my left hand. I grabbed his right wrist with my right hand, bent his hand holding the knife back, breaking his wrist, which allowed me to disarm him and bring him to his knees.

"I kneed him twice in the face, and he went down hard. I ended up with his knife in my right hand. Then a second guy – that guy over there – dressed identically, came at me from my right rear with an overhead stab. Luckily, he had to go around my open door to get me. I moved towards him, sidestepped him, and did a double-arm block of his knife hand. My move forced him off balance to his left. I turned into him with my right hand, which had the knife, and sliced him hard across his throat. That was all it took. He dropped the knife and went down holding his throat. I knew I had inflicted a fatal wound as soon as I saw him on the pavement. He bled out quickly. There's nothing anyone could have done to save him.

"While I was distracted with the second guy, the first guy got up, ran to the van, started it, and sped away. That's all there was to it. Unfortunately, I didn't have time to focus on the van or get a license plate number. It was an older model brown utility van. That's all I can tell you," explained Tzabar.

"Well, that's self-defense all the way. You'll be fine. Just tell the cops what you told me. I'll make sure that Gates takes your statement. Just have a seat and try to relax. This is going to take a little time. We'll get you down to the station as soon as we can. You'll be home tonight, I can promise you that," said Wade.

Wade approached Dakota, Gates, and Bill Hurd, who were gathered around the body with CSI Supervisor Lenny Spazzito. While Wade was speaking with Tzabar, Gates asked Dakota to examine the body and declare death.

“So what did Professor Tzabar tell you?” asked Gates.

Pretty much what he told Dakota and me over the phone before we called you. He came out to his car to drive home when he was jumped by two blacked-out guys, each with knives. They tried to kill him, but he managed to disarm and knock out the first attacker. Then he was attacked by the second guy. He blocked an overhead knife thrust and sliced the guy's throat with the first guy’s knife, and the second attacker went down.

“Down, and dirty, and over in seconds. Lyeb had no chance to disengage and was forced to defend himself. A straight Texas PC 9.31, 9.32 self-defense case, the way I see it, but you’re the detectives here,” explained Wade.

“Jesus, Mary, and Joseph, the guy's almost eighty. He takes them both on unarmed, disarms the first guy, and kills this fucker here? Absolutely amazing,” exclaimed Hurd.

“Like I told Dakota earlier, these two goons picked the wrong guy to mess with. Israelis are born fighters, and these Sayeret Matkal commandos are the best. You never forget your training, as shown by what Lyeb did here tonight,” said Wade.

“No shit. Tzabar doesn’t even have a mark on him,” said Det. Hurd.

“Well, thank God for that. Guys, I’d like to take a better look at the body if you don’t mind,” said Dakota.

Sure, here are some gloves, but I want Lenny to take photos and videos of the body in its current state before you do. Once that's done, he can work around the crime scene. Since you've already pronounced our John Doe dead, we won't need the ME to respond. Dr. Dyer can do his thing after the body is transported to the lab," said Gates.

As CSI Supervisor Spazzito was photographing the body, Dakota put on a pair of black latex surgical gloves and began to examine it. She immediately noticed matching black tattoos on the top of his left hand and the left side of his neck just below the ear, reading "666."

"Lookie here, people. That's an interesting tattoo. A biker, perhaps?" she asked.

"No, that's what's referred to as "The Mark of the Beast." It's normally associated with devil worship. I've seen it before," remarked Wade.

"Interesting," replied Dakota as she pulled up the man's hoodie and black undershirt, revealing his abdomen and chest. In the center of his sternum was a six-inch circle enclosing a pentagram with the face of the devil in the middle.

Wade, Gates, and Bill Hurd looked down at the man's chest. "That's a pentagram with a likeness of the devil in the center. I think this guy is a Satanist," remarked Wade.

"Let's get Lenny over here for a minute to get this. We'll do full photos at the ME's office during the autopsy," said Gates as she called the CSI supervisor over.

"The plot thickens," said Dakota as she waited for Spazzito to finish his quick photo shoot.

"This investigation is getting more bizarre by the minute," replied Gates as Dakota rolled up the sleeves of the man's hoodie, revealing more Satanic tattoos.

After Lenny Spazzito finished his initial photographic scan of the body, Gates slipped on a pair of latex surgical gloves and began searching the body. The man was missing, with no wallet, money, or identification. However, she did find a single piece of photocopied paper that featured a faculty directory photo of Dr. Tzabar with the caption, "Professor Emeritus Lyeb Tzabar, Ph.D., TX A&M, Hebrew Studies," and handwritten below it, "Teaches classes in Kirkham Hall. Hebrew Studies 101, T-TH 7:00 p.m. – 9:30 pm."

"Well, they did pretty quick research on Dr. Tzabar," said Gates as she carefully held up the photocopy paper by two corners and showed it to Hurd, Wade, and Dakota.

"Like I said, we're dealing with some person or people with intelligence. It took them a couple of hours after the news report to identify and do their intel on Lyeb. Then they had to select their hit team and deploy to surveil and wait for an opportunity to ambush him. These people move quickly," said Wade.

"Loose lips sink ships. This is our fault. We put Dr. Tzabar in danger. If I find out who blabbed to the press, I'll have them fired and prosecuted for obstruction of our investigation," said Gates angrily.

You've got bigger fish to fry. We don't know if they did a deeper dive into Lyeb. They might have his home address, too. We have one suspect on the loose. Undoubtedly, he's got a cellphone and has already told whoever sent them out here that their plot failed. You're going to have to assign a unit to watch his house or pay for a hotel room until we catch whoever is responsible for these crimes," suggested Wade.

“Given our current staffing issues, getting him a hotel room is better. We’ll bring him to the station, do an interview, then take him home to get a few of his things. Then we’ll find him a hotel,” said Gates.

“He’s also going to need campus police to provide full security when he’s on campus. I know Lyeb, and he won’t let this stop him from teaching his students,” said Wade.

“Sure, I’ll have Officer Paulson provide me with his chief’s cell number. I’ll get this sorted out tonight. In the meantime, I’ll stay here. Bill, take Wade and Dakota back to the Sandpiper, then head over to the ME’s Office and run some prints off the database (dead body) so we can get him ID’d. While Lenny and his team are working, I apologize to Professor Tzabar before driving him downtown for an interview. I’ll catch up with you two tomorrow. Thanks for your help and for being here tonight,” replied Gates.

Wade and Dakota said goodbye to Lyeb Tzabar, and Detective Hurd drove them back to the Sandpiper RV Park before heading to the Medical Examiner’s office, awaiting the delivery of their unknown assailant.

Chapter 16
Failure and A New Plan

Joshua was still trying to clear the cobwebs from his mind. The intense pain from his broken nose, along with the ringing in his ears, tormented him as he drove back to the now-occupied warehouse on Harborside Dr., which was home to the New Church of Satan. As he left the scene, he called "Priest" Bradford and delivered the bad news. Their attack had failed, and Curtis had likely been killed by their intended target, the Jewish Professor Lyeb Tzabar, in the parking lot at the Pelican Island Texas A&M campus.

Bradford was predictably upset because he had explicitly told them not to fail and to bring back a "trophy" of the professor's head in a sack. "Meet me at the church; it will be safe there. You can ditch the van inside because the cops will be looking for it," he ordered.

As instructed, when Joshua arrived at the warehouse, he honked his horn twice, and a corrugated metal door slid open, allowing him to drive inside. Unexpectedly, the interior of the warehouse was dimly lit. Joshua got out of the van as Bradford approached.

"So, tell me exactly what happened tonight," Bradford asked.

We arrived at the campus, parked in the lot just outside Kirkham Hall, and went to the building to find out where Tzabar was teaching. There were only two classes happening. We looked through the door windows at each classroom and saw the professor giving a lecture to a small class in the second room. Then we went back to our van and waited for him.

"Just after 10:00 pm, Tzabar stepped into the parking lot. He was the only vehicle remaining after all the students had left for the night. Coincidentally, we had parked our van near his car. Our plan was to split up and ambush him from two opposite sides at the same time. I was on his left side, and Curtis was on his right. Because the professor was next to his car, I went first. I tried to stab the old guy, but he dodged me. He grabbed my knife hand, and the next thing I knew, I was on the ground. He kicked me in the face and knocked me out.

"And Curtis?" the Satanic priest asked.

"Shit, I don't know. When I awoke, my knife was gone, and everything was blurry and out of focus. I saw Curtis on the ground with the professor standing over him with a knife. I just got up, ran to the van, and sped away. I don't know why he didn't run after me, except he's an old guy," explained Joshua.

"Yes, he *is* an old guy. So please tell me how two young guys let an old man get the better of you, no doubt killing one of you?" asked Bradford as the tone of his voice rose.

"I'm sorry, Bradford, I have no excuse," replied Joshua.

"I'm sorry, *Priest*! You don't ever refer to me as Bradford!" Bradford screamed at his assistant.

"Yes, I'm sorry, Priest. I swear that I won't make this kind of mistake again. Give me another chance. I'll kill him. I promise you I will kill him," declared the remorseful Joshua.

Bradford's voice softened. "Yes, we all make mistakes. Luck was on the professor's side tonight. There will be another chance. Where's the paper I gave you with the professor's photo and the address of the classroom building?" asked Bradford.

Joshua felt his pockets for the paper. "I...I don't know. Maybe in the van," he replied.

What the fuck! Thought Bradford as he began to panic, but he couldn't let his assistant see that. The Satanic priest struggled to stay calm, knowing how damaging Curtis's cellphone could be to him.

"Go back to the van, and retrieve it for me, will you?" asked Bradford, calmly.

"Yes, Priest. Give me a minute," Joshua said as he turned away from Bradford to head back to the van.

Joshua had taken no more than three steps when Bradford pulled the knotted garrote from his rear pocket and came from behind his errant assistant, throwing the garrote over his head and yanking it back tightly. At the same time, he kicked Joshua's legs out from under him. The hapless assistant reached up to grab the rope with both hands, but it was too late.

Bradford restrained his Satanic associate on the floor, tightening the rope so the knots pressed firmly against the man's carotid arteries and jugular veins. Joshua gasped for air, but he was quickly losing consciousness as the garrote cut off all oxygen-rich blood to his brain. His legs and feet kicked uncontrollably for thirty seconds before his body went limp. Bradford maintained pressure on the garrote for another two minutes to ensure death before finally releasing his grip. Joshua was no longer alive.

Bradford removed the garrote from Joshua's neck and ran to the van. He entered and frantically searched the vehicle's interior, failing to find the cellphone or the paper with the professor's information.

That's one loose end I won't need to worry about, but Curtis, the missing paper with the professor's photo, and his Kirkham Hall classroom address were potential problems. No doubt the police are carefully examining both, thought the Satanic priest with concern.

Bradford dragged Jacob's body to a large freezer, stripped him, and placed him inside. He put his former assistant's clothes in a black trash bag and later threw them into a nearby dumpster.

The Jewish professor damaged my efforts to make the police believe a white supremacist is responsible for the murders of the black Baptist minister and the Jewish Rabbi. I need to steer them back toward my false narrative. I must kill another minority clergy member quickly. The media frenzy will pressure authorities to keep searching for a white hater, but I must act fast. I will have my revenge on Father Fogarty, the Satanic priest.

The next morning, Bradford searched for Buddhist temples online. Although he didn't find a local one, he came across the closest option, the Zen Path of the Dharma Meditation Center. The spiritual center was located in the 500 block of Church Street at 5th Avenue. Since it was a weekday, Bradford knew he wouldn't be working at the Pleasure Pier that day.

Bradford found that the Zen Meditation Center was in Midtown, less than a mile east of his apartment. It was also less than two miles northeast of the Pleasure Pier and less than a mile east of his New Church of Satan.

It's centrally located, easy to get to, and escape the area afterwards, perfect! the Satanic priest thought.

Bradford jumped on his eBike mid-morning and pedaled to the Zen Meditation Center. The religious house was behind a Whataburger fast food restaurant in a mixed residential-commercial zone. It was a small, colored, single-story modest brick structure, shaded in the front by an enormous heritage oak tree. Parallel metal bars guided the visitor up its cement walkway from the street.

Bradford surveilled the meditation center for a hidden entry point. He parked his eBike in the rear westside lot of the Whataburger next to a line of tall, bushy cypress trees, and walked through the trees toward the Zen center. He saw a cyclone fence without barbed wire separating the two properties. Peering through the fence, he spotted a simple wooden door without any locking mechanism.

Here's how I'm getting in. He mused that I can easily pry back that locking hasp with a flat-bladed knife or a screwdriver.

If he needed an alibi, Bradford drove to the Pleasure Pier. He set his eBike's speed to 25 mph and headed for the pier. Using his phone's stopwatch, he could cover the 1.92-mile distance in less than three minutes.

Excellent, what's three minutes in an alibi? They'd have to give me the benefit of the doubt if I got caught later in any investigation. Now to pick the right day and time, he pondered.

Chapter 17
The Buddhist Monk

During his surveillance mission the previous day, Bradford observed the days and times when the Buddhist monk conducted Dharma, the teachings of Buddha. The tri-weekly teaching and meditation sessions took place on Tuesdays, Thursdays, and Saturdays after work from 7:00 p.m. to 9:00 p.m.

Buddhist monks are celibate and take vows of poverty, relying on their worshipers to donate funds to the Zen Meditation Center for maintenance, rent, and the monks' overall well-being. Bradford learned from googling the center that its resident monk lived there. Since it was a day off, he doubted any Buddhists who worshipped there would be present. There was a good chance that the Bhikkhu, or monk, would be alone. The name on the center's front door read "Bhikkhu Kassapa," which means "disciple of Buddha." He was a Thai monk.

Bradford prepared his kit for a late-night attack. He dressed in black and packed his black Satanic robe, a devil's mask with horns, gloves, zip ties, and a quart-sized Mason jar of ethyl alcohol into his black backpack. He had already planned out how he would get rid of the Buddhist monk.

Another spectacular ending for an undoubtedly hypocritical cleric, which will sufficiently terrify the people of Galveston. The media will go wild, reinforcing my white supremacist killer theory, Bradford confidently thought.

Bradford soaked a washcloth in chloroform and carefully placed it into a sturdy Ziplock bag before packing it into his backpack. His murder kit was ready. Bradford's eBike was fully charged, and he was now waiting for the sun to set.

As darkness covered the city, Bradford hopped on his eBike. He rode east on Market St. from his apartment to 5th Ave., then made a right turn. The Zen Center was just two blocks away. He passed by the building and saw a light on. Next, he turned right on Church St. and entered the rear parking lot of Whataburger, where he parked inside the trees to hide his eBike.

Bradford waited and watched the parking lot for a few minutes. Only four cars were there, all parked away from the restaurant. After observing the restaurant and lot for ten minutes, he saw no one visiting the place.

Must be a slow night. With no one in the lot or in the drive-through, this is the perfect time to move, the Satanic priest said to himself.

Bradford scanned the area one last time before tossing his backpack over the cyclone fence and climbing into the rear yard of the Zen Center. On the opposite side, he moved close to the rear wall of the building, unzipped his backpack, and took out his Satanic garments and black gloves. Before putting on the robe, devil's mask, and gloves, he listened carefully for any sounds from inside since he had no idea what the center's layout was. He heard nothing to worry him.

Bradford approached the back wooden door with a long-bladed pocket knife and slowly slipped the blade over the locking hasp until he felt it click open. He bent down and took out the Ziplock bag and zip ties from the backpack. He left the backpack, which holds the Mason jar of ethyl alcohol and the Ziplock bag, near the back door, put his knife away, and entered the center dressed as Satan.

The Satanic priest saw a faint light and detected the scent of incense. He heard a soft, deliberate chanting coming from the front of the building. He moved cautiously toward the source of the light and positioned himself behind the doorframe of the meditation room. From his concealed spot, Bradford observed Bhikkhu Kassapa in the brown robes of a Buddhist monk facing away and kneeling before an altar. The monk rocked back and forth while holding prayer beads, completely focused on the Buddha figurine.

The Satanic priest lowered his body as he approached the monk with the chloroform-soaked washrag in his right hand. The much younger and stronger attacker lunged at the frail, elderly monk, forcing the rag tightly against his nose and mouth. The monk gasped for air, inhaling the chloroform vapors directly into his lungs. Bradford twisted the monk's head upward to look into the face of Satan. The aging monk was too weak to resist much. Bradford smiled as he looked into his helpless victim's eyes, which were filled with terror. Bhikkhu Kassapa's body then froze in cardiac arrest as he collapsed backward against his Satanic attacker, his eyes open and fixed.

Now it was time to display the body of his victim for the police to find and document. He zip-tied the monk's ankles, knees, and arms together. Then he attached looped zip ties to the monk's hands, which were behind his back, to the looped ties that bound his knees together, keeping Bhikkhu Kassapa's body in the kneeling prayer position facing the altar as he had found him.

Bradford retrieved the Mason jar filled with ethyl alcohol and carried it to the meditation room. He soaked the deceased monk from head to toe in the highly flammable liquid. He removed his Satanic robe and devil's mask and placed them, along with his knife and Mason jar, into the backpack. He then took the chloroform-soaked washrag and the Ziplock baggie and positioned them on the back of the monk's legs so they would be burned in the fire.

"Your contrition will be achieved through the fires of perdition. All glory to you, my Satan!" exclaimed Bradford triumphantly as he used a cheap cigarette lighter to ignite the monk's religious robes.

As Bhikkhu Kassapa burst into flames, Bradford quickly exited through the back door. He threw his backpack over the cyclone fence and climbed over to his hidden eBike. He glanced once more from the cypress tree line to see if anyone was watching. Seeing no one, he got on the bike and silently sped away. His eBike, set at 25 mph, had him back at his apartment in less than three minutes.

Chapter 18
From Fire to Ritual

Fifteen minutes after Bradford returned home and was greeted by the twin black bronze gargoyles towering over his apartment duplex, the alarm sirens sounded at Fire Station 5, which serves the Midtown District.

"Station 5, Engine 5, Paramedics 5, and GEMS (Galveston EMS) – Structure fire reported in the 500 block of Church St. at 5th Avenue. Structure is fully involved."

The fire company, which had just finished a late dinner after responding to a major injury accident earlier that evening, hurried into their fire gear, manned their trucks, and blared sirens, with yelping and flashing red and blue LED emergency lights bouncing off everything the trucks passed on their way to the Zen Meditation Center from their station.

The evening had been otherwise peaceful until the sounds of multiple Galveston fire, EMS, and police units erupted through the historic Midtown neighborhoods. Bradford was already unpacking his murder kit when he heard the wailing and yelping of emergency vehicles. Although he could not see the responding units, he smiled with satisfaction, knowing that his updated plan would soon appear in the local news.

This ought to create some real controversy, he thought smugly as he hung up his black satin Satanic priest robe and devil mask in his closet.

Fortunately, because of the quick response of the fire units, the structure fire that completely engulfed the Zen

Meditation Center was quickly isolated and contained, preventing the fire from spreading to the neighboring Unitarian Universalist Fellowship Hall.

The quick-acting firefighters managed to keep the walls and roof from collapsing. Witnesses at the scene, who had called in the fire, told the fire captain that the fire seemed to have started in the front of the center. Firefighters who broke through the front door immediately found the body of a lone male, completely burned and strangely frozen in a kneeling position facing an altar. After removing their Scott air packs, the firefighters immediately detected the sharp scent of an accelerant. They reported this to the fire captain, who quickly called over the station's Arson Investigator for an initial analysis.

Engineer Pete Skogland, certified by the Texas Commission on Fire Protection, was guided inside the center by his teammates, who used their powerful flashlights to illuminate the charred, kneeling male body, frozen in death.

Skogland approached the body and started sniffing around the corpse, with remnants of charred clothing still attached to it.

Not gas but another highly flammable accelerant...perhaps some alcohol, he mused.

Skogland paid close attention to the burnt, kneeling form.

People don't die while kneeling, nor do they expire from being burned alive; instead, this occurs after they are already dead, and the fire consumes their bodies. We usually find them lying on their backs, crawling, after they die from inhaling toxic fumes from the fire, which also destroys their lungs. This seems very suspicious, he thought as he kept examining the body.

Skogland removed a metal expandable probe and illuminated the body's wrists, which he found fused with melted plastic. Then he checked behind the knees and ankles and found evidence of the same type of melted plastic.

"Zip-ties, I'm sure of it. We've got a murder scene here, fellas. You guys back out of here carefully. Don't touch anything," he warned his teammates before getting on his radio.

"Captain, we have an arson and a homicide here. Shut everyone down. Tell the cops to tape off this entire area and call GPD Homicide. We're going to need them to respond out here, ASAP. The media listens to us on their scanners, so please use only cell calls," Skogland directed.

"Copy, Pete. I'll get everyone rolling right now," the captain responded.

Gates Sullivan was enjoying a rare, peaceful evening at home when her department cellphone chirped. She looked at the display, which read, "9-1-1 Emergency Comm," and answered.

"Detective Sgt.. Sullivan, sorry to bother you tonight, ma'am, but GFD Station 5's captain and their arson investigator are declaring an arson with a possible homicide, and want you to respond," the supervising dispatcher said.

Gates closed the travel book she was reading. "Sure, what's the 20, Control?" the detective asked.

"The Zen Meditation Center, 500 block of Church St at 5th Ave, Sergeant," the dispatcher replied. Gates' eyebrow raised with intense curiosity.

"Control, can you check for me? Is that a religious place?" Gates inquired.

"Standby one, sergeant... Yes, our records show it's a Buddhist Zen Meditation Center. It states that meditation and prayers are held there three nights a week. A Buddhist monk is living on site, and we have him listed as the responsible person. His name is..., and I'm probably going to pronounce it incorrectly, but we have him listed as Bhikkhu Kassapa," said the dispatch supervisor.

"Copy, text me the spelling of his name with his contact info. Go ahead and call the number you have for him. Let's find out where he is. I'm en route, thirty-minute ETA.

"Also, roll my partner, Det. Bill Hurd, and CSI Supervisor Det. Leonardo Spazzito. Find out who the Midtown District Supervisor is tonight and give them my cell. I want a unified response on this one. One more thing, Control, zero info over the radio. All future comm via cell calls only. Let's keep our media friends in the dark as long as possible, " directed Gates.

"Will do," replied the supervisor, hanging up.

As Gates was driving to the scene, she received a text message from dispatch informing her that Sgt. Sergio Diaz, Unit Mary-10, was the Midtown District patrol supervisor. Det. Hurd and CSI Supervisor Spazzito, along with his team, were also en route. Gates had Sgt. Diaz on speed dial.

Sergeant Diaz and his patrol team were already on scene. The experienced supervisor had the area taped off, divided his patrol team between traffic and crowd control, and was conducting a neighborhood canvass for CCTV cameras.

Gates got out of her unmarked as the patrol sergeant approached.

“We’ve got to stop meeting like this,” he said wryly.

“Yeah, you gotta quit reminding me. What can you tell me?” asked Gates.

“Not much. The guy I spoke with is Engineer Pete Skogland. He’s Station 5’s arson investigator, a smart guy. He briefed me, “brief” being the keyword here.

“After they extinguished the fire, firefighters spotted one DB in the front room. They smelled an accelerant, found it suspicious, and called Skogland inside. The only other thing Skogland confided to me was that he could confirm both issues.

The big news for you and your team is that Skogland thinks it’s suspicious enough to justify calling you in. None of our uniforms has been allowed inside. We’ve been the isolation and containment crew until now,” explained Diaz.

“Okay, thanks. Point Skogland out for me,” said Gates.

“Guy in the red fire helmet with 'Arson Investigator' on it. His turnout jacket also has his name,” replied Diaz, pointing toward the front of the burned structure. Gates put on a pair of latex surgical gloves and started walking toward the building when Det. Bill Hurd arrived. Gates waved him over.

“What gives, Gates?” Hurd asked.

“We’re just about to find out. Glove up, get your flashlight, and come with me. We will get briefed by the Station 5 Arson Investigator,” replied Gates.

Gates and Hurd met Arson Investigator Pete Skogland at the front entryway. They identified themselves.

“It’s going to be wet, ugly, and potentially dangerous inside. The structure isn’t sound for obvious reasons. Let’s get a few helmets and turnout jackets first. Once Gates and Hurd were geared correctly up, Skogland directed them inside, leading the way with his flashlight illuminating the interior. He turned left into a large room with an altar.

“That’s why you’re here,” he said, illuminating the kneeling, black, charred, frozen body of a male. The skin had been completely burned from his head and face. The man’s face, reduced to a blackened skull, was frozen in a white toothed grimace; the nose was gone, and the orbits of where his eyes once were looked into what appeared to be cooked brain matter.

It was a horrific scene, and the stench of burned human flesh was nearly overpowering. Bill Hurd momentarily turned away, gagging. He pulled a handkerchief out of his rear pocket and held it tightly to his mouth.

“Your first crispy critter, I take it? Calm down and take slow, measured breaths,” said Skogland. Reaching into his pocket, he retrieved a small plastic container of Vicks VapoRub and handed it to the detective.

“Take some of this and stuff it into each nostril. You’ll find it works pretty well in masking the stench,” the arson investigator offered.

“Thanks. Stupid me. I left mine in my car. I wasn’t expecting to see a body in this condition. I’m good,” replied Hurd, trying to hide his embarrassment.

“So Pete, what makes you think this is a homicide?” asked Gates.

Skogland ran down the homicide elements as he perceived them. A distinct odor of an accelerant, possibly an alcohol based fluid, the very unusual position of the body – kneeling instead of prone.

“Now the big one,” he said while using his metal probe and flashlight to point to the body’s wrists, back of his knees, and ankles. “What do you guys make of this?” he asked the homicide detectives.

Gates and Hurd looked closely at the body parts, perplexed. “You got me. What are we supposed to be looking for? Everything is burned to a crisp,” said Gates.

“Look closer, here,” said Skogland, pointing to thin lines of melted plastic in each area. “That’s not burned skin, bone, or charred clothing; it’s plastic. What would plastic be doing in these strategic spots?" he asked rhetorically.

The arson investigator could see the lights turning on in each homicide detective's head. “Plastic...Thin plastic...Jesus Christ, zip-ties?” exclaimed Gates.

“Damn... zip-ties!” repeated Bill Hurd.

“This man was bound together in zip-ties and then murdered?” asked Gates.

"And then the place was lit up to cover up the murder, that's what you think, Pete?" asked Hurd.

"I'm an arson investigator, not a homicide detective or an ME. That's for you all to figure out. I'm just telling you what I see from my perspective and experience," replied Skogland.

"So, who's our vic?" asked Gates.

"I have no idea. Our guys only found one person in the structure. Neighbors outside told my captain that a Buddhist monk lives here and conducts meditations several times a week. Maybe you can start there," replied Skogland.

"We've got our records unit attempting to contact the monk listed as the responsible person for the meditation center," said Gates, who was checking her cell phone text messages. "His name is Bhikkhu Kassapa. Since this crime scene is both an arson and a homicide scene, we can bifurcate a search of the structure. Just tell Det. Spazzito, our CSI supervisor, where he and his team can go, and what they can touch and what they can't," replied Gates.

"Fair enough, but I suggest we clear the building for tonight and check it tomorrow. Your team can post a guard to keep people out. Tomorrow will be a better chance to test the structural integrity of this place. I don't want anything falling on you or your team. That wouldn't sit well with our boss," replied the arson investigator.

"Makes sense. I'll gather our people together and advise. How does 10:00 am tomorrow look for a meeting here, and perhaps a search of the premises?" asked Gates.

"Sounds like a plan. I'll cover our vic with a plastic tarp and tell my team not to throw water in this direction. We'll stay out of the building until tomorrow. See you all then," said Skogland, and he went to find a plastic tarp.

Gates and Bill Hurd stepped outside the burned-out Zen Meditation Center, removed the loaned fire department turnout gear and helmets, and handed them over to the Station 5 fire captain. Gates then gathered Det. Lenny Spazzito, his CSI techs, and patrol Sgt. Diaz, along with his patrol team, received a quick briefing.

Gates started, "People, here's the deal. GFD has told us it's too dangerous to poke inside the building. They want things to cool down first. A fire truck will stay out here just in case something reignites. Arson Investigator Skogland has told them not to put any more water on the front room where our only victim is located.

"The place is isolated, contained, and taped off. Sgt. Diaz, I'd like you to assign a unit to stand guard at the front to ensure no one enters the crime scene, which includes the building and the surrounding area, both taped off. We've coordinated with Skogland to return here tomorrow morning at 1000 hours. GFD will test the building for structural integrity. If they say it's safe to enter, we'll call the ME to stand by, and Lenny and his team will handle their responsibilities.

"In the meantime, Det. Hurd and I are heading back to the office to prepare an affidavit for a search warrant for the center. We'll have the night duty judge sign it, and it should be ready by tomorrow. Bring your helmets, several disposable coveralls, rain boots, and expect to get dirty. Any questions?" the homicide supervisor asked. There were no questions, so Gates and Hurd cleared the scene and drove back to the office.

On the way back to GPD, Gates called Wade. Wade and Dakota were enjoying a relaxing late evening before the fire, sipping glasses of chilled Garrison's Whiskey outside their RV at Sandpiper RV Park, when his cell phone rang. The display read, "Gates." Wade showed the screen to Dakota, who asked, "What in heaven's sake now?" and Wade responded.

"You're calling to invite us over for a later dinner on you, right?" Wade asked, joking.

"You wish, ranger," replied Gates sarcastically.

"That's former ranger to you, emphasizing the operative word 'former." What can I do for you?" asked Wade, waiting for the shoe to drop.

"Bill Hurd, and I just left a knocked down structure fire in Midtown over at Church, and 5th..." she started to say before Wade interrupted.

"Good choice; the fire service is a much better job than cop work. Should have done it myself. Better pay and more days off. Notice how firefighters always have a good-paying side job?" Wade continued before he was interrupted by Gates.

"Will you knock it off and let me finish?" the homicide supervisor chided.

"Okay, okay. You and Hurd just cleared a fire, and...?" asked Wade.

"It wasn't just a fire; it was an arson of a Buddhist meditation center, a religious center, and a homicide. We think our clergy killer just took out another priest or monk or whatever religious person Buddhists use to pray or meditate with," replied Gates.

“Jesus, another one already? This guy is going to kill more people than cancer,” said Wade, who had put Gates on speaker phone so Dakota could listen in.

“Yup, single vic found inside the center, burned to a crisp. We haven’t ID’d him yet, but Bill and I think it’s the monk who resides there and offers meditation sessions to believers three times a week. Dispatch and records haven’t been able to raise him yet. He’s listed as the responsible person for the center.

“And here’s the kicker: the arson investigator found the victim in a kneeling position, facing an altar with his wrists, knees, and ankles all zip-tied together to keep him there. For example, for shock value, he was purposely displayed for yours truly to find. According to the investigator, "there was an odor of some type of accelerant,” explained Gates.

That makes three in as many weeks. The press is going to have a field day with this. A Buddhist priest or monk? My best guess is he’s Asian. Great, a black minister, a Jewish rabbi, and now an Asian Buddhist priest. It kind of strongly challenges our white supremacist misdirection theory,” replied Wade.

“What are you two doing tomorrow morning around 10:00 am? We could really use your expertise. We’re meeting with GFD Arson Investigator Pete Skogland at the scene. We’ll bring you two extra helmets and clothing if you can come. Just an hour, ninety minutes max of your time—wanna do it?” pleaded Gates.

Wade looked at Dakota, who raised her glass of Garrison’s and nodded affirmatively. “We’ll be there, but only under one condition; afterward, it's lunch at Gaido's on you," Wade replied with a chuckle.

"Man, you're a tough sale. Deal. See you at Church and 5th tomorrow at 1000 hours," said Gates.

"Done and done. Dakota and I will come on empty stomachs. You'd better break out your unit's expense account, " replied Wade before hanging up.

Satanic priest Bradford D'Ablo Natas was ecstatic. Tonight at midnight, he would perform a special Satanic ritual called the Celebration of the Black Angel. He had called on one of his loyal female followers, "Debra," who he knew was infatuated with him, along with two new assistants eager to impress him, to help with the ritual. The trio was thrilled to be part of the event.

At 11:00 p.m., Bradford carefully packed his black satin Satanic robe and devil's mask into his backpack and left his apartment on his eBike to head to his New Church of Satan. However, his strong curiosity about what was happening at the crime scene of the Zen Meditation Center on the 500 block of Church Street was overwhelming, so he had to make a detour to see what was going on.

Bradford was dressed in his usual black pants and wore a black hoodie with the hood pulled over his head as he pedaled slowly up 5th St. toward Church. He noticed that the police had blocked off the intersection so that he couldn't pass by the Zen Center. From what he could see, the front and roof of the center had suffered significant fire damage.

Bradford reversed course and rode around the block, traveling north on 5th Ave. to Post Office St. He turned left, heading west on Post Office St., and made his next left on 6th Ave. and cut through the Whataburger restaurant parking lot, reconnecting with Church St. Although the police had also sealed off the street in front of the Zen Center, Bradford became quietly gleeful when he saw that much of the center was a total loss.

The old wooden structure burned far better than I imagined. It's pretty much a goner. No way the cops are going to be getting any forensic evidence out of that crime scene linking the monk's murder to anyone, let alone me.

Now they've got a black minister, a Jewish rabbi, and an Asian Buddhist monk. Sure looks like a white supremacist is killing off these hypocritical child rapists to me, he thought with an air of confidence.

The confident, covert Satanic priest left the scene heading to his leased, once-abandoned warehouse that now housed his New Church of Satan on Harborside Dr. at 15th Street, just a few miles away. Tonight's ritual would be the Celebration of the Black Angel, which Bradford eagerly looked forward to.

Upon arriving at the warehouse, Bradford unlocked the heavy chains securing the front sliding corrugated metal doors, entered the building, and locked the doors behind him. He had only thirty minutes to prepare for his followers. The Satanic tribe was known as the Yezidis. Ancient Middle Eastern Satanic history notes that the Yezidis believed in a figure akin to Lucifer. Like the legendary lost tribes of Israel, the Yezidis had separated themselves from the larger tribes due to unresolved conflicts. They became doctrinally distinct from all other groups.

Since Bradford was a faithful orthodox follower of what was called the "True Satan," he had decorated his temple in keeping with the style of the historic Yezidi temples. Bradford's Satanic followers entered his temple through portals featuring images of a lion, a snake, a double-sided axe, a man, and a portal adorned with a comb, scissors, and a mirror.

The lion symbolized strength and dominance, the snake represented procreation; the axe signified potential for good or evil; the man represented the god; and the comb, scissors, and mirror stood for pride.

Tonight, Bradford would wear two different Satanic garments. First, his black satin robe with blood-red inner lining, representing the Prince of Darkness, while he was delivering his sermon. However, for the Celebration of the Black Angel ritual, he would wear an ornate cloak with a colorful design of a peacock – a form taken by Satan in the Yezidi liturgy. In ancient times, followers did not dare to utter the name of Satan (Shaitan) for fear of prosecution. Instead, they referred to Satan as Melek Taus – the Peacock King.

Bradford unlocked the front sliding doors at 11:45 pm, and the Satanic followers who had gathered outside began to filter in. He immediately spotted Debra in the crowd and pulled her aside; she was hard to miss. The curvy young woman in her early thirties was of medium height and had a striking figure. She had long platinum hair that reached her mid-back and piercing blue eyes. Her skin was as white as porcelain, and she wore a black, form-fitting nylon jumpsuit that accentuated her figure.

Bradford's two new assistants, Cleve and Marcus, arrived shortly after Debra and Bradford led the three into a back room. There, Bradford explained the Black Angel ceremony, a sexual ritual. Debra was excited to obey her Satanic master, and the two assistants were eager to participate.

Bradford first donned the multi-colored Peacock Robe, then put on his black satin robe of a High Satanic Priest and placed his devil's mask over his shaved head. He grabbed his six-foot silver metal priest's staff, with a pentagram bearing the devil's likeness, and walked out to take his position before the altar, honoring the Angel of Darkness, Lucifer, the God Satan.

The altar was made of a large, flat, heavy wooden surface, fourteen feet long and eight feet wide, painted black and covered with a large black tablecloth. On top of the altar sat a large black square box with tall, silver candlesticks behind it, illuminated. Suspended from the ceiling above the altar was a large, silver pentagram featuring the likeness of Satan in its center.

Three stairs led up to the altar, perfect for tonight's visually striking and shocking ceremony. A single red spotlight shone on the altar, highlighting the pentagram above and the altar below. Red lights mounted on the floor surrounding the inner sanctum of the church illuminated the black curtains.

Dressed as Satan, the Angel of Darkness, Bradford activated a recorder, allowing flute music to sound in the room. He then began his sermon by reading a passage from the Al-Jilwah – the Satanic *Black Book.*

After the Satanic priest had read from the Black Book, on cue, a loud gong sounded, the flute music stopped, and Bradford's two assistants, dressed in hooded black satin robes, stood on either side of Debra, who was also dressed in a hooded black robe. The trio entered the chamber and walked to the altar.

Bradford now invoked the Third Enochian Key – The Satanic Bible and encouraged his faithful followers to witness the *Celebration of the Black Angel.* After reading from the Satanic Bible, the gong sounded again. Assistants Cleve and Marcus approached their Satanic priest, standing on either side of him, and carefully unbuttoned and removed his black satin robe, now revealing the brightly colored Peacock Robe, which mirrored the feathers of the bird, symbolizing the god Satan.

Now displaying his Peacock Robe, which was secured from neck to ankles with Velcro fasteners, Bradford climbed the stairs and took a position at the center of the altar next to the raised black box. His Satanic assistants then returned to Debra and helped her up the stairs. Debra approached the Satanic priest and then turned to face the crowd. In an instant, she shed her black robe, revealing her entire naked body. The gathered followers gasped in pleased surprise. Debra's ample breasts and erect nipples were striking. Even more remarkable, as she slowly turned, was a black tattoo of a large pentagram covering the area from just below her breasts to her shaved crotch, along with the large black tattooed bat-like wings of Lucifer that extended from her shoulders to her lower back.

The Satanic priest and Debra faced each other. Bradford tore open his Peacock Robe and extended it outward and away from his naked body like the wings of a bird, which was an ancient symbol of Satan. Assistants Cleve and Marcus shouted in unison, "Behold the Black Angel, Lucifer. Hail Satan!" In response, the followers exclaimed, "Hail Satan!"

Bradford's large, erect penis pointed towards Debra, who took a step forward, fell to her knees, and took the Satanic priest's penis into her mouth and began to copulate him, pumping in and out as Bradford cupped Debra's head in his hands, directing her and later cupping her breasts. The followers were mesmerized and excited by the erotic display.

After several minutes of oral intimacy, Bradford withdrew his penis from his female follower's mouth. He then directed her to the black box above the altar, so she was now bending over it, facing away from him, with her rounded buttocks facing his still erect shaft.

As the Satanic priest approached his willing slave from behind, he exclaimed, *"Behold, those who follow me will be rewarded with all of Hell's pleasures, including the pleasures of the flesh."*

Bradford's assistants led the chant, *"Hail, Satan! Hail Satan!"* as the personification of the Black Angel, Lucifer, entered Debra from behind, and the pair coupled intensely. Debra groaned with pleasure as the assembled followers chanted, *"Hail, Satan! Hail, Satan!"* until Bradford and Debra climaxed, he pulled out, and she lay prostrate and exhausted upon the altar.

The excitement and fervor of the sexual ritual caused couples to tear off their clothes and engage in sex, while single men looked for and got chances to join in threesomes for the next half hour.

This is the effect I've been looking for. When word spreads in the underground community, my church congregation will grow like no one expects. Now that the rewards have been shown publicly, Bradford thought, *It's time to give*

Cleve and Marcus a taste of the reward to pre-approve my next murder.

The sex-driven crowd barely noticed that their Satanic priest had left the altar with his sex slave, and his assistants had to go to the private back room.

Once secluded in Bradford's private chamber, he pulled Debra aside and whispered in her ear. She smiled and kissed Bradford passionately on the mouth. Then the Satanic priest faced his two assistants.

"I have a crucial and secret assignment for each of you that will let you show your loyalty and fidelity to your priest. This assignment will send you into darkness with me. Will you accept it without any questions or hesitation?" Bradford asked the men.

"Yes, priest." The men replied in unison.

"I will call on you for a mission tomorrow night. You must promise me now that you will be ready. Do you promise so?" Bradford asked.

"Yes, priest." The men replied.

"Very well. Enjoy your time together. I will check on my followers and lock up after you all leave. Debra, you have my promise that you'll be well rewarded for your loyalty today," Bradford said as he left the trio to indulge in their pleasures.

Chapter 19
Hell has no fury like a pissed off reporter

Gates and Bill Hurd picked up Wade and Dakota at the Sandpiper RV Park and drove them to the Buddhist Meditation Center for their 10:00 a.m. meeting with GFD Arson Investigator Pete Skogland. CSI Supervisor Lenny Spazzito and his team were already there, unpacking their gear and putting on their white disposable jumpsuits that read "FORENSICS" in bold black letters.

Gates and Bill Hurd introduced Wade and Dakota to Skogland. "Pleasure to meet you both. Nice to have a Texas Ranger and an experienced forensic pathologist on scene," said the arson investigator as he shook their hands. Once everyone had the proper safety gear, the arson investigator gathered them for a briefing.

Okay, people, here are your basic safety guidelines, most of which are common sense. Don't lean against walls or shake anything like a beam or wall frame. If you want to pick something up from the floor, call me and let me check it out first. Always look up before you move into any area, and then look all around your feet. Even though the electricity is off, don't touch any wires. I'm sure that almost all of you will be interested in the front room where the DB is. Who's going to be your finder for the search warrant?" Skogland asked.

"That will be me, Pete," replied Gates.

"Fine. You all know your search and evidence protocols, so work with Det. Sgt. Sullivan on any recoveries and recordings. I'll take you to the DB and point out again what I found that I believe provides us with the elements of arson and murder. Take all the photos, videos, and measurements you want," Skogland concluded before turning to Gates.

"Gates, it's your call when you want the ME's people out here. Let's go see our DB," said the arson investigator, leading the group into the front room.

The firefighters carefully built a small tent-like plastic tarp over the incinerated male figure kneeling on the floor facing the altar to shield the body from water dripping off the roof all night.

"Have you got an ID on our vic?" Skogland asked Gates.

"Yes, we are fairly certain the victim is the resident Buddhist priest Bhikkhu Kassapa from Thailand. He's the individual our department has identified as responsible for the center. Once we involve the ME, I believe we can obtain a positive ID with DNA," said Gates.

For the benefit of the CSI team, Wade and Dakota, Skogland pointed out the melted plastic zip-ties fused into the Buddhist priest's wrist bones, behind the knees, and ankle bones. Dakota took a close look at the locations of each pair of zip-ties. She saw that Skogland had a telescoping metal probe.

"Pete, can I borrow your probe for a minute?" the pathologist asked.

"Sure thing," replied the arson investigator, handing over the probe.

Dakota took the probe in her latex-gloved hands and asked Lenny Spazzito to photograph the body's condition, focusing on the placement of the melted zip ties first. After the CSI supervisor finished his photo scan of the body, Dakota began probing around the melted zip ties. Then she returned the probe to Skogland and started physically examining the charred skin on the victim's face, frozen in terror.

When Dakota leaned in to sniff the head of the body, Bill Hurd kept his mouth closed and turned away. Dakota noticed the detective's adverse reaction.

"You gonna be okay, Bill? She asked.

Bill's face was pale as he looked back at Dakota. "With all due respect, doctor, how the hell do you have the stomach to do that? My stomach's churning just watching you," the detective asked.

"No disrespect taken, my friend. It just comes with the job. And no disrespect to you and Gates, but you must remember that death is my business; you are occasional visitors." Addressing the group, Dakota shared her opinion.

"As Pete will tell you, the hottest spot in this room is where your victim is. See his skin and how deeply it's charred? This indicates that the fire started here, with our suspect setting him on fire using an accelerant. I can still smell it on him. The fire then spread throughout the room and to the adjoining areas, eventually reaching the roof and engulfing the entire structure."

"Wow, you're good, doc; very good," exclaimed Skogland.

Dakota smiled, "Well, I try, Pete; I try. You made a good call early in the game, Pete. You know your job," said Dakota, complimenting the arson investigator. "You definitely have a homicide here. The priest was zip-tied in this kneeling position as a display for us."

Wade patted Dakota on the back and smiled, "I'm impressed, Dr. Shannon," he whispered in her ear.

"Well, what do you think, Wade?" asked Gates.

"I think, just to cover all the bases motive-wise, your team should search the center and the priest's quarters for evidence of theft. Finding any point of entry will probably be fruitless but be thorough. Check with the officers on Swing Shift who responded and see if anything has come up in their neighborhood canvass. I saw a Whataburger behind the center. Those fast-food places usually have CCTV cameras, so maybe you'll get lucky.

"There's not much more that Dakota and I can do now. I want to return to our RV and review the murder book again. I keep thinking we're missing something," said Wade.

"Sure thing. Bill and I will give you guys a ride back to the Sandpiper. We need to return to our office. I have to inform our chief that we've got another clergy killing, this time an Asian Buddhist priest; another minority. He's not going to be happy," said Gates.

Gates and Hurd dropped Wade and Dakota off at their RV and returned to CID. No sooner had they walked through the door than their secretary, Sally, waved them over to her desk, handed Gates a stack of call slips, and gave them a heads-up.

"Chief wants to see you both at your earliest convenience. He's already reviewed last night's Watch Commander Report, which mentions the arson and possible homicide at the

Buddhist Zen Center. I wouldn't keep the Old Man waiting," the secretary suggested.

Gates and Hurd looked at each other. "I'm going to the John to freshen up. You put on a tie. Meet you by the elevator in ten," said Gates, and the pair split up.

Twelve minutes later, the detectives entered the foyer outside the chief's office. "He's expecting you, go right in," said the chief's secretary. Hurd adjusted his tie, and the pair entered the chief's office, standing at attention in front of his desk. The Commander of CID and the department's Press Information Officer (PIO) were already seated.

"Please be seated," the chief said as he started the conversation. He noticed their unhappy faces and wanted to begin by comforting his detectives.

"First off, I brought you here so I, the CID Commander, and our PIO can stay ahead of the curve on what the press calls the Clergy Killings. Your boss, Captain Hazen, told me that you two have been working hard on these murders and have already contacted a retired Texas Ranger, a forensic pathologist, and a local professor of Hebrew studies to consult on these cases. Those were smart moves. However, I've heard that there was a subsequent attack on the professor at Texas A&M's campus, and one of the attackers was killed."

"Yes, sir, unfortunately, that's correct. Professor Tzabar was forced to defend himself and killed one of his assailants. The other suspect got away. We have been unable to locate him, but we have a BOL out for his vehicle," Gates replied.

"Now, I've got one pain-in-the-ass local reporter pushing a divisive racial narrative that we have a white supremacist serial killer on the loose. He's scaring the crap out of our minority and Jewish communities. What can you two share with us on this third homicide?" the chief asked.

Gates began carefully and directly, understanding her chief's pressure.

"Our third victim is tentatively identified as Bhikkhu Kassapa, a Buddhist priest who was the resident cleric at the Zen Meditation Center. Our records indicate that he is from Thailand. The priest was incinerated in the fire, so we'll need to wait for DNA confirmation from the ME's Office to verify his ID.

"Our investigation, supported by GFD's arson investigator and our consulting pathologist, Dr. Dakota Shannon, indicates that the priest was zip-tied in a kneeling position facing an altar and then set on fire. The fire consumed most of the center, so any other direct evidence of the fire scene will be negligible. Of course, the priest's body is also a crime scene, so we will be able to recover evidence of the zip-tie restraints there. Both Arson Investigator Pete Skogland and Dr. Shannon detected the odor of some alcohol accelerant. That makes this arson and a homicide. Our CSI team, led by Supervisor Lenny Spazzito, is currently at the scene. After I have Spazzito's report, I'll have more for you later, Chief," Gates concluded.

"What about this narrative about a white supremacist killing off our clergy that this reporter from KWAV-TV 4 is pushing?" asked PIO Frank Fitsimmons.

"Although on its face, with all three clergy vics being either minorities or Jewish, all three of our consulting experts are advising that this is intentional misdirection from our real killer," said Gates.

"How so?" Asked the PIO.

"Our Hebrew religious and cultural expert, Dr. Tzabar, found a passage in Rabbi Abramson's Tanakh open to a section referencing a sexual assault that had nothing to do with the Rabbi's upcoming Saturday sermon. Next, one of the attackers that Dr. Tzabar killed in self-defense had tattoos that our expert, former Texas Ranger Wade Justus, identified as Satanic. Ranger Justus and Dr. Tzabar have been profiling our killer and believe he is possibly a Satanist who has a history as a sexual assault victim, possibly from a religious figure like a priest or cleric," Gates explained.

"I see. Is there any way we can pin this profile down further? We really need something to counter this reporter's inflammatory false narrative." Remarked the chief.

"I can assure you that my team and I are fully engaged in that angle. Unfortunately, these things take time," replied Gates.

"Yes, I'm sure you're doing everything you can, but time isn't a luxury we have. The murder of this Asian priest feeds into the media's wild white supremacist narrative. Some people naturally latch onto a "crazy racist" storyline. In the meantime, I want you and your team to know you have our full support, and this comes directly from the Mayor. He's a fair and straightforward guy and hates "political policing," as you know. Just keep going and keep us all updated. That's all, detectives," said the chief, wrapping up the meeting.

"Sir, yes, sir," said Gates. Gates and Hurd did an about-face and left the chief's office.

"Well, that was short and sweet. At least we're still employed," remarked Bill Hurd in the elevator on the way back up to CID.

"Could have been much worse, but at least we know that, for now, we have the support of our administration and the Mayor. My take on the meeting was to continue doing what we're doing and keep everyone informed—no surprises," replied Gates.

As the elevator doors opened, Gates and Hurd found themselves blindsided by KWAV-TV 4 reporter Johnny Costa, who was in the hallway outside of CID with a cameraman. Costa shoved a microphone into Gate's face.

"Detective Sergeant Gates, what can you tell us about last night's firebombing of the Zen Meditation Center on Church Street? Can you confirm that someone was found dead inside the center?" Asked the reporter.

Geeze Louise. How the hell did this asshole get inside the stationhouse? Thought Gates as she took a deep breath to compose herself before responding.

"We can confirm a fire at the Zen Meditation Center last night. However, there is no evidence that the center was firebombed as you assert. Galveston Fire arson investigators and our GPD CSI team are currently attempting to determine the nature and origin of the fire.

"We can also confirm that a body has been found inside the center. However, due to the intense fire, the victim was nearly incinerated. Therefore, we are working with our Medical

Examiner's Office to identify the person. This may take a few days," replied Gates guardedly.

"Is there any truth to the rumor that the body found inside the center is the resident Buddhist priest, an Asian from Thailand?" pressed Costa.

"As I said, we are trying to identify the victim, so we can't confirm a name, position, or race of the person right now," replied Gates, trying to steer the conversation away from the racial narrative she knew the reporter was aiming for.

Costa wouldn't let it go. He continued to push his narrative with the detective.

"But, if the victim *is* identified as an Asian Buddhist priest, this will make three clergy killings in three weeks, two of which were minorities, as well as one Jewish Rabbi. Can you confirm that homicide detectives are currently working on the premise that the killer is a lone wolf white supremacist serial killer with a strong racial and antisemitic motive?" asked Costa, pointedly. Gates was ready for this. She needed to thwart this divisive narrative – nip it in the bud. Gates looked past Costa and stared directly into the camera lens.

"Look, your continued comments claiming that any of these killings of our beloved religious figures are inaccurate or based on wild speculation with no factual basis. You need to stop pushing this divisive narrative.

"While it is true that a black minister and an Orthodox Jewish rabbi have been found murdered, our homicide team, along with external, independent consulting experts, has been developing a profile that dismisses your highly speculative theory.

"However, since this is an ongoing investigation, I cannot discuss anything about our investigation with the public now. Our department's PIO will continue to provide the media with updates as approved by the Office of the Chief of Police. Thank you, we've got to get back to work," said Gates with finality. She then moved past reporter Johnny Costa and his cameraman with Hurd into CID, closing the door behind them.

"Well, that went well," laughed Bill Hurd.

"F-ing ahole. I'll bet that put a bee in his bonnet," replied Gates.

"You can bet Costa's heading straight down to the chief's office right now for a comment," said Hurd.

Gates reached her desk and picked up the phone, dialing the chief's office. "I'm one step ahead of him. I'll give PIO Fitzsimmons a heads-up and let him know what I told Costa. Everyone's on the same page," replied Gates.

Wade and Dakota enjoyed a relaxing three-mile jog along the beach. Desi ran in and out of the water, chasing the local seabirds and barking happily. Despite occasional interruptions due to the clergy killings investigation, the couple cherished their special time together. The investigation was something they could work on as a team. It brought back memories of when they first met while investigating Nashville's infamous "Sleeping Beauty Murders."

The couple turned around at the Pleasure Pier and returned to the Sandpiper for a shower. Wade said he wanted to get back into the murder case involving the Baptist minister's homicide. "I just can't help feeling that we might have missed something there," he had said.

Wade, Dakota, and Desi returned to their RV. They took showers and felt refreshed. Desi was exhausted and happy to lie outside on her bed in the shade of the awning, chewing on a large bone Wade had brought her.

While Dakota read an eBook, Wade went back into the minister's murder book, starting with photos of the scene where he was found hanging above his pulpit. Wade reviewed the images of the pulpit, recalling Professor Tzabar's discovery of the Tanakh passage that shifted the investigation away from a white supremacist killer.

Maybe, just maybe, there's a theme here, the retired Texas Ranger pondered as he viewed CSI Supervisor Lenny Spazzito's enhanced images of the pulpit and the open Tanakh. As Wade read the open pages carefully, he spotted a curious passage in Revelation 12:9 that read,

"The great dragon was hurled down – That ancient serpent called the Devil or Satan, who leads the whole world astray."

A clear sign that Satan is the deceiver of humanity. The pentagram and 666 tattoos found on the deceased suspect who tried to kill Lyeb, and now this new reference to Satan. No way our killer is a white supremacist, Wade pondered, who then wrote a note to himself to have Gates check with Minister Jefferson's assistants or any congregants about the topic of his Sunday sermon on the day he was murdered.

Wade next examined the CAD—Computer Aided Dispatch Incident Summary. The CAD offered a detailed timeline with timestamps for every piece of information related to the police response to an incident, from the initial 9-1-1 call, the complaint taker's details, the dispatched call for service, to all units responding, from beginning to end.

Wade noted that the incident started from a 9-1-1 call to the Galveston PD 9-1-1 Emergency Center. He mentioned that the caller was "anonymous." The call came in at 18:06 hours, with the reporting person telling the 9-1-1 operator, *"I am reporting suspicious circumstances—maybe a man hanging at the First Southern Baptist Church on 23rd Street at Sealy Avenue,"* before hanging up. The caller's phone number was listed as "unavailable." He did not give a name, even though the complaint taker asked him twice.

Wade thought about his Texas Ranger mentor Matt Fremont's wise advice about investigations, *"When stymied, all investigations begin at the beginning... At the beginning..."* Wade pondered. *"At the beginning... What am I missing?"* he wondered as he looked over the CAD.

Anonymous caller who refused to ID himself or provide his location. Not all that unusual. Sometimes people don't want to get involved but want the police to know about something.

However, the CAD notes indicated that the caller repeated the same information verbatim to the complaint taker before hanging up. The complaint taker listed as "B. Rosarios, #1618," noted, "Voice sounded synthesized, metallic, possibly recorded."

The CAD documented "Unlisted phone number" and timestamped the call into the 9-1-1 center at 18:06 hours.

"I am reporting suspicious circumstances—maybe a man hanging at the First Southern Baptist Church on 23rd Street at Sealy Avenue,"

Wade reviewed the images in the murder book taken of the outside of the church and asked himself, *Who just walks past a church and looks through the windows? How could he see the minister hanging inside the church? You couldn't. He had to be inside...*

Wade went outside, where Dakota was lounging in a chair next to Desi, reading her eBook. "Hey, I've got a minute to look at something. Do I need a fresh set of eyes?" he asked.

Dakota devoured murder mysteries and was in the middle of one now. "From one murder mystery to the next. Sure, be right in," she said, closing her Kindle Fire.

Dakota noticed Wade had the murder book for the Baptist minister spread out on the kitchen table. "What are you working on, Ranger?" she asked.

"The CAD. I've reviewed this CAD, reconciling the anonymous caller's information with the 9-1-1 complaint taker. The CAD shows that the RP was anonymous and used an unlisted phone. More suspiciously, the complaint taker noted that the call sounded synthesized and metallic, as if it were recorded. The same information was repeated word for word. See here?" said Wade, passing the CAD report to Dakota and pointing to the entry.

"Can you make anything from this?" Wade asked.

Dakota carefully looked at the page, reading everything about the initial 9-1-1 call.

"I see what you see. What's so suspicious about an anonymous caller? Don't police get those all the time? These days, not many people want to get involved, especially with a dead person. He's reporting he saw a possible dead body hanging inside the church," Dakota replied.

"Yes, but now look at these photos of the outside of the church. How can anyone from that sidewalk see through those narrow louvered windows into a dimly lit church? Call came in at 18:06 hours," replied Wade.

"Good point, cowboy. I don't think he could see inside unless he was up against those windows looking in," said Dakota.

"I'm just not buying the whole crazed white supremacist, racist, Jew hating suspect angle. I went back over the images of the pulpit and found that the Rabbi's Tanakh was open to Revelations.

"I've been going over the images. Look here, said Wade, showing Dakota the open passage in Revelation 12:9.

Dakota read the passage aloud: "The great dragon was hurled down—that *ancient serpent called the Devil or Satan, who leads the whole world astray."*

"Well, I think you're definitely on the right track. Your buddy Lyeb Tzabar was saying the same thing about the killing of Rabbi Abramson; not that the killer was a Satanist, but that he wasn't a white supremacist in his opinion..." Dakota stopped talking as her eyes shifted back to the CAD report.

"Wait...What was the date of the Baptist minister's murder?" Dakota asked.

"The 6th, April 6th," replied Wade.

Dakota pondered the date. *April 6...the 6th...1806 hours...the 6th at 6:06 pm...606 on the 6th...the 6th at 606...*

It struck them like a bolt of lightning as they looked at each other and exclaimed in unison, *"6-6-6, 666," Mark of the Beast!"*

"This is far too coincidental to pass up. I've got to call Gates," said Wade, picking up his cellphone and dialing the detective.

Gates was reviewing the Supplemental Reports from Swing Patrol Supervisor Sgt—Sergio Diaz's patrol team officers after the arson fire and homicide at the Zen Meditation Center. An officer had noted that the Whataburger restaurant had CCTV facing the Center. He contacted the manager, asking him to preserve the digital video file for homicide detectives. Gates' cellphone rang. It was Wade, and she answered it.

"What are you up to? I've been reviewing the Baptist minister's murder book and have some things to discuss," Wade asked.

"Well, since you asked, I've been dodging asshole reporters and reading supplements. How's your vacation going? I hope we haven't screwed it up too much so far," said Gates.

"Luckily, I found the right girl to spend time with. Vacation is going well. We enjoy the beach, and your investigations keep the brain cells from atrophying," replied Wade.

"Well, if you were here in late summer, you'd be changing your tune. You'd be swapping shirts three times a day—like living in Florida," said the detective, chuckling. "What's on your mind, Ranger?" she asked.

"A couple more things that strengthen our suspect profile argument favoring a Satanist rather than a white supremacist killing your clergy. Can you pull out your CAD report for the 9-1-1 call that triggered the police response?" asked Wade.

"Sure, give me a minute," said Gates, accessing the electronic file on her PC and bringing up the first page. "I'm here, what do you have?" she asked.

"Look at the date and time of the first call into the 9-1-1 call center and then the complaint taker's notes of the call," said Wade.

"Okay... anonymous caller reporting a possible man hanging inside the church... Call taker writes, "phone unavailable... exact call information repeated twice... voice sounded synthesized, metallic, and possibly recorded..." Gates replied.

"Do you see the date and time of the call?" Wade prompted.

"Sure, the 6th at 1806 hours, okay...what?" Gates asked.

"Dakota figured this out, so I must give her the credit. How about "6-6-6," April 6 at 606...666. The Mark of the Beast, Old Mr. Satan. Remember the 666 and pentagram tattoos on the DB that Professor Lyeb Tzabar took out the other night? Dakota and I think our killer is a Satanist, not a crazy racist, Jew-killing white supremacist.

"It's all deliberate misdirection to throw us off the trail. The 9-1-1 complaint taker noted in the CAD that the caller sounded "synthesized, metallic, and possibly recorded."

That's right there. It was recorded. Our guy used a recorded, synthesized voice, so we couldn't identify him. He killed Reverend Jefferson on April 6th and then called in the death exactly at 6:06 pm," Wade continued.

"Now pull up pictures of the outside of the Baptist church. Observe the distance from the sidewalk to the narrow louvered windows. There's no way a citizen could see inside the church from the sidewalk. He would have to be right up against the windows or inside the church," said Wade.

Gates brought the images and saw that Wade was right.

"That's pretty good, Wade. You've convinced me. I will share this new information with my boss and our chief. That's a boost for them. It will definitely create some resistance to keep that reporter Johnny Costa at bay," replied Gates.

"Sounds good to me. Let me know how it all works out," replied Wade, ending the call.

As soon as Wade hung up, Gates called Bill Hurd into her office and told him what Wade and Dakota had found.

"You're calling the chief on this, right?" said her partner.

"Just watch me before we do that, chain of command. Let's walk down to Commander Garcia's office. We give him the 4-1-1 first and let him decide who will tell the chief. Come on," said Gates, standing up from her desk.

The two homicide detectives entered the CID Commander's office, where Gates spent ten minutes updating their boss. Commander Garcia decided to inform the chief and the department's PIO personally.

Coming out of the office, Gates told Hurd about the Supplemental Report from one of Sgt. Diaz's officers are documenting the CCTV at the Whataburger behind the Zen Meditation Center.

"Let's drive over there and see what we can find. It might be helpful," suggested Gates. Thirty minutes later, the two investigators arrived at the restaurant. Gates and Hurd circled the establishment, noting that CCTV cameras covered all four corners of the property. They entered the restaurant and introduced themselves to the manager.

"Yes, I made sure to keep a copy of the videos from that night. The officer was particular about that," the manager said as he led them into his office at the back of the restaurant. Inside the office was a forty-inch monitor split into eight camera feeds. Four screens showed the establishment's interior, while the other four displayed all four corners of the restaurant, including the surrounding area and parking lots.

"How far back do you want me to go?" the manager asked. Gates presented the CAD report documenting the first 9-1-1 call about the fire, including timestamps. She noted the time of the 9-1-1 call and instructed the manager to return in thirty minutes. The manager was happy to comply.

"Sit at the desk, Sergeant. This is the joystick. You can select any of the cameras and control them from here. You can adjust the speeds by touching this icon, freeze the frame by clicking here, and even zoom in and out using the control knob on the stick. It's really pretty simple. Give it a try," he suggested.

“Let’s watch all the cameras to see what’s moving about. If we see something interesting, we can log the timestamps and go back for a closer look,” Gates replied.

After the first ten minutes, Gates and Hurd started watching the videos and noticed that the Whataburger was having a slow night. Aside from the employee cars parked in the back, no one had entered the parking lot or gone through the drive-thru. Five minutes later, a man dressed in all black, carrying a black backpack and riding an eBike, drove into the rear of the lot next to the employees' cars and stopped. The individual brought his bike up to a line of trees that separates the restaurant’s property from the backyard of the Zen Meditation Center.

“Hey, look at this guy,” Gates said to her partner.

“Yeah, I see him. Why isn’t he going into the restaurant?” Hurd asked. The subject pulled his bike into the tree line and disappeared one minute later.

“Auto burg perp?” asked Hurd.

“I didn’t see him scope out any of the vehicles there. Maybe he’s taking a leak. Keep watching,” said Gates. Then two detectives watched the tree line where they had seen the blacked-out subject disappear for another fifteen minutes.

“That’s way too long for taking a leak. No activity at the vehicles either. Where the hell is he?” Gates asked rhetorically. Five minutes later, the figure dressed in black reemerged from the tree line, wearing his backpack and walking his eBike. The subject carefully scanned the parking lot, returned on his bike, and quickly rode away. Gates captured the timestamp when the subject left.

"Let's keep watching," said Gates.

Ten minutes later, the homicide detectives saw a bright glow through the tree line and smoke drifting over the trees. Gates wrote down the timestamp and paused the video to review the CAD report. Check the CAD timestamp for the 9-1-1 call reporting the fire. It's very close to what we're seeing here," she said, pointing out the timestamp on the video. Let's go back and take a closer look at eBike Boy.

Gates reversed the videos of the rear parking lot facing the employee cars and the cypress tree line until the man dressed in black with the backpack on the eBike entered the parking lot and stopped next to the tree line. Then she zoomed in on the subject and froze the video frame with its timestamp.

Gates called out to the manager who was working at his desk. "Does your surveillance system have the ability to print screenshots?" she asked.

"Sure. Just tell me what you want printed. Save the screenshots, keep the timestamps, and make me a list. I'll print them out for you. I can also store everything—videos and screenshots—on a flash drive and give it to you. I'm used to doing that for the cops when we have auto burglaries," said the manager.

"Awesome, that will work fine for us," replied Gates as she zoomed in on the blacked-out subject straddling the eBike and froze the frame for a screenshot.

"What have we here?" she asked rhetorically as she and Det. Hurd examined the enhanced image of their potential arson and homicide suspect. Although it wasn't clear enough for identification, they confirmed he was a white male.

Gates took a screenshot, recorded the timestamp, and let the video play until the person in a black hoodie got off his eBike and stood beside it. Then she paused the frame, zoomed in again, and took another screenshot with its timestamp.

“See how close he is to this Toyota Tundra pickup? I think Lenny Spazzito in CSI can determine his height using photogrammetry. All we need is the Tundra’s specifications, then we can compare measurements," explained Gates.

“Sweet,” replied Hurd.

Gates next zoomed in on the eBike, capturing its battery pack's “RAD” logo. “The logo says 'RAD,' use your phone and Google RAD eBikes and tell me what comes up,” said Gates.

Hurd pulled out his iPhone and began typing. “Chinese make, not cheap either, about $1,600 a pop,” he replied.

“Copy. Please find all the bike shops in the county that sell them. That’s a follow-up for the future. Let’s see what we missed the first time around,” remarked Gates as she and her partner played through the video until the subject in the hoodie reappeared from the tree line, pushing his eBike.

“Here we are, my friend. Pray tell, what kind of backpack are you wearing?” Gates asked rhetorically as she zoomed in on the suspect as he rode out of the parking lot. Unfortunately, she was unable to identify the backpack type.

Gates called the manager. “Here’s our list of screenshots and timestamps. We will need you to create two separate files, one for all the videos from CCTVs 1 and 3, and one for these screenshots. Can you do that?”

"One hundred percent, Sergeant Gates, can do," replied the manager, smiling.

"Great. We'll grab some chow out front, and you can bring us the flash drive, " Gates said.

"Tell the gals out front it's on the house. Just happy to help out. Heard someone died in that fire. Poor soul," replied the manager.

"Thanks, but we'll pay for the chow. It's the least we can do," offered Gates.

Detectives Gates and Hurd had lunch, received the flash drive from the manager, and headed back to CID. It was almost 5:00 p.m. Bill Hurd turned on the TV in the office to watch the local news on KWAV-TV 4, just in time to see their friend, reporter Johnny Costa, standing in front of the Galveston Police Department.

"In tonight's news, I've been reporting the developing story for the past three weeks on the Galveston Clergy Killings.

"We now have confirmation from GPD Homicide that last night's suspicious fire at the Buddhist Zen Meditation Center has claimed one life. Current speculation is that the victim of the fire, believed to have been set by an arsonist, could be Thai Buddhist priest, Bhikkhu Kassapa, the resident cleric.

"This makes the third death of a cleric in as many weeks. As you may recall, three weeks ago, First Baptist Church's well-regarded black minister, the Rev. Jacob Jefferson, was found lynched inside his own church after Sunday services. The following week, orthodox Jewish Rabbi, David Abramson, of the old Congregation B'nai Israel Temple, was discovered deceased in his office following the Shabbat. It is believed that he was the victim of a toxic gas.

"Now we have the highly suspicious death of an Asian, believed to be the resident Buddhist priest of the Zen Meditation Center. All three deaths, two of which have been classified as homicides, have taken place in the City's historic Midtown District. All three deaths strongly suggest that the motivation behind them is racism and antisemitism.

"When I interviewed Galveston PD Homicide's lead investigator, Det. Sgt. Gates Sullivan, about last night's arson and suspicious death, she was tight-lipped about the circumstances."

The story then cut to an edited clip of Gates' interview with Costa.

"Detective Sergeant Gates, is there any truth to the rumor that the body found inside the center is the resident Buddhist priest, an Asian from Thailand?"

"As I told you just now, we are attempting to identify the victim, so right now we can't confirm a name, position, or the person's race," replied Gates. The camera returned to reporter Costa.

"The GPD administration has been equally cautious in providing any additional information, potential leads, or any criminal psychological profile of the suspect or suspects, citing an ongoing investigation.

"So right now, we are left to wonder, just who is stalking and systematically murdering Galveston's religious clergy? What is the motive? Is it racism and antisemitism? We have no answers right now, just a sense of foreboding as we await the next assault upon our clerics. This is investigative reporter Johnny Costa, KWAV-TV Channel 4 News."

Bill Hurd turned off the set. Gates was seething.

"You know they say that television makes you look twenty pounds heavier, but I think you look slender," remarked Hurd, joking.

"Up yours, Bill. That prick Costa is a real a-hole," replied Gates.

"Well, what did you expect after you shut him down this morning – and appropriately so, I might add," said Hurd.

"We've got a serial killer to find. I don't have the time nor inclination to fence with that POS, that's POI Fitzsimmon's lane," replied Gates.

"Well, if it's any consolation, after the chief, Commander Garcia, and Fitzsimmons catch this broadcast and include the info you got from Wade and Dakota, the Chief's Office will shut down that idiot and his BS inflammatory story, pronto. I'll bet my next paycheck on it," replied Hurd, trying to calm his agitated partner.

"Thanks, Bill, we'll see. It's after five, and I'm heading home for a stiff drink and some late-night studying," said Gates, putting all three murder books into her expandable, rolling briefcase and heading for the door. Remember that you've got the night call duty tonight. I'll be available if you need me."

"Copy that. Just take it easy. Tomorrow is another day in paradise. Catch you in the morning," replied Hurd, waving Gates out the door.

Chapter 20
A Pleasant Walk On the Beach

Wade and Dakota were enjoying a cold beer inside the RV. Dakota turned on the TV to catch the local weather report on KWAV-TV 4 when Gates' media nemeses, investigative reporter Johnny Costa's spray-on tan face and one-hundred-dollar haircut, appeared on the screen. True to form, the reporter was hell-bent on spewing his disconcerting false narrative about a racist, antisemitic serial killer terrorizing the minority and religious communities.

The couple watched in disgust as the peacock Costa put their colleague Gates Sullivan front and center and accused the Galveston PD's administration and their Homicide Unit of withholding information about the killer.

"How do these jerks like Costa get away with this crap show? Gates, Bill, and their whole team are working their tails off to catch this creep," exclaimed Dakota.

"The best revenge against POSs like Johnny Costa is to do everything we can to help Gates and Bill catch this guy. If our theory that the real killer is a Satanist is correct and we catch him, Costa will have egg all over his orange spray-tanned face," replied Wade.

"I'm sure you're right, Wade. This whole thing about dumping on GPD and our friends drives me to work even harder. I still have plenty of time before starting my new job in San Antonio. In the morning, why don't you call Gates and tell her we're available to spend more time on these cases," said Dakota.

Wade was impressed. *This one's a keeper*, he thought. Wade got up from the dinner table, went over to Dakota, and gave her a big kiss and hug.

"You're my gal, Dakota. I like your fighting spirit," he exclaimed with a smile.

"Thanks, Wade. It's the right thing to do," replied Dakota.

The couple had dinner after the sun set, and it got dark. Desi was whining about going outside for her evening walk on the beach. Dakota put the dog's harness and leash on and was about to leave when Wade warned her.

"Hey, sweetie, it's pretty dark outside, and we already know there's at least one creep out there. Let's say we arm ourselves before we go on our walk. Better to have a gun and not need it than to need a gun and not have one," said Wade.

Dakota paused, dropped the leash, and went into the back bedroom. She opened her portable gun safe, took out her Glock 48 9mm semiauto, and tucked it into a wide belly band holster that she fastened under her loose Vanderbilt U. Medical School T-shirt.

"Good to go!" she remarked as Wade strapped on his Nichols Custom Combat .45 caliber 1911A semiauto pistol. The couple, carrying small tactical flashlights, walked outside with Desi and headed for the beach for a quick walk and a potty break. After returning to the RV, the couple watched a John Wayne western for the night.

The next morning, detectives Gates Sullivan, Bill Hurd, and Lenny Spazzito had breakfast together at Miller's Seawall Grill on Seawall Blvd. while watching the morning news on Houston's FOX News affiliate KRIV-26 when GPD's Chief of Police, CID Commander Garcia, and department PIO Frank Fitzsimmons briefly appeared on screen for a quick press conference. The chief, dressed in full uniform, began the conference.

"Ladies and gentlemen of the press and Galveston residents, we have called this press conference out of necessity to protect our community members and residents. At the end of the event, we will not be answering any questions for now.

"Recently, a so-called investigative reporter has been claiming that the suspect in the murders of three members of our local clergy was motivated by racism, bigotry, and antisemitism to kill our clerics. The term "white supremacist" has been loosely and irresponsibly thrown around on public television. We are here to publicly oppose this divisive, self-serving, false narrative in the strongest terms.

"The local reporter, whom I will not name, has no facts or evidence to support his false claims. He has intentionally tried to embarrass our homicide investigators and team members, who are working hard to find the killer and bring him to justice quickly.

"As some of you understand, in an ongoing investigation like this, we, as police officers sworn to protect the public, cannot violate our promise to keep you safe by sharing highly confidential information with the media that could allow the killer to interfere with the investigation. At this

moment, I will say this: Our investigation team now has solid evidence indicating that these murders were not motivated by racism, bigotry, or antisemitism.

"No so-called white supremacist is stalking and killing our City's clergy, and we challenge any reporter who asserts otherwise to provide us and you, the public, with factual evidence to support their claims. In other words, either put up or shut up!

"Therefore, we ask you to please dismiss all these irresponsible and wildly speculative reports that aim to inflame and divide our communities.

"As your Chief of Police, I assure you that the men and women of the Galveston Police Department will identify and bring this killer to justice. I promise that whenever we have information to share that doesn't compromise our investigation, it will be shared with the news media, you, and the public. This concludes our press conference. We will not be taking any questions at this time. I appreciate your understanding. Now, please let us do our jobs."

"Well, that was a mic drop moment. Geez, Louise. I know one set of tail feathers the chief just singed. Good for him," exclaimed Bill Hurd.

"Put up, or shut up? My mother used to say that. It's a classic," said Lenny.

"I don't know when I've seen the chief that pissed. I think spray tan Costa will find another news story to work on for a while. Hopefully, this public bitch slapping by the chief buys us some important time to ID this guy before he kills someone else," offered Gates.

The three detectives returned to CID, where Bill Hurd busied himself checking all of the eBike shops in Galveston and the surrounding county that sold the RAD brand to gather lists of owners. CSI Supervisor Lenny Spazzito was working on cracking the cellphone found on the body of the man Professor Tzabar had killed in self-defense. Gates was poring over the three murder books for anything else they might have missed that could help identify their killer.

Wade called Gates late in the morning to tell her he and Dakota had seen reporter Costa on TV the night before and were willing to give up some vacation time to assist with the homicide investigations. Gates mentioned the chief's morning press conference and guessed that the now-embarrassed reporter might have received enough criticism to back off the story for a while.

"Great news. One more thing. I've been thinking more about my involvement in the Sleeping Beauty Murders in Nashville a few years back. The serial killer in those murders was a guy named Brennan, Jeremy Brennan. A real smart killer who was stalking and strangling rising female Country Western stars in the city," he explained.

"Yes, I remember your involvement in that case. As I recall, you and your son Hunter, a TBI Special Agent, "replied Gates.

"Exactly. Compared to this one, you should query VICAP, the Violent Criminal Apprehension Program, out of the National Crime Information Center – NCIC. VICAP aims to link cases that may be cross-related across different jurisdictions and help law enforcement catch and track serial killers.

"VICAP is essentially a national repository and an analytical tool within NCIC. You can input the basic facts of our suspect's methods in our killings to see if there have been any similar MOs nationwide. Maybe something will come up," suggested Wade.

Gates thanked Wade for his offer and the VICAP suggestion, saying she would call if she needed more consulting help. After she hung up, she briefly shifted her focus and began to compile a list of facts about the killer's methods for killing each of the three fallen clergy members to submit as an inquiry into NCIC's VICAP.

Overall, the day moved slowly for the GPD homicide and CSI detectives. Wade and Dakota spent the day driving along the coast with Desi, checking out the beaches and seafood restaurants. The couple went back to the RV after dark.

A few miles north of the Sandpiper RV Park, Bradford met with his eager assistants, Cleve and Marcus, at the New Church of Satan on Harborside Drive. Bradford had watched the Galveston Police Department's morning press conference, where the Chief of Police had pretty much dismantled his white supremacist killer misdirection ploy. The Satanic priest was visibly angry.

"What the fuck! All the meticulous planning, the work, the would be perfect scheme – destroyed in one fucking press conference!" Bradford exclaimed.

Of course, Cleve and Marcus had no idea what their priest and mentor was ranting about, so they stayed silent while Bradford vented. After several minutes of uncontrolled outbursts, Bradford calmed down. He had devised a new plan that his assistants could actively participate in.

He would still have his revenge on his abuser, Father Fogarty. Out with the old and in with the new plan. I can still keep the cops off balance. Fine, so the killer isn't a white supremacist, but he is stalking and killing clergy.

They can't possibly protect them all. I'll kill another one and completely overwhelm the Galveston Police Homicide Unit. While they are working overtime to solve four homicides, I'll strike down Father Fogarty and make him pay heavily for his vile sins against me and his God. Satan will have his pound of flesh! Hail Lucifer, hail Satan! Thought the myopically fixated Bradford.

Bradford had seen several commercials for the Galveston Sea of Christ's Prophecy Evangelical Church in the Midtown District. The church's charismatic pastor, Rev. Patrick Steiner, a German-born evangelist, was gaining recognition as a religious leader among younger people.

The Satanic priest has been researching Rev. Steiner and noted that his ministry had grown substantially. Steiner was part of the New Age movement of evangelism. He built his reputation and popularity through social media platforms like Instagram, Facebook, and TikTok. His Galveston Sea of Christ's Prophecy Evangelical Church was conveniently located on Seawall Blvd. at 11th St. Ave., just east of the Galveston Jetty and the beach. He often delivered sermons on the beach, where he frequently baptized new converts into Christ in the Gulf's shallow waters near the jetty.

Rev. Steiner was young, handsome, charismatic, and hugely popular. The perfect target for Bradford's next spectacular homicidal act. Bradford decided that he and his assistants would kidnap the evangelist, take him to the beach, and crucify him right where he preached and baptized his followers. *How shocking would that be!* the crazed Satanic priest mused.

Now it was time to motivate his assistants. Bradford drew the two over to him in front of the altar.

"How was your time with Debra?" he asked Cleve and Marcus, smiling.

"Awesome," replied Cleve.

"Like no other woman I've been with before," said Marcus.

I'm glad you both enjoyed yourselves. More women like Debra and others will follow if you demonstrate your loyalty to your priest. As I mentioned and promised earlier, tonight you'll join me on a special mission—a Satanic one—to remove a religious hypocrite from our community, an evangelical preacher named Rev. Patrick Steiner. Have you heard of him?" Bradford asked. Both young men nodded affirmatively.

"Who hasn't heard of him? He's all over TV and social media. His church is down by the beach," said Cleve.

He has thousands of followers. Lots of cute girls go to his church. He preaches there and even baptizes people in the waves," replied Marcus.

"Exactly. Evangelical Christians are the enemies of Satan, do you agree?" asked Bradford.

"Yes, priest," replied Cleve.

"Yes, they are all enemies of Satan," said Marcus.

"Will you both join me on a mission blessed by our god Satan to vanquish this purveyor of false prophecy?" asked Bradford.

"Yes, priest," the men said in unison.

"Excellent, then we strike when darkness falls," replied the Satanic priest.

Bradford learned from his Instagram posts that Rev. Steiner often worked at his church at night after regular hours. He planned to use one of his assistants' vehicles. Cleve had a pickup truck, which would be perfect not only for transporting the disabled preacher but also for carrying a large wooden cross that the Satanic priest had built for the evangelical preacher's crucifixion. The Satanic priest brought his black satin robe, devil's mask, silver metal priest's staff, and his backpack with a murder kit.

The trio, dressed in hoodies and all in black, drove to the Galveston Sea of Christ's Prophecy Evangelical Church and parked across the street on Avenue M, watching the premises. Eventually, the lights were turned off, except for one at the back of the building. Bradford turned to Marcus.

"Get up next to the building and see if you can see Steiner inside," he instructed.

"Yes, my priest," replied Marcus, exiting the truck and stealthily approaching the back of the church. Marcus carefully moved toward a window and looked inside, immediately recognizing Rev. Steiner, who was placing some items in a cabinet. Marcus returned to the truck to report that the preacher was inside the church.

"What was the preacher doing?" Bradford asked Marcus.

"He was placing some items inside a cabinet. It looked to me like he was getting ready to leave soon," the assistant replied.

"Very well," replied the priest, opening his black backpack and pulling out a pair of black gloves, several long black plastic zip ties, a roll of duct tape, a small flashlight, and a clear plastic Zip-Lok bag containing a black washrag soaked with chloroform.

"Marcus, you will go with me to the back of the church, where we will wait for the preacher to exit through the rear door over there. We will stay hidden in those bushes nearby. We'll approach from behind him. I'll hold him, and you place this chloroform-soaked rag over his nose and mouth while you hold his legs tightly. We'll bring him to the ground. The chloroform will take effect quickly, and he'll be unconscious in seconds. Once he's down, we'll secure his arms behind his back and his ankles with these zip-ties and tape his mouth so he can't call out or scream. Do you understand?" Bradford asked.

"Yes, my priest. I can do that," replied Marcus. Bradford then turned to Cleve, who was in the driver's seat.

"Cleve, watch the back of the church carefully. When you see the blinking flashlight, drive the truck to us and park as close as you can. Then get out and help us load the preacher into the truck bed. We'll cover him with the tarp and Marcus; you'll jump into the bed to watch over him. I'll be in the cab with you, Cleve, and will guide you to drive onto the beach to a spot I've picked.

"Once we reach the spot, we'll quickly assemble the cross. Then we are going to nail this enemy of Satan to the cross and set him on fire to cleanse and absolve him of his sins. We drive off the beach and out of the area, and I'll call 9-1-1 to report the fire. It will be a spectacular sacrifice to our god, Satan, for which each of you will be amply rewarded," explained the maniacal priest.

Cleve and Marcus were incredulous of their priest's plan and anxious, but were intent upon pleasing their Satanic master.

It was just past 9:00 p.m., and Desi's internal clock went off. She howled while looking closely at Wade and Dakota. It was time for her walk and potty before bed.

Wade looked at Dakota and chuckled. "You can set your watch by this dog. That's the 'Hey, it's past nine and potty time' howl," said Wade.

Dakota saw that Wade was reviewing the Buddhist priest's murder book, so she offered to take Desi for her evening walk and constitution.

"Okay, you know the drill—dog harness, leash, cellphone, tactical light, and gun. I really appreciate it. Desi loves her walks. I need to finish this last review. Remind Desi not to pull you along while you're walking her," Wade cautioned.

"Sir, yes, sir, Sergeant Justus." After she got Desi out of the RV and closed the door, she replied, "We're going to walk to the jetty and back."

Bradford and Marcus stealthily approached the rear of the church and waited in the darkness. Minutes later, Rev. Steiner emerged from the back door, closed it, and locked it behind him. As he turned to walk to his car, the Satanic priest and his assistant enveloped the preacher from top to bottom.

Bradford used his technique of pressing the chloroform-soaked washrag against the reverend's nose and mouth, causing him to lose balance backward. Marcus tackled Steiner's lower legs, bringing him down like a pack of jackals attacking a wildebeest. Steiner's attempts to breathe and struggle only worked against him as he inhaled the chloroform fumes. He was unconscious within seconds.

Bradford and Marcus rolled Steiner onto his stomach, quickly zip-tied his wrists and arms behind his back, then secured his ankles together. Bradford tore off a piece of duct tape and pressed it over the preacher's mouth to stop him from calling out when he woke up.

Bradford pulled the small flashlight from his back pocket and blinked it three times at Cleve. The driver's assistant was ready, darting across the street, over the sidewalk, and into the back of the church, where Bradford and Marcus had the evangelical preacher hogtied. The trio quickly tossed Steiner into the truck's bed, shut the tailgate, and Marcus jumped into the rear bed as Cleve and Bradford entered the cab.

"Go, go, go! Get to the jetty quickly!" yelled Bradford as Cleve hit the gas and the trio sped around the corner, onto Seawall Blvd., then quickly turned right onto the Galveston Jetty.

The Galveston Jetty was about three-quarters of a mile south of the RV park. Dakota knew she and Desi could usually cover that distance and return within thirty minutes. That night's spring weather at the beach was cool, in the low sixties. Dakota wore running shorts, her Vanderbilt U. T-shirt, a zip-up nylon athletic jacket, and running shoes. As usual, her Glock 48 9mm pistol was securely strapped to her body in the wide Velcro holster inside her suit top. She could easily reach the weapon by drawing it up her top.

Following his Satanic master's instructions, Cleve took a dirt side road from the jetty onto Porretto Beach and drove toward the water until Bradford told him to stop about twenty yards from the shoreline. The three of them got out of the truck and carried the unconscious Steiner and the large wooden cross from the truck bed, placing each on the sandy beach.

Bradford pulled his backpack out of the cab and removed his black satin Satanic priest robe and devil mask. Then he grabbed a large hammer and three half-inch by ten-inch metal tent stakes. He put on his priest's costume, getting ready for his planned crucifixion ritual, and approached his assistants, who were dressed as their god, Satan.

"Use your knives to cut the zip-ties, then lay him onto the cross so we can secure him on it before he awakes," ordered the Satanic priest, anxiously.

Cleve and Marcus used their eight-inch fixed-blade Buck knives to cut the zip ties from the reverend's wrists and ankles. Then they dragged him over to the cross and laid him on it.

"Hold his arms down while I hammer his wrists into the cross. Then we'll do his ankles. When the preacher wakes up, I want him to see the real god, Satan, before he is consumed by fire!" Bradford exclaimed.

"Yes, Satan!" replied the enthralled assistants, holding their victim's arms down against the wooden beam.

Bradford placed the substantial tent stake against Steiner's left wrist and looked at his assistants in the dark.

"Cleve, hold his arm down, and Marcus, keep the tent stake steady over his wrist so I can drive it in," he ordered. The two men obeyed the commands, and Bradford began pounding the stake through the preacher's wrist into the beam of the wooden cross. The intense pain woke Steiner, who looked up into what seemed to be the face of a living Satan and screamed in terror through the duct tape. The preacher started kicking his legs, causing Marcus to lie over the man's legs to keep him down and against the cross.

Cleve held Steiner's right arm against the wooden beam so Bradford could quickly hammer the reverend's wrist to it. Now Steiner's upper body was secured. Next, they moved on to the preacher's ankles. Holding the screaming minister's legs to the vertical support beam required both assistants' strength. Bradford saw Steiner struggling so fiercely against them that he couldn't nail him to the cross.

"This isn't working while he's conscious. Hold him down. I'll get the zip ties from my pack, and we'll secure his ankles to the cross with them. Then we'll burn him!" Bradford exclaimed. The priest ran to the truck, grabbed the zip ties, and the trio managed to attach the terrified victim to the cross.

Once Pastor Steiner was securely tied to the cross, Bradford returned to his backpack, grabbed a Mason jar of gasoline, and went back to the tormented minister. Wearing his Satan mask, he bent down, stared into his face, sneered, and triumphantly raised the open jar toward the night sky.

"All those who preach to the False Father in Heaven are enemies of the true god, Satan, and are child rapists. You have all stolen their innocence and virtue. These are crimes that you, Reverend Steiner, must atone for tonight. I now bathe and anoint you with Satan's holy water," Bradford said as he slowly poured the gasoline over the minister from his head to his feet.

The evangelical pastor's screams were muffled by duct tape over his mouth. His attempts to escape were useless. The toxic gasoline fumes made him dizzy, and his head spun.

Dakota led Desi from the RV park past the closed Galveston Island Beach Patrol office toward Stewart Beach, heading south to the Galveston Jetty. A quarter moon partially lit the beach. As they crossed onto Porretto Beach, Desi immediately sensed movement in the darkness ahead, freezing, leaning forward against her leash, and peering into the semi-darkness. Then Desi bared her teeth and growled.

Dakota saw the dog's behavior instantly shift from playful to protective. "What's the matter, girl? What do you see?" she asked.

Desi kept scanning ahead, growling, then started pulling Dakota forward. The sixty-pound pit bull was strong, requiring Dakota to use both hands to hold her back. Dakota looked ahead and saw three dark, upright figures and what appeared to be another figure on the sandy beach, but she was too far away to tell exactly what she was seeing.

Desi pulled Dakota another twenty yards forward to a spot where Desi suddenly froze again, continuing to growl. "Stop, Desi, stop!" Dakota commanded. As the dog froze again, Dakota switched the leash from her left hand to her right, took her tactical light out of her left pocket, and turned it on, illuminating the area just beyond them.

What Dakota saw shocked her. A figure in a devil mask and black cloak stood next to another man who was impaled on a large wooden cross, flanked by two men dressed in black with hoodies pulled over their faces.

As soon as Desi saw the frightening figures, she began barking loudly, warning them of her imminent attack to protect Dakota.

My Lord, protect me! Dakota muttered to herself as she quickly assumed a defensive stance. *"Stay, Desi, stay!" she ordered the dog.* She held Desi close, worried the protective dog might attack the men. When she saw that Desi had obeyed her command, she released the leash and drew her concealed Glock 48, holding it in the low-ready position.

Bradford, Cleve, and Marcus were startled by a sudden bright light that illuminated them, revealing them in an act of violence against the minister. The light was too intense to identify its source, but hearing a barking dog and seeing a single light, the trio naturally assumed that someone walking their dog had stumbled upon them.

The Satanic priest, who had already murdered three clerics, could not afford to be identified or have his plan to kill a fourth cleric foiled. *"Kill them! Kill them, now!"* he ordered Cleve and Marcus as he drew a knife.

The Satanic followers drew their knives, spread out, and charged at Dakota and Desi. The Satanic priest also moved toward the pair with his knife raised.

Dakota's previous Air Force weapons training kicked in. She issued a single, deadly warning to back off: *"Stop, I'm armed and I'll shoot!"* she exclaimed, but all three men ignored the warning and kept moving quickly toward her.

Dakota raised her 9mm and fired a controlled pair of shots at Cleve on her left, then turned and delivered two more shots at Marcus on her right. All four shots hit each man center mass, knocking them down. Desi lunged forward and hit the Satanic priest square in the chest at twenty miles per hour. Bradford went down as if a 300-pound NFL nose tackle had hit him. When the priest hit the sand, Desi grabbed his right arm, which was holding the knife, biting through the robe, clothing, and flesh. She shook Bradford like a rag doll, dislodging the knife.

Dakota scanned the nearby area and saw that both of her attackers were down and not moving. She looked ahead, where she heard screams and saw Desi fighting with the figure dressed as the devil.

"Off, Desi! Off, off! Come here! Come to me!" she commanded the dog, who released her grip on the Satanic priest and returned to Dakota's side. The distance between Dakota and the devil figure was thirty yards, creating a safety zone between them. Dakota also knew that if needed, she could command Desi to re-engage the figure as a prelude to deadly force. She had already mortally wounded two of her attackers and knew that she was a physician, after all. She decided to de-escalate.

When Desi returned, holding his right arm, the devil figure quickly got off the ground. He stumbled past the man tied to the wooden cross and reached the pickup truck. Seeing the man on the cross and the attacker in the devil costume, she connected the dots.

My God, it's the clergy killer! I can't let him escape! she thought to herself. As Bradford struggled to start the truck with his wounded right hand, Dakota screamed at the top of her lungs, *"Stop, I'll shoot! Stop, stop!"*

The truck started, and its engine revved loudly as Bradford began to drive off the sandy beach. In response, Dakota emptied the remaining ten rounds from her Glock 48 magazine, unsuccessfully trying to hit the right front and rear wheels. She could hear and see the impacts of her rounds hitting the sand and the vehicle as the Satanic priest managed to escape on the dirt access road.

"Damn, double-damn!" Dakota yelled in frustration as she watched the clergy killer speeding up the access road in a cloud of dust.

Dakota told Desi to stay in a low stance while she approached each of her fallen attackers with her gun out and checked if they were alive. Both were clearly dead. Then she went to the moaning man and saw he was impaled on a large wooden cross with tent stakes and zip-ties. She took the duct tape off his mouth so he could breathe easier and speak.

"My Dear God, thank you. Thank you, you saved my life. Who are you?" moaned the gasoline-drenched preacher.

"I'm a physician. Take it easy, you are wounded. I'm going to call for help.

Dakota dialed GPD's 9-1-1 line and reported the attack, shooting, and the injured minister. She also provided a detailed description of the suspect, dressed as the devil, and the pickup truck he used to escape. Fortunately, she had seen a sign while walking that identified the beach as Porretto Beach. The dispatcher reassured her that police, paramedics, and an ambulance were on their way. Her next call was to Wade.

Wade's phone rang, and he saw it was Dakota. "What's up? How's the walk going?" he asked.

Dakota told him about witnessing the attack on the minister, the attackers—one of whom was undoubtedly the cleric's killer—and having to kill two of her assailants in self-defense. Wade was incredulous.

"What? Are you okay? What happened to Desi? Have you called the police?" Wade asked in a rapid-fire stream of questions. Dakota quickly filled Wade in on the situation, including Desi getting a solid bite from the Satanist and the suspect escaping in the pickup truck.

"When the officers arrive, tell them who I am and that we're working on the cleric killer investigation. Have one of them pick me up and take me to you. I'm calling Gates right now. I'll be there as soon as possible," said Wade, hearing sirens approaching Dakota over the phone.

Exhausted, Gates Sullivan had just finished a warm bath and was looking forward to some quiet reading when she heard her cell phone ringing in her bedroom. She hurried over to it. The display showed, "Wade Justus," and she answered.

"Gates, you won't believe it, but Dakota just tangled with the cleric killer and a couple of his goons on the beach not far from here. She just called me. She shot and killed two of them, but a guy dressed as Satan managed to get away. Cops are on the way. I asked her to ask one of the cops to pick me up and take me to her," said Wade.

Before Gates could respond, her phone rang, and she saw "9-1-1 Emergency Dispatch" on the display.

"Hold on a second, Wade. I gotta take this call," replied Gates quickly. The supervising dispatcher was reporting a shooting with two people down on Porretto Beach, just off the Galveston Jetty. A woman reporting as the shooter, an injured male, and a dog at that location, with uniforms, fire, and EMS en route. The dispatcher also provided Gates with a description of the suspect vehicle.

"Copy, en route. Tell the uniforms to seal off everything and get that vehicle description out as a BOLO immediately. I also want a full callout for CSI. From here on, handle only cell phone traffic, got it?" Gates ordered. She hung up and returned to the line with Wade.

"Wade, I'm twenty minutes out. I'll pick you up. I gotta call Bill Hurd. Be outside waiting for me when I pull up," said Gates, hanging up.

Dakota had Desi on a leash and was tending to Pastor Steiner when the cavalry arrived. Thinking ahead, Dakota had already taken off her athletic jacket, placed it on the sand away from her, and set her empty Glock 48X on top of it so the police wouldn't think she was still armed.

Dakota saw the police cars' lights flashing and sirens blaring as they sped down the Galveston Jetty and onto the dusty access road to the beach. She stood up, away from the injured pastor, raised one hand in surrender while holding onto Desi with the other. *"Sit, Desi, sit and stay,"* she ordered, understanding how confusing the light and noise were, and threatening the officers approaching with drawn guns would be to the dog.

"I'm Dr. Dakota Shannon, your RP, and I'm unarmed. She pointed to two bodies. "We have two down and deceased over there, and this man needs medical help right now. He's been nailed to that cross, so you'll need something to free him. My gun is empty and on top of my jacket over there. I'm a physician and I can help," she explained.

Swing shift Sergeant Sergio Diaz approached Dakota and told his men to reholster their weapons.

"I know of you, doc. You and that Texas Ranger Wade Justus are consulting on the cleric killer investigation, right?" Sgt. Diaz said.

That's right, Sergeant. One escaped—the guy dressed as Satan. He's in a dark-colored Toyota Tundra pickup truck, probably with some bullet holes. Did dispatch give out the BOLO?" Dakota asked.

"Yes, but we're short-staffed tonight, so we're spreading the word across the county. This is occupying my entire Midtown patrol team right now. We've got the Sheriff, DPS, and Texas A&M campus police working on it. Are you okay? What the hell happened here?" asked Diaz.

"Yes, I'm fine. I was walking our dog on the beach when she suddenly alerted to something ahead. As you can see, it's pretty dark out here. We literally stumbled onto the preacher being crucified by three men, one of whom was dressed as the devil, wearing a black cape and a mask with horns.

"Before I knew it, they divided up and engaged. I drew my Glock in self-defense and shouted a warning that I was armed. It didn't seem to matter. Then they charged at me with knives. I shot the closest two. Our dog Desi broke free and attacked the guy dressed as the devil. I took down both men, and Desi knocked the devil guy off his feet. I think she got in a pretty good bite, too. I heard him scream and saw him holding his arm as he ran to a pickup truck parked just off the access road on the beach," Dakota explained and continued.

"Seeing how he was dressed and what they had been doing to the preacher, I had a good feeling they were the clergy killers. I didn't want him to escape, so I emptied my magazine at the truck's tires. Unfortunately, I missed with every round, but I'm pretty sure that truck's got some holes in it. He sped up the access road onto the jetty, and that's the last I saw of him. I called 9-1-1 right away to report it. Then I checked on the two guys that I shot. They were both dead. After that, I tried to render medical aid to the preacher," said Dakota.

"I'm trying to establish our crime scene. Aside from checking on the decedents, putting your gun down, and treating the man on the cross, did you touch anything or walk anywhere else?" asked Diaz.

"No, I got Desi back under control and waited for you while I was tending to him," replied Dakota.

"Okay, the firemen and paramedics are working on the preacher. The scene is stable, so I will ask you to sit in my car. You are not being detained, but homicide is en route, and they're going to want to interview you. You good with that?" asked the sergeant.

"Sure, I'm an ME and a forensic pathologist; I know the drill," replied Dakota, accompanying the sergeant to his unit, where she sat in the front passenger seat with Desi in the back.

Leaving Dakota in his patrol car, Sgt. Diaz approached the two bodies and shone his flashlight on them and the surrounding area. He noticed fixed-blade knives next to each man. He observed that both had fallen face-first, each with two exit wounds in their backs. *Nice shooting,* he muttered to himself.

Sergeant Diaz noted that the scene was filled with evidence and ordered his men to tape off a fifty-yard square area for the CSI team.

Bradford Natas sped away from the Galveston Jetty and turned left, heading south on Seawall Blvd. He was in full panic mode. The wounded Satanic priest swerved right on 18th Street and traveled all the way up to Harborside Drive before he slowed down to catch his breath. I've got to ditch this truck before they find me! his mind screamed.

Bradford pulled into the historic Galveston Immigration Stations just past the intersection and exited. He was bleeding heavily from Desi's vicious dog bite to his right forearm. He quickly moved to the right side of the truck and saw four obvious gunshot holes in the right rear quarter panel and rear door. He returned to the vehicle, grabbed his devil mask panel from the floorboard, and a second Mason jar filled with gasoline.

The wounded Satanic priest removed his priest's robe, soaked it with gas, threw it into the truck's cab, and set it on fire. The vehicle immediately burst into flames. He pulled a plastic zip tie from his back pocket and tightened it around his bleeding forearm, just below the elbow, to act as a tourniquet. Then he hobbled toward his New Church of Satan, about a quarter mile away on Harborside Drive, like a wounded animal.

I'll tend to my wounds and lay low here, preparing for my revenge against Father Fogarty tomorrow night. Everything I need for my final act of retribution is right here. No one will be able to stop me from getting my revenge! He thought.

Gates and Wade arrived in her unmarked sedan with blue lights flashing at the end of the access road behind the line of police and emergency vehicles. They got out of the car just as Pastor Steiner was being loaded into the ambulance.

"Wait a minute, fellas. This won't take long," Gates said to the crew.

Gates bent down to speak to the pastor. "Where did you come from to get here?" she asked.

"The last thing I remember was leaving my church on Seawall Blvd., when someone grabbed me from behind and pushed a foul-smelling rag against my nose and mouth. The next thing I knew, I was on that cross, having my wrists nailed to the beam, looking up and seeing Satan. Then he doused me with gas and told me I would burn for my sins," Pastor Steiner replied weakly with tears in his eyes.

"Seeing Satan, how so?" pressed Gates.

"He wore a devil's mask with horns. To me, he was Lucifer... the Dark Angel... Satan," rasped Steiner.

“Okay, detective, he’s lost a lot of blood, we’ve got him on a drip. You’ll have time to talk with him later. We need to get him to the ER now,” one of the paramedics said as they pushed the evangelical minister into the back of the ambulance.

"Gates... Gates, down here!” CSI Supervisor Lenny Spazzito yelled from the beach. The area was illuminated by the headlights of two GPD SUVs and the overhead lights from the paramedics' fire truck. Gates saw Lenny on the beach, standing over one of the bodies and waving excitedly.

“I’m going to find Dakota. You go to your people,” said Wade.

Wade approached Sgt. Diaz’s patrol car and lovingly embraced Dakota. Desi barked excitedly in the back seat, eager to get out and see her owner. Wade opened the rear door, freeing Desi, who jumped on him uncontrollably. Like Dakota, the pit had been through a lot.

Dakota briefed Wade on what happened and Desi’s part in protecting her from their attackers. Wade knelt to pet Desi, saying, “Good girl, good girl,” while rubbing her ears.

“So you actually saw the guy, and he was dressed like a devil?” asked Wade.

“Yes, one of the scariest things I’ve ever seen. They were all hell-bent on killing both of us. I warned them I was armed, but it didn’t matter; they all came at me at once. I had to shoot,” Dakota replied.

Wade looked down at the beach where the two bodies lay and then back at Dakota. “Well, it looks to me like you took care of business. They’ll never hurt anyone again. Straight self-defense. Sorry you had to go through that,” Wade said as he hugged Dakota, pulling her closer.

Gates headed down to the beach, where CSI Lenny Spazzito was standing with a smile.

“You’re smiling in the middle of a crime scene? What are you so happy about?” she asked.

Lenny held up two cell phones in clear plastic evidence bags and showed them to her. “This is why. Each one of these DBs had one on them. Remember, we got one off that DB who Dr. Tzabar killed? Well, I cracked it this afternoon using our Detego Global software. I’m eager to return to the office to explore these two devices. I’m sure there’s a connection here. Hopefully, something that will lead us to our clergy killer,” he replied.

Gates examined the yellow numbered evidence plaques on the beach, identifying various pieces of evidence. Close to each deceased attacker were eight-inch fixed-blade Buck knives. An additional four-inch folding knife was found yards away from the bodies. Near the large wooden cross was an empty Mason jar that reeked of gasoline and a backpack.

Lenny called out to Gates, “I’ve already photographed all of that evidence, but don’t open that backpack until I get there. I haven’t touched it yet,” he cautioned. Gates waited until her CSI supervisor was beside her with his digital camera and opened the backpack. Inside, she found a Zip-Lok baggie containing a black washrag and some zip-ties.

After Lenny had photographed the items, Gates carefully opened the baggie to examine the rag. “Jesus, that’s chloroform, consistent with this guy’s MO. Just what the preacher told me. That’s how he gets control over his victims,” said Gates, closing the baggie.

Sergeant Diaz approached Gates. “Just want you to know that GFD is responding to a vehicle fire at the Galveston

Immigration Station on Harborside Drive. An adjacent district unit is already there, and he reports it's a Toyota Tundra pickup truck with some bullet holes in it. Looks like our perp dumped the truck and set it on fire. He's on the lam. Looks like you guys have got this. Can I free up a couple of units to begin a search of the area?" the patrol sergeant asked.

"Absolutely, Sergio. We're fine here. I need one unit to keep the curious away," Gates replied.

"Great, I'll pull all of my people but one. If he's wounded, maybe we get lucky," he said as he walked off.

Bradford cleaned the puncture wounds on his right forearm caused by the dog's bite using warm water, then applied some antibiotic ointment and a compression bandage from his basic first aid kit. The wounds were inflamed and painful. He took three pain relievers and lay down to rest for the night. I hope that damn dog didn't give me rabies, he thought.

Gates allowed Dakota to return to the RV with Wade for an interview the next day. A uniformed officer gave Dakota, Wade, and Desi a quick ride back to the Sandpiper RV park. By 3:00 a.m., the crime scene was cleaned up, and Gates, Bill Hurd, Lenny, and his CSI team returned to the station. The police search for the clergy killer was unsuccessful.

Chapter 21
A Race Against Time

Lenny Spazzito worked tirelessly throughout the night using the Detego Global forensic software to unlock both decedents' phones. At 9:30 a.m., he staggered into Gate's office, exhausted but smiling.

Gates was watching the morning news. KWAV-TV 4's meteorologist had a map of the Gulf Coast near Galveston highlighted and was starting his weather report.

"Get ready for some high winds and a lot of precipitation late this afternoon and throughout the evening. The National Weather Service is reporting an approaching freak Spring tropical storm scheduled to come ashore at Galveston sometime just before dark and continue through the wee hours of tomorrow morning.

The Saffir–Simpson Hurricane Wind Scale indicates that wind speeds could reach just below Category One levels, ranging from fifty to sixty miles per hour, with the storm bringing between four and eight inches of rain locally. Small craft are advised to be out of the water by no later than 1:00 pm today, and those with boats in docks should ensure everything is securely tied down. Heavy thunder and lightning are also expected."

"Good morning, Lenny. You look like the cat that ate the canary. I hope you have some good news to report. Coffee?" the homicide supervisor asked.

"Yes, please, it's mother's milk." Well, the Detego Global software worked flawlessly. I've now cracked all three encrypted cellphones. The guy named Curtis Cain that Dr. Tzabar killed at Texas A&M, and the two men, Cleve Wright and Marcus Foster, who attacked and tried to kill Dr. Shannon, were all using burner phones.

I was not only able to access their contact lists, phone calls, text messages, and photos, but also extract their GPS tracking data. One name that kept recurring was "Natas." Besides themselves, all three suspects were communicating with this "Natas" guy. I'm thinking he might be our clergy killer," said Lenny.

That's great news, Lenny! You and the Detego software have made the breakthrough we needed. Thanks for your excellent effort. I'm thinking that once we catch this sicko and everything is settled, a nice seafood dinner at Gaido's is on me. FYI, now that we have a live victim and I get the chance to interview him today, I'll have more to include in my VICAP inquiry," replied Gates.

"Okay, I'll send you all the cell phone data before I go home this morning. I need a few hours' rest, and I'll be back this afternoon to get back to work," replied the CSI supervisor as he walked out of Gates' office.

Gates immediately called her partners Bill Hurd and Wade Justus. They agreed that Gates would pick up Wade, Dakota, and Desi. She would take Desi to her house, where Desi could spend time with her dog. Then, she would bring the group back to CID, where she and Det. Hurd could interview Dakota. They could then collaborate on a criminal profile to send to NCIC/VICAP.

Once Gates, Wade, and Dakota arrived at CID, Gates and Hurd conducted the video interview with Dakota. At the same time, Wade compiled a list of the killer's MO to be added to Gates' list for entry into the NCIC/VICAP system electronically.

Gates sent Bill Hurd to the hospital to conduct a video interview with Pastor Steiner. By mid-afternoon, Hurd reported back with additional details about how the pastor had been assaulted. With this new information and what Dakota had told them, Gates contacted the FBI Behavioral Science Unit and personally spoke with one of their profilers.

The homicide supervisor told the BSU profiler, *"We're in a race against time, here. We have three murdered clergy members in as many weeks. Our killer is due to hit again any day."* Gates requested a rush job through their VICAP system to see if they could find any matches for similar homicides nationwide. Then the waiting game began.

Bradford tossed and turned all night. The throbbing pain from the deep dog bites to his right forearm kept him awake. The strongest pain reliever he had was Tylenol, which wasn't cutting it. He decided that nothing and no one would stop him from his planned encounter between Father Fogarty and Satan.

In the morning, he got into his former assistant Marcus's car and drove to Our Lady of the Blessed Ascension Catholic Church on the 2000 block of Church Street to observe the elder priest's activities. He entered the church's foyer and read a schedule indicating that Father Fogarty would be holding evening confessions from 6:00 pm to 8:00 pm. that night.

The hypocrite is scheduled for confession tonight. This is my best chance to catch him, Bradford thought. The Satanic priest left the church and drove back to the New Church of Satan to prepare his attack on the Catholic priest who had wrecked his life.

Gates, Wade, and Dakota had been poring over at least fifty pages of phone numbers, text messages, and GPS tracking data from the three cell phones police had recovered from the three deceased suspect assailants. There was definitely a pattern developing that they wanted to explore further.

"This Natas guy is coming up in all three cellphones through calls and text messages back and forth. I know there's a connection here," remarked Gates.

Wade pulled up a Google Earth Pro map on Gates' laptop, inputting the GPS coordinates from all three cellphones, and placing yellow pins on the map for each recurring set of coordinates. The GPS coordinates matched locations outside Kirkham Hall on the Texas A&M campus, where Dr. Tzabar was attacked, Pastor Steiner's church on Seawall Blvd., and Porretto Beach, next to the Galveston Jetty, where Dakota and Desi had their deadly confrontation with two suspects and the suspected Satanic clergy killer.

Then Wade discovered that all three deceased suspects had been to a specific location in the vicinity of Harborside Drive and 15th Street.

"Look here, Gates," said Wade, calling Gates' attention to his Google Earth Pro pin map and pointing to the intersection.

"Lenny's download data from the cellphones indicates that all three of our suspects have been to this location on several occasions recently," he said. Gates looked at Wade's map.

"Yes, I see, interesting. Can you enhance that image?" she asked. Wade improved the image and switched the mapping mode from "overhead" to "street level view." He then positioned the icon right in the middle of the intersection.

"Let's walk down the street to see what's so interesting," he replied.

The only notable location was a seemingly abandoned warehouse at the northeastern corner of the intersection.

"Why the hell would these three guys be so interested in an abandoned warehouse? Gates, can you assign a patrol unit to drive over there and check the place out? Maybe you can get us an address. I also see a couple of residences directly east of the warehouse. Could your officer contact the owners there to see if they know anything about this place?" he asked.

"Sure thing," replied Gates, getting on the phone to dispatch. We'll know what's up soon enough," she replied.

Dakota had been hovering over Wade and Gates as they looked at Wade's map, then she looked down at Lenny Spazzito's data pages.

"Natas...Natas. What a unique, or allow me, a rather strange name. Natas...","" Dakota remarked. Then Dakota stopped in mid-sentence.

"Jesus Wade, Natas, it's a semordnilap. Of course!" Dakota exclaimed loudly while pointing out the name "Natas" that kept appearing in the data sheets.

“A what?” asked Wade.

“You know, a semordnilap – a word that becomes a different word when spelled backwards; like the word 'stressed' spelled backwards is 'desserts,' get it?” said Dakota.

“Oh,” replied Wade.

Sure, look, “Natas” spelled backwards is the word “Satan,” see?” said Dakota, pointing again to the name “Natas.”

“Oh, got it. Damn!” replied Wade.

“Yes, it does for Christ’s sake!” exclaimed Gates, excitedly.

“So, now we at least have his last name. That’s a start,” said Wade.

“And an unusual one at that,” said Dakota.

By 4:00 pm, the weather had begun to change noticeably. The clouds overhead had darkened, blocking the sun, and the winds had picked up. Gates’ office phone rang, and she answered. It was dispatch.

“Sergeant Sullivan, patrol reports from the field about your warehouse on Harborside Dr. and 15th. According to neighbors, the property was leased to a guy who holds meetings a few times weekly. They say what's unusual is that the meetings happen at midnight. The attendees seem to be in their twenties to forties. The neighbors describe them as dressed oddly, usually in dark clothes. The officer tried to look around the property, but it was locked up tight. Here’s the address on Harborside Drive. There is no sign or name on the building,” said the dispatcher, giving Gates the address she had written down. Gates thanked the dispatcher and hung up.

"So, we have an address linked to all three deceased suspects, two of whom we know are connected to Natas, and a third whom we strongly suspect knew him. What we don't have is his full name, but we do have Natas' cellphone number. I'll ask Lenny when he returns on duty to see what he can do with Natas' cellphone number," said Gates.

CSI Supervisor Lenny Spazzito walked into Gates' office at 4:30 pm.

"There's a bad storm brewing out there, I can feel it," he said.

Gates filled Spazzito in on the afternoon's events. "Can you do anything more with this guy Natas' cellphone number?" she asked.

"Well, depending on the phone he's using, I might be able to identify his cellphone service provider. From there, if we had his full name, we could get a judge to sign a telephonic search warrant to track him through triangulation. It's not easy, but I'll go to my office and focus on it," replied Spazzito.

"Alright, Lenny. Thanks, I'll let you know when we get Natas' full name," said Gates. Spazzito was walking out the door when Gates' cellphone rang. The display read, "FBI, Washington, DC."

"Detective Sergeant Gates Sullivan," she said into the phone. It was the FBI Behavioral Science Unit profiler Gates had called earlier. Gates put the call on speaker.

"Sergeant Sullivan, you mentioned it was urgent, so I wanted to call you before I headed home. Based on your inquiry, we found a single hit through VICAP. If you check your emails, I also sent you the data. Our search parameters were "clergy, homicide, hanging, crucifixion, zip-ties, bondage, and fire."

"Several years ago, a member of the Catholic clergy, a brother, was found murdered in a small border town in Pueblo, New Mexico, at La Nuestra Señora del Desierto, "Our Lady of the Desert" Catholic Church. His name was Brother Boyd Chester. The victim was found hanging, bound to a staff as if he were crucified. He was also set on fire; he was burned alive,

"Was he a local?" asked Gates.

"No, I've sent you the victimology. He was a brother transferred from the Catholic Archdiocese in San Francisco, California," the Special Agent replied.

"I really appreciate you calling me personally on this. This will be very helpful," said Gates.

"Well, you said it was important, and lives were on the line, so we're here to serve. Good luck with your hunt, and call me if there's anything else we can do," replied the agent before hanging up.

Gates looked at her watch; it was just about 3:00 pm Pacific Standard Time in San Francisco. She Googled the San Francisco Catholic Archdiocese and found the phone number for the Office of the Archbishop before dialing it.

An administrative clerk for the Archbishop answered the phone. Gates identified herself, explained the purpose of her investigation, and asked for someone who could provide information about the former Brother Boyd Chester. There was a moment of silence on the line. Gates put the call on speaker so Wade and Dakota could hear.

"You say that you are investigating the serial murders of clergy in Galveston, Texas? I'm sorry to be a bit skeptical, but the Catholic Church is understandably very protective of our clergy. Can you email me a copy of your identification to verify who you say you are, detective?" the clerk asked.

I'd be happy to do that. Could you give me your email address? In the meantime, please speak with one of your superiors to find out the name and position of the person responsible for administration and what we refer to here as human resources. I am facing a strict deadline, which could be a matter of life and death for another clergy member in Galveston. I'll wait on the line while you confirm receipt of my identification," Gates pressed.

Gates photocopied her Galveston PD ID card and her business card, then scanned the documents to the email address the clerk provided. Five minutes later, the clerk returned to the phone.

"Sergeant Sullivan, we have your identification. The person handling administrative tasks is Father Michael. I am transferring your call now," replied the clerk, passing Gates' call. After several rings, Father Michael answered the line.

"This is Father Jonathan Michael. How can I assist, detective?" he asked. Gates repeated the details of her investigation, informing the priest that she needed to learn more about the former Brother Chester. The priest's tone immediately shifted to one of defensiveness.

“Well, I’m sure you understand the Church’s stance on protecting our clergy’s privacy. Is Brother Chester under investigation for something?" he asked.

Wade whispered to Gates, “He doesn’t even know that Brother Chester is dead? Press him,” he advised.

“Father Michael, I’m curious why you didn’t ask me why I called all the way to the San Francisco Diocese instead of just calling Our Lady of the Desert, Catholic Church in Pueblo, New Mexico. Clergy assignments shouldn’t be private since they are published at every church. Are you implying that Brother Chester might have been involved in some disciplinary matter?” Gates bluffed. There was a moment of silence on the line as the perplexed priest struggled for an answer.

“Well...ah.....The Church is precluded from discussing disciplinary matters,” Father Michael stammered.

“So, apparently, Brother Chester *was* involved in something disciplinary while assigned in the San Francisco Diocese?” Gates pressed. More silence on the other end of the phone.

“Detective... Sullivan, the Diocese cannot confirm whether Brother Chester was the subject of any disciplinary action. Furthermore...,” Father Michael said, but he was abruptly cut off by Gates, who now went for the sucker punch.

“Father, with all due respect, you *are* aware that Brother Chester was brutally murdered in a very bizarre way one year after the San Francisco Diocese apparently transferred him to Pueblo, New Mexico, right?” Gates asked. More silence followed.

"Detective Sullivan, are you telling me that our Brother Chester was murdered in Pueblo, New Mexico? If so, this is the first I've heard of it," the upset priest replied.

"Unfortunately, that's precisely what I'm telling you, Father. We believe that Brother Chester's murder is somehow connected to a series of clergy murders here in Galveston. You know we have Catholic churches here as well. So, if you can confide in me, strictly confidentially, about the circumstances of his assignment in the San Francisco Diocese and his reassignment to Pueblo, it might help our investigation.

"Look, Father, we're working in the dark here. Someone is killing our clergy, and we've lost three in as many weeks, with another minister brutally attacked just last night. We believe another attack is imminent, and I'm asking for your help. Another clergy member's life is at stake—maybe a Catholic priest," explained Gates, pulling out all the stops.

I appreciate your concern, detective, but disciplinary matters are strictly confidential. I'm afraid that, given the circumstances you've just described, specifically the murder of one of our Brothers, I'll need to personally consult with the Archbishop before releasing such information. If you can provide your contact details, I'll work on this. I understand the urgency involved. I promise to call you as soon as I hear from the Archbishop," Father Michael replied.

"Fair enough, Father. Yes, please call me as soon as you hear from your Archbishop. You have my business card with my office and mobile numbers," said Gates, before hanging up.

Lenny Spazzito checked in just before 6:00 pm.

“Gates, I’m having trouble getting tracking data from Natas's cellphone number. I retrieved information from the other three phones because we had their owners' IDs. I’ll need Natas’s full name if I’m going to be able to help you,” said the CSI supervisor.

“Copy, Lenny. I’m doing my best. You’ll know when we know,” replied Gates.

The time passed slowly. By 7:00 pm, 5:00 pm Pacific Standard Time, a fierce storm had made landfall in Galveston. Winds reached up to 35 mph, and rain hammered the city. Gates turned on the local news just in time to see the weather report. The KWAV TV-4 meteorologist was reporting live from the beach.

“As seen from the sea behind me, our tropical depression is heading toward Galveston. As predicted, rain accompanied by moderate winds reaching 35 mph struck our shore late this afternoon during the start of the evening commute. Our Doppler radar shows this is just the beginning. We expect the storm's full force to hit the city by 10:00 pm, and the storm should last well into the early morning hours of tomorrow. If you're commuting now, be especially careful of flooding on our highways and boulevards. Hydroplaning can cause serious accidents. This is Meteorologist Bob Cummings with KWAV TV-4. Sports is next.”

“Maybe the incoming storm will keep Mr. Natas home tonight,” offered Dakota.

"Me too," replied Gates. We can use the extra time to gather more information about this guy. I don't know how the San Francisco Archbishop will handle our request for information on the former Brother Boyd Chester," replied Gates.

"I hate to be the pessimist in the group, but this Natas seems way too goal-oriented to let something like a storm stop him. This sicko might use the storm as a cover. I mean, the cops will be busy with accidents for sure. Galveston isn't Houston. Your department only has so many cops on a swing shift. I hope he'll back off tonight," said Wade.

At 7:45 p.m., Gates' cellphone buzzed. The display only showed a 415 area code. From her previous call, Gates recognized the area code from San Francisco and answered, placing the call on speaker.

"Detective Sullivan, even though it's a bit late out there for you, I wanted to get back to you on the issue of Brother Chester. I'm using my personal cellphone because I didn't want to use an in-house landline," the priest said softly.

Gates raised an eyebrow, immediately skeptical.

"Yes, Father. Thank you for calling me. Do you have a decision for me?" Gates asked hopefully.

"The Archbishop has carefully reviewed your request. Unfortunately, Brother Chester was murdered. While he is allowing me to share some details about his reassignment to Pueblo, New Mexico, he has also instructed me not to disclose any information regarding the Church's internal investigation," the priest explained.

"Oh, I see. That is indeed unfortunate. I'm afraid the Archbishop's decision could put Catholic clergy here in Galveston at risk. If something terrible happened and a member of your clergy was harmed, our office might have to publicly reveal that we warned you and asked for the San Francisco Diocese's cooperation, but got none," replied Gates, baiting the priest. There was a brief pause on the line before Father Michael responded.

"Detective Sullivan, are you a Catholic?" the priest asked.

"Yes, Father, I am," replied Gates.

"Then, Catholic to Catholic, I must confess that I disagree with the Archbishop's decision. We are here to protect our flock and do God's important work, not to mitigate, cover, or protect the wicked. I have read our internal investigation, and what Brother Chester was accused of doing was horrible – a serious breach of a sacred trust and a mortal sin.

"As a Catholic, you must give me your firm promise of non-disclosure if I am to discuss anything further with you. Do you give it, Detective?" asked Father Michael.

"Yes, you have my word, Father," replied Gates.

"Do you have a pen and paper to write notes? I want no recordings of our conversation. Is that clear?" the priest insisted. Gates grabbed a legal pad and a pen, ready to write.

"Brother Chester and one of our former priests, Father Charles Fogarty, were transferred out of the Diocese following an internal investigation over inappropriate behavior with several minor students in our parochial school system here," Father Michael explained.

"Inappropriate behavior – define what you mean by that?" asked Gates. There was a moment of silence on the line.

"Father Michael, are you still there? What type of inappropriate behavior?" pressed Gates. The priest cleared his throat and spoke quietly.

"Unfortunately, by rumor only because we were unable to get full cooperation from the minors, but the gist of the activity was of a sexual nature," Father Michael replied.

"Were the police involved?" asked Gates.

"Yes, in the file were business cards from San Francisco Police Department Inspectors John McKenna and Robert Mells," replied the priest.

"Can you give me the business number on their cards?" asked Gates.

"Certainly," replied Father Michael as he provided the numbers Gates wrote down.

"Do you know if anything came from the police investigation?" asked the homicide supervisor.

"The notes in the file show that the police were also hampered by a lack of victim cooperation and had to shut down their investigation," said the priest.

"So we know where Brother Chester ended up. What happened to Father Fogarty?" asked Gates. Father Michael lowered his voice.

"Signs in the file indicate interference from higher authorities in our chain. Apparently, Father Fogarty had some influence within our Diocese. There is a letter from Cardinal Santos stating that, due to a lack of cooperation from the complainants—which means the accusations of sexual misconduct could not be substantiated—Father Fogarty would not be removed from his duties as a priest. He was to be reassigned out of the San Francisco Diocese," explained Father Michael.

"Can you tell me where Father Fogarty was reassigned?" asked Gates.

"Our records show he was sent to one of our churches in your city, Our Lady of the Blessed Ascension," replied the priest.

Gates, Wade, and Dakota all glanced at each other. Wade immediately looked up the church's address, pulled it up on his Google Earth Pro map, and pointed out the location to Gates. The church was on the 2,000 block of Church Street in Midtown, right in the middle of the areas where all of the previous clergy killings had taken place.

"Get the report on Fogarty," Wade whispered to Gates.

"Do you have access to the Church's internal investigation of Father Fogarty?" asked Gates.

"Unfortunately, no. Father Fogarty's file is unavailable at my level. This is disturbing because I am our Diocese's human resources director. I'm afraid this is all the useful information I can share with you. I wish I could do more," the priest replied.

"Is there a list of complainant minors?" Wade whispered in Gates' ear.

“Yes, but in no way can you contact any of them. It would come right back to me. The only other source of a list would be the San Francisco Police. There are six in the file,” replied Father Michael, reading the list slowly to Gates, who wrote every name down.

“Well, Father Michael, I truly appreciate your honesty with me. I understand and respect your stance. I promise you that this conversation never happened. I will try another way to learn more about Father Fogarty. May Our Lord bless you for the help you've given tonight,” said Gates as she hung up.

“Let’s call those two SFPD inspectors. Try their cell numbers first. I’m sure their detective office is closed right now,” Wade suggested.

Gates dialed the cell number for Inspector John McKenna. The recording announced, “The number you have dialed is no longer in service. "

“No dice for McKenna. I’ll try Inspector Robert Mells,” replied Gates, dialing the cell. The number is no longer in service recording responded.

“Damn, both numbers are down. What are the odds?” Gates exclaimed.

“Gates, this investigation was years ago. Chances are, those two inspectors are retired, and these cell numbers were department phones. Try the Bureau of Inspectors line,” said Wade. Gates dialed the BOI office number, which was automatically transferred to a second number. The phone rang and was answered.

“Bureau of Inspectors, Night Desk, Inspector Swanson. How can I help you?” said a male voice.

Gates identified herself, stated the purpose of her call, and asked to speak with Inspector John McKenna or Robert Mells.

"Detective Sergeant Sullivan, John McKenna retired and passed two years ago. Captain Mells retired four years ago and is a good friend of mine. I just happen to have his personal cell number. Ready to copy?" he asked.

"Sure, Inspector Swanson, go," replied Gates, who wrote down the cell number, thanked Swanson, and hung up. Her next call was to the new cell number. The phone rang four times before it was answered.

"Bob Mells, who's this?" the former Captain Mells asked.

Gates identified herself and explained the nature of her investigation.

"I understand that you and your former partner, Inspector John McKenna, worked on a serial child predator case about twenty years ago involving a couple of clergy members from the San Francisco Archdiocese. The persons of interest were Brother Boyd Chester and Father Charles Fogarty. Would you happen to remember that case, Captain?" she asked.

There was a pause on the line before the retired inspector spoke. "You say Galveston PD in Texas, and you're working a serial murderer of clergy out there?" Mells asked.

"Yes, our guy has already killed three of our clergy members and nearly killed another. We have a person of interest we're working with, whose last name is Natas. Does that name mean anything to you?" Gates asked.

"Natas, you say... no, that name doesn't ring any bells, but I remember Brother Chester and Father Charles Fogarty—two real deviates. My ex-partner, John McKenna, and I worked on those cases at least twenty years ago. That one really sticks in my craw. John and I were so pissed about how that case was swept under the rug that we kept copies of the files.

"As I recall, there were at least six or eight victims, all of them kids. No, wait, one of them was a kid when they first groomed him, and then they continued to abuse that poor guy until he was in high school. The kid couldn't take it anymore and finally called it in," Mells explained.

"Why did the cases go away?" Gates asked.

"We couldn't get any of the kids to testify. They were too scared, and their parents didn't want their children to go through the court process... You know, testifying and everyone finding out. We also didn't find the Catholic Church very cooperative, but John and I made sure we exposed those two to their superiors. John was my senior at the time. He was a great cop. He retired before I did and kept copies of the files just in case those two ever showed up again.

"John caught the cancer. He gave me the files the year before he died, so I might be able to do something. We made a pact—if those two surfaced on another case, I'd go to the DA with the files and push for prosecution. I kept in touch with a couple of parents for years afterwards. Rumor was that they transferred Brother Chester to some dusty shithole in Arizona or New Mexico. Father Fogarty got sent to your state, but I don't know where. A few years ago, I saw on the national news that Chester was murdered in his church in some bizarre fashion," Mells said.

"That's correct. Brother Chester was found hanged, partially crucified, his penis was cut off, and he was burned alive. No one was ever arrested for that homicide," Gates replied.

"Holy shit! Well, that child molester got what he deserved. His penis was cut off? That's definitely a revenge sign. Maybe he messed with the wrong migrant kid, and the family took action. What about the priest? Do you know anything about him?" Mells asked.

"No, that's what we're trying to find out from you. Anything else about Fogarty that you've heard over the years?" asked Gates.

"No, just that the San Francisco Diocese sent him packing to another church in Texas," Mells replied.

"When you and your partner worked Father Fogarty, about how old was he?" Gates asked.

"Ah...he was in his thirties. He ought to be in his sixties now. I know I have his DOB in my files," replied Mells

"Okay, can you access what files you have? I'm in a time crunch. We're concerned that our clergy killer is set to strike again. I'm looking for any connections between what you and McKenna were working on and Fogarty," replied Gates.

"Sure thing. You've got me motivated. Can you hold on for a few so I can get my files, or can I call you back? Just give me your numbers," said Mells. Gates gave the retired police captain her office and cell numbers and hung up.

Gates accessed her Texas Department of Transportation database from her PC, searching for Texas driver's licenses and ID cards belonging to Charles Fogarty. She found two matches for Charles Fogarty: one was a man in his early thirties in McKinney, and the other was a man in his mid-sixties in Galveston. She examined the address on the DL carefully; it was the same as the one listed for Our Lady of the Blessed Ascension Catholic Church on Church Street.

"Bingo, got Father Fogarty's address! Our Lady of the Blessed Ascension Catholic Church on Church Street," exclaimed the homicide supervisor, as he printed out the priest's driver's license with a photo. "Now we know where he lives and what he looks like."

Satanic priest Bradford Natas was holed up in his New Church of Satan on Harborside Drive when he heard noises outside. He peered through a crack in the corrugated aluminum siding and saw a uniformed police officer on the property. Bradford hid in a dark corner inside the building, waiting and watching. The officer pulled on the front sliding door, which was secured with a thick lock and chain. Satisfied that the building was secure, the officer moved on.

Bradford's thoughts were racing inside his head. *Are the police on to me? Have I somehow been identified in the clergy killings? Are detectives preparing arrest and search warrants for me? They are too close to me now. I must strike Father Fogarty tonight while there's still time. In the meantime, I've got to rig this place so any evidence of me and my killings is destroyed. It must be a cleansing by fire.*

The Satanic priest packed his kit for his final act of revenge—this time against the evil Catholic priest who had destroyed his life. Bradford found another backpack. He was out of chloroform and lacked the strength in his right arm to physically take down the priest, so he placed his revolver in the pack as an incentive, along with gloves, zip ties, a black satin sack, his Satanic priest's robe, and a devil's mask with horns. Then he went into the closet in his private office and took out a five-foot wooden dowel along with his six-foot ornamental stainless steel Satanic priest staff topped with a six-inch pentagram engraved with the likeness of Lucifer. He set the items next to the front sliding door.

Next, he went to the back of the building, where he had three five-gallon cans of gasoline, and brought them to his former assistant Joshua's van, which had been hidden inside the building since Natas had strangled him to death.

Bradford sealed and locked all of the van's windows to prevent gas fumes from escaping. Then he took Joshua's frozen body out of the freezer and placed it inside the van through the rear doors.

Now, the difficult part — devising an incendiary device, mused the depraved Satanic priest.

Natas used a simple Boy Scout fire starter and glued the spark maker to one side of the van's sliding door, securing the metal striker with duct tape to the opposite side of the door. Natas opened and closed the sliding door several times to ensure the striker contacted the fire starter and produced a good spark.

Satisfied that his ignition "switch" would work, Bradford took a table cover, rolled it tightly into a long, thin strip, and soaked it in gasoline. Next, he placed all three gas cans into the van side by side and opened their lids. He then connected all three gas cans with the table cover, inserting sections of the tightly twisted fabric into the cans' openings so that the rope-like part acted as a fuse. Finally, he locked both rear doors, leaving the unlocked side sliding door as the only way for anyone to open the van.

Whoever opens the van's sliding door is in for a big surprise. The explosive fire erupting should be enough to quickly spread through the church, destroying any evidence linked to me. Now, it's time to go and take care of Father Fogarty, thought the human devil.

The Satanic priest grabbed his backpack and ran through the pouring rain to the street where Curtis's sedan was parked, the same one that the woman on the beach had killed. Bradford started the car and set out for his planned kidnapping of Father Charles Fogarty.

Chapter 22
The Wrath of God

Our Lady of the Blessed Ascension Catholic Church was just a mile and a quarter from Natas' New Church of Satan. The satanic priest drove slowly through the pouring rain and flooded Midtown District streets as the storm raged outside, thunder crashing and lightning occasionally blinding Bradford.

Back at the Galveston Police Department's CID office, Gates, Wade, Dakota, and now Bill Hurd huddled around a conference table, trying to piece together the deadly puzzle as the horizontal raindrops hit the office windows.

"Geeze Louise, that's one hell of a storm. I can't imagine anyone in their right mind would be out there looking to kill another clergy member tonight," Det. Hurd remarked.

"Well, it's really a matter of perspective, Bill. You have to consider how serious and determined Natas is to kill another clergy member. So far, he's been right on schedule, killing one clergy member each week. This storm would be the perfect opportunity. Think about it for a moment: cops are busy with accidents, street flooding, and power outages. What better time to strike?" said Wade.

"I agree. Deflection and redirection. You know..." Dakota's remarks were interrupted by Gates' cellphone buzzing. Former Captain Robert Mells called, and the detective sergeant answered.

“Sergeant Sullivan, Bob Mells calling. I’ve got a name for you. The kid John McKenna and I felt so bad about was a boy named Bradford Cirelli. He suffered the worst. Fogarty had groomed him in elementary school at St. Margaret's, and then Fogarty and his assistant, Brother Chester, repeatedly sexually assaulted Bradford until he was a sophomore at St. Ignatius High School. I’ll never forget the look on that poor kid’s face as he told us what those two vile pieces of shit did to him,” Mells explained. Gates wrote down the name, “Bradford Cirelli.”

“Thanks, Bob. This is a big help. Do you know approximately how old Cirelli would be today?” Gates asked.

“I can do better, here’s his DOB,” the retired inspector replied, providing Gates with Cirelli’s date of birth.

Wade, Dakota, and Bill Hurd were listening to the conversation on speaker. “Public records request, name changes. Ask him how you can access that,” said Wade.

Thanks, Bob. It’s already past 5:00 pm in San Francisco; do you have any tips on how I can access the City and County of San Francisco’s Public Records database?” Gates asked.

“What would you be looking for?” Mells asked.

“Court records on applications for a change of name, from Cirelli to Natas,” replied Gates.

“Ah, good thinking. That makes sense. Okay, you didn’t hear this from me, but as you know, the police department always has 24/7 access to any municipality’s database. Here’s the SFPD BOI’s access entry code and password. You can access it remotely. It’s our general access code so it won’t be traced back to anyone, just the BOI," said Mells, giving Gates the code and password.

Gates wrote down the access code and password. "Thanks so much for all your help, Bob. If there is ever anything I can do for you in the future, just name it," said Gates.

"Sergeant, I'm only going to ask for one favor from you. If you get your man, or you get to burn that bastard priest, call me and let me know. Good hunting," said Mells, hanging up.

After hanging up, Gates immediately accessed the City and County of San Francisco's Public Records database. The website responded, "We are closed. Our hours of operation are 9:00 am – 5:00 pm, M-F." To the side of the site was a scroll-down menu. Gates scrolled until she found "City Departments Access" and clicked on "SFPD." Two boxes appeared: "Access Code" and "Password." Gates entered the code and password Captain Mells provided, and the website opened.

Gates clicked on the "Court Records" submenu and then "Request for Change of Name." She selected it, and a template appeared, prompting her to enter a name and date of birth. Gates typed in "Bradford Cirelli" along with his date of birth and waited as her request loaded into the system, and her records search began. Two minutes later, her PC beeped. She moved her mouse over the highlighted box and clicked it. A single response appeared.

Bradford Cirelli, with a matching date of birth, applied for a name change to "Bradford D'Ablo Natas" with the CCSF Superior Court on his eighteenth birthday. Three months later, the court approved the name change.

"Hot dog, got him. Here's our guy, Bradford D'Ablo Natas," Gates exclaimed, sharing her computer screen with Wade, Dakota, and Bill Hurd, then hitting "print" to record her records check.

"Oh, that's rich, D'Ablo – the devil and Satan spelled backwards to 'Natas.' "Boy, that's right in your face, isn't it?" said Dakota sarcastically.

"Let's go for a DL and some records," suggested Det. Hurd.

"That's where I'm headed next," replied Gates, now entering Natas' full name and DOB into Texas and the National Crime Information Center databases. Both systems returned "No Records On File."

"Wow, nothing in Texas or in NCIC. No DL or ID; not even a parking ticket," said Gates, to the surprise of the foursome. This was not Gates' first rodeo. Wade Justus had trained her well. Gates then queried Galveston City and County Records and again came up empty; "No Records Revealed," each database responded.

"This guy is a ghost," said Hurd.

"Look, we know Natas exists. Maybe he's not from here," said Gates.

Wade closely followed Gates' investigative method. He knew she was on the right track, so he pulled up his Google Earth Pro map of the city on his iPad.

"Nope, he's local. I can tell. Look again at the pinned locations for his victims and the warehouse on Harborside Drive. Natas knows the area well. See how close everything is? Hell, you could easily bike or jog to each spot. We've already caught him on the Whataburger CCTV cameras. We know it's him now. He doesn't have a driver's license, but he doesn't need one. He used his assistants' vehicles to reach Dr. Tzabar at Texas A&M and to kidnap the pastor, taking him to the beach below the Galveston Jetty. He's from here, for sure.

"Keep digging locally, Gates. He's gotta be living nearby, and I bet it's in the Midtown District. It's in the middle of everything," said Wade, confidently.

Gates switched screens and visited the website. "City of Galveston – City Resources." The city's homepage resembled the City and County of San Francisco municipal site. A scroll-down menu on the left side listed "Licenses, Permits, Utilities, and Departments." Gates clicked on "Utilities," and a form read, "Name, DOB, address, and utility type."

Gates typed Natas's full name, date of birth, and "utilities – all," leaving the address blank. She clicked "Search" and waited as the program loaded and searched. Her PC beeped, and she looked at the highlighted response, "One file. Click to Open." Gates clicked on the open file and read, "Bradford D'Ablo Natas," with the correct DOB, "Electricity," with an address on the 1700 block of 17th Street.

"We are rocking and rolling now, people. Search Warrants time!" exclaimed Gates, showing Wade, Dakota, and Bill Hurd the return.

Gates and Bill Hurd agreed that, to speed things up, they would each write search affidavits, one for the warehouse on Harborside Drive and the other for Natas's residence in the 1700 block of 17th Street. Wade used his Google Earth Pro Street View program to obtain descriptions of each location.

"My God, look at the Natas' apartment building on 17th. It's got evil-looking gargoyles on twin pillars over his apartment, said Wade.

"The perfect place for him," remarked Dakota.

"Wade, can you take screenshots of both locations and email them to me? We'll need them for the search warrant briefing for our troops," said Gates.

"Sure thing," replied Wade, making the images.

"I'm calling the on-call DA, the magistrate, and our SWAT Commander to give them all a heads-up. It's gonna take everyone at least two hours to muster and gear up to hit these two places tonight," said Gates, now switching to an Affidavit of Search template on her computer.

Barnard Natas pulled up to the rectory of Our Lady of the Blessed Ascension Catholic Church in heavy rain. The strong winds had knocked palm fronds from the line of palm trees in front of the building. The Satanist's ruse was that he had been hurt in a car accident.

Natas opened his backpack, took out the revolver, and hid it in his waistband behind his black hoodie. Exiting the vehicle, he grabbed his backpack and walked through the pouring rain to Father Fogarty's front door. He set the backpack out of sight beside the door and knocked. When no one answered, he knocked louder.

Father Fogarty was in his bedroom, on his computer, communicating with another child predator in Sweden over a dark website. The two were exchanging images of child pornography – men having sex with underage boys and girls. The priest was so focused on sharing pornographic images that he didn't hear Bradford's initial knocks. However, the loud knocking at his front door finally caught his attention.

Father Fogarty answered the door still dressed in his black priest's clerical attire: a black shirt with a white tab collar and black pants. A gust of wind and cold rain blew inside as the door opened, causing him to shiver. He looked outside to see a man about forty, dressed in dark clothing with a hood, holding his right arm and clearly in pain.

"Father, father, please help me. I was just in an accident, and I think my arm is broken. I'm in a lot of pain. I need an ambulance. I'm a Catholic – can you please help me?" Bradford pleaded.

The surprised priest was taken off guard. "Yes, my son, wait here, and I'll call you an ambulance," said Father Fogarty as he shut the door.

"Father, it's freezing, and I'm soaked to the bone. May I please wait inside while you call, Father?" Bradford pleaded.

Father Fogarty reassessed the man who appeared to be in obvious pain. "Of course, my son, sit right here," the priest said, guiding Bradford into the living room and settling him into a recliner. Fogarty turned to walk across the room, where a telephone sat beside the sofa. As soon as the priest looked away from Bradford, the Satanic priest retrieved his hidden pistol, approached from behind the Father, and pressed the gun to the side of his head.

"Not so fast, you fuck. I've got plans for you. Come back and sit in the chair," he ordered the priest at gunpoint. Father Fogarty immediately believed that this was a home invasion and began to plead for his life.

"Please...Please don't kill me. There is a little money here in my apartment. I can give it to you. Just don't do anything rash...Please don't hurt me, I am a priest," said the priest.

Bradford laughed. "I'm not here to rob you, you vile piece of shit. I'm here to ensure your day of atonement for your sins. Don't move, or I will kill you right here," Bradford said as he walked to the front door with his gun aimed at the sinful Catholic priest. Bradford briefly opened the front door, grabbed his backpack, and closed the door shut. From the pack, he pulled out a set of zip-ties.

"Stand up and place your hands behind your back," the Satanic priest ordered. Fogarty complied, continuing to plead for his life. Bradford secured the priest's hand behind his back, sat him in the chair, and removed the hood over his head, revealing his face. "You don't remember me, do you?" he asked the priest.

Father Fogarty examined the now much older, shaved-headed Bradford closely. "Should I know you, my son?" the elderly priest replied.

"So, you don't remember me, huh? Well, we've got some catching up tonight before you atone for your sins," Bradford said snidely.

Back at the Galveston PD's CID office, Gates and Bill Hurd finished and submitted their affidavits for search warrants for Natas' apartment on 17th Street and the warehouse on Harborside Drive. The on-call DA reviewed and approved them, calling the detectives to tell them to present them to the magistrate. Gates had emailed both affidavits to Judge Mallory and was waiting for his call.

Gates had already spoken with GPD's SWAT Commander Jeff Sedwick, explaining the nature of the search warrant operation. The Commander had authorized two squads of operators and a Bearcat armored vehicle. Gates called Sedwick back, informing him that the DA had approved both warrants. Considering the circumstances and exigent conditions, it was certain that Judge Mallory would approve both warrants. The SWAT Commander was assembling his team to gear up at the station. An operations briefing was tentatively scheduled for 11:00 pm.

Gates' PC beeped with an urgent email from Judge Mallory, scheduling a Zoom meeting with both detectives in ten minutes. Gates clicked the "meeting accepted" button, letting the judge know she and Bill Hurd would be online and waiting. Moments later, Judge Mallory's image appeared on screen. Gates clicked the video and microphone buttons to start the three-way video call.

Detective Sergeant Sullivan and Detective Hurd, your affidavits are in order, and I approve both searches. Just remember that these are search warrants only – not arrest warrants. However, I'm sure you also understand that anything you find in plain view could provide the grounds for probable cause to arrest your subject, Bradford D'Ablo Natas," the jurist explained.

"Yes, your Honor," both detectives replied in unison.

"Very well, raise your right hands and be sworn in," said the judge. Both detectives raised their right hands on screen.

"Do you both swear and affirm that the information incorporated into these Affidavits of Search is the truth, the whole truth, as best as you know and understand it, so help you God?"

"Yes, your Honor," Gates and Hurd replied.

"Then so be it. I'll email your warrants back to you. You have ten days to produce the Return of Search Warrants. Good luck and good hunting," replied the magistrate before ending the call. Gates immediately picked up the phone and called Commander Sedwick.

"Pete, this is Gates. Judge Mallory approved both search warrants. We'll meet you and your team in the patrol briefing room in fifteen minutes," said Gates.

Father Fogarty unexpectedly came face-to-face with the victim of his repeated sexual molestations and assaults. Now restrained, with a gun in his former victim's hands and alone, describing the elderly cleric as scared was an understatement.

As hours passed, what was forecasted as a tropical storm had intensified into a Category One hurricane with winds now gusting to sixty miles per hour. Continuous lightning and thunder rattled the sky. Outside, as the violent tempest howled, Bradford confronted his childhood rapist, revealing his identity. The storm's noise drowned out the visibly upset victim's loud voice.

"I trusted you as a mentor and a man of God. I thought that you were my friend. I loved being an altar boy, getting closer to your God. You promised my parents and me that you would get me into St. Ignacius. But you breached your trust. You groomed me, you evil fuck. You took my youth and innocence. You and Brother Chester destroyed my life!" Bradford screamed at the priest.

"Bradford... please, I... we... didn’t mean to harm you. I only wanted to help you get into St. Ignacius, which I did...” Fogarty’s voice trailed off.

‘Liar! You’re fucking lying, bastard. Now, like Brother Chester, you'll pay for your sins!” Bradford yelled back.

“Get up from that chair. You are going to your place of atonement,” exclaimed Bradford, pointing the revolver at Father Fogarty.

Assuming his former child victim was about to kill him right then, the priest started sobbing uncontrollably and begged for his life.

"Bradford...please, please. Don’t kill me here,” the priest sobbed, pleading for his life.

“Shooting is too good for you. I have other plans. We’re going for a ride,” Bradford replied, grabbing his backpack and signaling Father Fogarty to the door. “You’re going to walk straight to my car. If you try to escape or scream even once, I’ll shoot you where you stand,” he warned.

Bradford opened the door and pushed Father Fogarty out, pressing the revolver’s barrel into the small of his back. “Move!” he commanded. The wind blew the partly open front door open, slamming it against the living room wall. Bradford ignored the noise, focusing intently on his cleric prisoner.

Once in the car, Bradford opened the front passenger door on the right and pushed the priest inside. He put the revolver in his pocket, seat-belted the priest, and quickly sat in the driver’s seat with his backpack between them. Bradford reached into the backpack, removed the black satin hood, and put it over Father Fogarty's head. As the predator priest cried openly, Bradford drove away toward the Pleasure Pier.

Gates Sullivan, Bill Hurd, and Wade worked hard to piece together their deadly puzzle. The search warrant operation briefing, involving uniformed officers and SWAT, was scheduled for ten minutes from now in the patrol briefing room. Gates picked up her desk phone and called dispatch.

"This is Homicide Det. Sgt. Gates Sullivan. I need a Swing shift patrol unit for a welfare check at the rectory at Our Lady of the Blessed Ascension Catholic Church in the 2,000 block of Church Street. The welfare subject's name is Father Charles Fogarty, who resides in an apartment there. Contact the unit and give me an ETA," she directed the dispatcher.

A minute passed, and the dispatcher reported that a District Mary FTO unit would be at the rectory in fifteen minutes.

"Copy, control. Inform the unit via MDT (Mobile Data Terminal) that Father Fogarty is a potential assault victim, with our clergy killer still free. Use all caution. I'll be in a briefing. Here's my cell number. Have the unit call me for a status update."

Gates, Bill Hurd, Wade, and Dakota walked into the patrol briefing room and found SWAT Commander Sedwick, twelve fully equipped SWAT officers, and Sgt. Sergio Diaz and his five-officer District Mary patrol team were waiting. Gates immediately joined the briefing.

"Ladies and gentlemen, for those of you who haven't met us, I am Det. Sgt. Gates Sullivan, and immediately to my right is Det. Bill Hurd. We are with CID's Homicide Unit. The man and woman to my left are retired Texas Ranger Wade Justus and forensic pathologist Dr. Dakota Shannon. Both Ranger Justus and Dr. Shannon have been brought in as consultants for the investigation of what is now called the serial murders, Clergy Killings."

"Tonight, we will conduct a joint operation with SWAT and the District Mary uniformed patrol units, executing simultaneous search warrants at two locations in Midtown," Gates explained as she showed Wade's Google Earth Pro Street images of the apartment building and warehouse linked to Natas.

"Location No. 1 is an apartment in the 1700 block of 17th Street. The premise on the left is linked to our person of interest, Bradford D'Ablo Natas. Location No. 2 is a warehouse at the corner of Harborside Drive and 15th Street, associated with Mr. Natas.

"SWAT Commander Pete Sedwick will serve as the OIC of the tactical operations, and I will oversee the investigation. Supervisor Lenny Spazzito and his CSI team will arrive after each scene has been secured to assist with the search, identification, and recovery of evidence.

"As you know, our clergy serial killer has murdered three clergy members and seriously injured a fourth in as many weeks. We strongly believe that his next attack is imminent. We have identified his next potential victim as Father Charles Fogarty of Our Lady of the Blessed Ascension Catholic Church on the 2,000 block of Church Street in Midtown," Gates explained as her cellphone buzzed, and she answered.

"Sergeant Sullivan, Officer Bill Bowers, Unit 6-2-Mary-1. We are at the Our Lady of the Blessed Ascension rectory.

There is no sign of Father Fogarty, and we have suspicious circumstances here, ma'am. We found the front door wide open, with no one inside. Also, we found a laptop in the bedroom, and there was a child porn website on the display. No one would leave their apartment unattended with the front door unlocked and wide open," the officer reported.

"Copy, Officer Bowers. Lock the front door, seal it with crime scene tape, and stand by for further instructions," Gates ordered. Gates had a worried face.

"What's up?" asked Wade.

"The Mary unit I sent to the church rectory for a welfare check on Father Fogarty just checked in; not good news. The priest wasn't in his apartment, the front door was wide open, and there were signs that he had been inside," replied Gates.

"How so?" asked Wade as the room buzzed with conversations from the assembled officers.

"The officer said they found the lights on, and a laptop in his bedroom was open to a kiddie porn site. We need to speed this operation up, " said Gates as she turned back to the officers.

"People, we just received news from a Mary District unit I sent to the church's rectory to check on Father Fogarty. The unit reports the priest is not at home under suspicious circumstances. I now think our killer is out there and may have even kidnapped the Father. That said, I'm going to turn this briefing over to Commander Sedwick," said Gates, stepping away from the podium so the SWAT Commander could brief the officers.

Commander Sedwick stood behind the podium. "Okay, everyone. Sergeant Gates told you that we will conduct simultaneous search warrants at both locations. Alpha Team will serve at the apartment on 17th Street, and Bravo Team, with the Bearcat, will hit the warehouse on Harborside Drive. Sgt. Diaz, we will split your Mary units between the two sites. SWAT will breach, enter, and secure, while the Mary units will maintain inner perimeter security if our suspect or associates try to flee on foot.

"As in any operation, we will assume that our person of interest, Mr. Natas, is armed and extremely dangerous. This storm tonight is a real bastard, so everyone needs to stay alert with their heads on a swivel. You all have to bring your A-game tonight. Sgt. Gates has told me that this Natas guy likes to play with fire, so for God's sake, watch out for booby traps. The first sign of gas fumes, I want everyone to disengage past the inner perimeter. Then we wait for the fire team to check and clear it.

"Once both premises are secured, CID can enter and do their thing. Any questions?" asked the commander.

"Alright, saddle up and lock and load. We leave here in ten, dismissed!" said Sedwick. The officers exited the patrol briefing room and headed for the parking lot to get into their vehicles.

Gates gathered the foursome together. "Wade and Dakota, you're with me. We're going to the warehouse. Bill, I want you to take the 17th Street apartment, let's go," she said.

Bradford pulled up in front of the Pleasure Pier in the pouring rain that hammered the windshield so hard his wipers couldn't keep up. He quickly scanned his surroundings, drove the car up the pedestrian ramp, past Bubba Gump's Restaurant, under the "Pleasure Pier main covered entrance," and stopped between the Pelican Bay Gift Shop and the closed Security Office. He was directly in front of the carousel. His kidnap victim, Father Fogarty, blinded by the black satin hood, felt the car come to a stop.

"Where are we?" he asked.

"None of your fucking business. You'll find out soon enough," smirked Bradford. Unbeknownst to the Catholic priest, Bradford, who was the manager of the Pleasure Pier's carousel, had spent the past week preparing the ride for the ultimate human sacrifice to Satan. His lifelong psychological nemesis and rapist, Father Charles Fogarty, was to be crucified, beheaded, and burned to death as a final act of atonement at the hands of the Satanic priest.

The Satanic priest had crafted a Rube Goldberg-style death device for himself, featuring a four-foot razor-sharp blade mounted horizontally on a spindle. Bradford had fixed the spindle so the blade would lower three inches with each carousel rotation. He would seat and secure the priest on the gilded bench of a chariot that was not on a pole, allowing the blade to make direct contact with the priest's head and neck.

Bradford grabbed his backpack, exited the driver's side, and headed to the trunk. He took out the wooden closet dowel and his six-foot stainless steel Satanic priest's staff. Then he ran around to the passenger side. *"Time to go!"* he yelled at the priest, unbuckling and forcefully pulling him out of the car. The Satanic priest grabbed the elderly cleric by his shirt collar and pulled him forward into the covered carousel.

Bradford shoved Father Fogarty into the gilded chariot and pushed him onto the seat. He placed the wooden dowel into the chariot and his backpack on the floor. Then he took out a pair of snips from his pack and the revolver from his waistband, pressing the weapon against the priest's forehead.

"Don't even think about doing anything crazy, or I'll blow your brains out! Lean forward slowly," he said, and Father Fogarty complied. With his support hand, Bradford used the snips to cut the zip ties restraining the priest's wrists. He put the snips away and picked up the doweling. "Put your arms up!" Bradford commanded. Fogarty raised his arms as ordered. The Satanic priest then placed the dowel behind the priest's shoulders and ordered him to grab onto each end. Again, the terrified priest did as he was told.

Bradford aimed the revolver at Father Fogarty's head and moved behind the chariot so the priest couldn't see him. He quietly tucked the gun into his waistband and then zip-tied the Father's wrists to each end of the dowel, creating a makeshift cross. Bradford returned to the front of the chariot to face the sexual predator, now holding a large, thick plastic zip-tie. "Stretch out your legs and cross your ankles," he commanded. Father Fogarty complied, and Bradford quickly secured his ankles and legs tightly with the zip-tie.

"What in God's name are you doing?!" exclaimed the frightened Catholic priest as lightning lit up the sky, thunder rolled, and the sharp horizontal rain soaked both men.

"You're the Catholic priest. Doesn't this position look familiar to you?" said Bradford with a maniacal laugh. "Now, don't move off that bench. I'll be watching, and if you move even an inch, I'll shoot you dead, right here!" Bradford threatened again, pointing the revolver in Fogarty's face. The Satanic priest then disappeared.

The convoy of SWAT teams, uniformed officers, and detectives pulled out of the Galveston PD parking lot, split up, and headed toward their assigned locations. Galveston Fire and EMS had been notified of the operation. They had pre-staged two blocks from both sites in case any officers or civilians were injured during the operation.

Team Alpha, led by Det. Bill Hurd, in his unmarked unit, took the lead. District Mary Patrol Supervisor Sgt. Sergio Diaz followed him. Sergio Diaz was with eight uniformed, heavily armed SWAT operators in marked units and an unmarked SWAT van. The group pulled up one block short of Natas' two-story apartment and waited until they knew the Bravo Team had arrived at the warehouse on Harborside Drive.

Galveston PD dispatch had already been notified of the special operation, and all units had switched to their Tactical Channel, with an experienced dispatch supervisor managing the radio traffic. SWAT Commander Jeff Sedwick was riding shotgun in the Bearcat armored vehicle, which was filled with operators behind Gates, Wade, and Dakota, with two Mary units behind them.

As the Bravo Team arrived at the warehouse, Commander Sedwick radioed only for emergency–restricted radio traffic. The dispatcher copied his transmission, and three loud beeps were heard over the Tactical Channel.

The SWAT Commander then radioed to all units, *"Execute, execute, execute!"* Simultaneously, all the officers bailed out of their vehicles in the pouring rain and cautiously approached the buildings in single-file line formations, with breachers leading each group.

Alpha Team ascended the steps to Natas' 17th Street apartment. Holding a battering ram, the lead breacher loudly knocked on the front door and announced, *"Galveston PD, we have a search warrant. Open the door!"* After waiting five seconds without a response, the breacher rammed the door, splintering it into pieces, then moved aside for the entry team to enter the dark apartment. *"Clear!... Clear!... Clear!... Clear!... Clear up!... Clear down!"* the entry officers shouted as they searched room by room, securing the apartment. No one was home. Sgt. Diaz radioed, "Code-4 at location one. No one here."

Moments later, the lead breacher for Bravo Team loudly knocked on the corrugated metal sliding doors of the Harborside Drive warehouse and announced their presence and intent, *"GPD! ... Search Warrant, open the door!"* When there was no response, the SWAT operator behind him removed the channel locks from the back of the lead operator's assault vest and quickly cut through the metal chain.

The officer slid open one of the doors and stepped aside as a four-person entry team stormed in, gun lights flashing and green LED laser designators sweeping the interior of the building. The two breachers immediately followed inside, along with Commander Sedwick. *"Clear!... Clear!... Clear!... Clear!"*

Sedwick yelled, "Now take your time, boys. Clear this entire building yard by yard." While the entry team systematically searched the warehouse's nooks and crannies, the breachers approached an older model dark van parked inside the building.

"Hey, doesn't this look like that van from the attack on that Jewish professor over at Texas A&M we had the BOL (Be On the Lookout) for?" one operator said to his partner as he approached the van and illuminated the cab with his tactical light.

"Yeah, older model dark-colored van," replied the partner, who started trying the driver's side door. "Locked," he said as he moved to the rear to try the rear doors. "Go try the other side," he suggested to his partner, who split off and went to the van's right side.

The partner tested the right front passenger door and found it to be locked as well. "Also locked," he said as he started to open the right-side sliding door to the van. "Hey, this one's unlocked......" The operator's sentence abruptly ended in a fiery explosion that threw him and his partner apart to opposite sides of the warehouse. The van was instantly engulfed in flames.

The warehouse visibly shuddered. The explosion totally surprised Wade, Dakota, and Sgt. Gates Sullivan.

The SWAT Commander immediately shouted to his operators, *"Extract Donnelly. I've got Marquis!"* as he grabbed the body drag strap at the top of the downed officer's assault vest and pulled him backwards out of the now engulfed warehouse.

"Jesus!" Gates exclaimed as she, Wade, and Dakota leapt out of the unmarked vehicle and sprinted toward the burning warehouse along with the uniformed officers at the perimeter. “We need fire and EMS here, now!” one of the officers shouted over the radio.

At that moment, CSI Supervisor Lenny Spazzito arrived in the Forensics van with his technicians. “My Lord in Heaven!” he exclaimed. His technicians exited the van and sprinted to the now fully engulfed building to support the blast-stunned officers staggering away from the warehouse.

Dakota ran to SWAT officer Donnelly, who was critically injured by the force of the blast, with every inch of his exposed body suffering third-degree burns. Dakota quickly checked his vitals as Galveston Fire and EMS arrived. She looked at Officer Marquis, whom Commander Sedwick had pulled to safety. The officer was unconscious but not burned. “I’m a doctor. Stabilize and transport these two immediately,” she ordered the paramedics.

Dakota approached each officer, supported by a colleague, and quickly checked them for concussion and burns. All were in shock and needed transport to the hospital, but fortunately, none were in serious condition.

The Station 5 Fire Captain arrived with his paramedic team. He had already activated a General Alarm for a two-station response. “This entire area is unstable and needs to be evacuated. Move across the street to that parking lot and establish a triage station,” he ordered. Of course, all this happened in high winds and driving rain.

Dakota approached the Fire Captain. “Captain, with all due respect, these men are in shock. These conditions could prove catastrophic for them. I suggest you put them all into that Bearcat and a patrol unit or two and get them to the hospital

ASAP." The captain looked around, assessing the officers' condition.

"You're right, doctor. That's a much better idea," he said, turning to Commander Sedwick.

"Evacuate your men, Commander. Fire will handle the scene. Leave a couple of uniforms for perimeter and scene security," he directed.

Commander Sedwick wasted no time. "Listen up, men. We are evacuating all wounded to the Bearcat and a couple of patrol units. Transport everyone to the hospital, stat!"

As the officers headed toward the Bearcat and patrol units, Detective Bill Hurd radioed to Gates. "Henry 10, this is Henry 20. Natas' apartment is clear. No sign of him, but we have strong evidence here, enough to establish PC to arrest him," the detective advised.

"What have you got, Bill?" Gates asked.

A roll of hemp rope, identical to the one used to hang Rev. Jefferson, an empty chloroform bottle, zip-ties, and a RAD eBike that exactly matches the one from the Whataburger CCTV footage of the Zen Center homicide. Here's a lead: we also have recent pay stubs from Gulf Entertainment – owners of the Pleasure Pier. Natas works there, but the pay stubs only specify the location," the detective replied.

"Jackpot! Nice going, Bill," replied Gates as CSI Lenny Spazzito approached her.

"Gates, Wade, I gotta speak to you right now. This can't wait. Come over to the van," exclaimed Lenny, excitedly as he started walking to the CSI van. Wade and Gates quickly followed behind the CSI Supervisor.

“Get inside,” said Lenny, opening the side sliding door. Once all three were inside, Lenny showed them his laptop, which displayed a map of the Midtown district.

I finally managed to get Natas's cell service provider and a signal from his phone. Look here, Natas! He’s at the Pleasure Pier right now!” he exclaimed.

“Are you sure?” Wade asked.

“As sure as it's raining outside. The pin popped up as soon as I got his signal. No doubt about it, he’s at the Pleasure Pier," replied Lenny.

“Thanks, Lenny. We gotta run. We’ll hook up later,” said Gates as she and Wade bailed out of the van. Gates ran to Commander Sedwick, and Wade headed to Dakota, supervising the loading of the shocky SWAT officers into the Bearcat.

“Natas is at the Pleasure Pier. We gotta go. He’s probably got the priest and is going to kill him for sure,” exclaimed Wade.

“Go, Wade. I’m going to the hospital with these officers. We’ll meet up later. Be careful, sweetheart.”

“Careful is my middle name. Love you, sweetie,” replied Wade, as he kissed Dakota and began to jog away.

“No, it’s not, Wade Justus. I know you. Be careful. That’s an order!” Dakota yelled back.

Gates met with Commander Sedwick and said, "Jeff, we've got Natas' cellphone signal. He's at the Pleasure Pier, no doubt with the priest, and he's gonna kill him for sure. We have no idea where he's specifically located. Mount up, everyone. Wade and I are heading out now," she said.

"Copy that," replied the SWAT Commander, immediately radioing all remaining units to converge on the Pleasure Pier, Code-3.

Given the inclement weather and flooded streets, the Pleasure Pier was at least a ten-minute drive from both search warrant locations. All units shut off their sirens several blocks from the entertainment pier for tactical reasons.

Bradford stepped out of a storage room at the carousel's center, dressed as Satan himself. His devil mask with horns covered his head and face, and his black priest's robe billowed like a sail in the gale-force winds behind him. In his right hand, the Satanic priest held a six-foot stainless steel staff, topped with a large pentagram bearing an engraved image of Lucifer. His left hand grasped a large three-gallon metal pail filled with gasoline for the carousel's generator. Tucked into his waistband was a bright yellow civilian version of a TASER electronic control device that fired two electrically charged darts. He would use the device to ignite the gasoline-soaked priest.

Bradford stood before the traumatized Father Fogarty, dressed in all his Satanic regalia, a terrifying sight to behold. It was to be a final, deadly confrontation between the terrified Catholic priest and the devil. The victim of years of child and teen sexual abuse, who, due to the priest's breach of a sacred trust, had turned to Satanism, had things to tell his former tormentor.

"In the name of God and all that is holy, please... I beg of you, Bradford... spare me. Allow me to atone for my sins... sins of the flesh. Please spare me, don't kill me, my son," the Father pleaded.

"The time for your verbal atonement has long since passed, you fuck! You destroyed my trust. You stole my innocence. You ruined my life! Now your atonement will come out of the fires of hell, where I will send you. You are going to burn for your sins against me and your God," Bradford yelled out over the sounds of the crashing thunder and the heavy rain colliding with the thin metal cover of the carousel.

The Satanic priest leaned his metal staff against the corner of the chariot and, with both hands, grabbed the pail, ready to thoroughly soak the priest with gasoline from head to toe. However, as Bradford tossed the pail forward, Father Fogarty kicked it with his zip-tied legs, causing the gas to soak them equally.

"Awe, my eyes...my eyes!" screamed Bradford in pain as some of the gas penetrated through the eye slits in his devil mask. The Satanic priest pulled away from the priest.

Gates and Wade arrived at the Pleasure Pier and saw a vehicle parked on the pedestrian walkway leading into the entertainment zone. Wade unholstered his 1911-A .45 caliber pistol in the car and press-checked it to ensure a round was chambered. He reholstered and checked his two extra magazines of .45 ammo. *Good to go!* he said to himself. Gates saw Wade checking his weapon and did the same.

As numerous police units converged at the base of the Pleasure Pier, Wade looked at his protégé and said, "Do you know your Bible? In Peter 5:8, he warned*, "Be alert, and of sober mind. Your enemy, the devil, prowls around like a roaring lion looking for someone to devour."*

Gates responded with an intense look, "No, but I got a passage for you. Mess with me, devil, and I'll kick your ass! Now let's get this murderous bastard."

The pair exited Gates' unmarked sedan with guns drawn and cautiously moved up the pedestrian walkway behind SWAT operators and uniformed officers. As they reached the vehicle parked under the entryway, they saw a figure dressed as Satan, holding a metal pole in one hand and the remote control to the carousel in the other, screaming. The helpless Father Fogarty was on the carousel, clearly restrained in the gilded chariot seat. The priest saw the approaching officers and yelled, "Help me, help me! He's going to kill me!"

Simultaneously, Wade, Gates, and the accompanying officers raised their weapons, aiming at the Satanic figure, illuminating him with their bright gun lights and painting him with green and red laser beams.

"Bradford Natas, Galveston PD, step away from the carousel and get on the ground, now!" Gates yelled over the roar of thunder as heavily armed officers surrounded the Satanic priest in a semi-circle.

"For the love of God, save me! He's poured gas all over me and is going to burn me to death*!"* pleaded the weakened Father Fogarty.

Natas yelled back at the officers, "You think I'm the devil? He's God's devil! This hypocrite ruined my life! He and Brother Chester raped me as a child and a teen. He stole my innocence; he took my life! Well, now it's his turn to atone for his sins – for the evil he has done to me and many other kids. This unholy priest is going to burn in the fires of hell!"

The ride slowly spun when Natas pressed the carousel's cable remote button. "God in heaven, save me. I repent for all my sins, Father in Heaven," the priest cried out.

"Stop the carousel, stop the ride now, Natas!" yelled Wade.

As the ride rotated, the four-foot razor-sharp horizontal blade in the spindle lowered closer and closer to the priest's head after each rotation. Wade spotted the device.

"He's got a blade that drops each time the carousel turns. It's going to decapitate the priest. We've got to stop that carousel from turning!" the former Texas Ranger yelled to the officers.

The storm was now directly overhead, at its highest crescendo, with the thunder crashing and lightning striking the tumultuous waters on either side of the Pleasure Pier.

"Natas, stop the ride now, or we'll shoot. I swear to God we will. Turn it off, now!" Gates ordered.

The demonic Satanic priest was unfazed, pulling the TASER out of his waistband with his right hand while holding the stainless steel staff with the pentagram high into the air. Natas stepped closer to the rotating carousel as the gilded chariot carrying Father Fogarty approached him.

Natas aimed the TASER directly at the priest and yelled, "Go to hell, you fuck. Burn forever in the underworld for your sins!"

Just as the Catholic priest and Natas were aligned, a massive bolt of white lightning shot downwards from the dark clouds and struck the Satanic priest's metal staff. Natas's gas-soaked black robe ignited while simultaneously electrocuting him. The vapors from Natas's and the priest's clothes caused Father Fogarty to ignite.

Both men screamed as they burned alive. Natas crumpled to his knees; the electrified metal staff fused to his hand, which he held high toward the sky. The Jesuit priest, fully engulfed in flames, twisted back and forth inside the chariot seat, restrained by the crossbar and zip-tied legs as if he were on a burning cross.

Wade rushed toward the cabled remote box to turn off the ride. However, when he reached the box, he saw it was fried from the lightning's massive electrical charge. Two uniformed officers hurried to the carousel and jumped on to break the horizontal blade and spindle, but they were on the opposite side of the device. As they feverishly worked to get to the blade, the carousel kept rotating, dropping the blade lower and closer to the burning and screaming priest's head.

The blade reached the flaming Father Fogarty before the officers, decapitating the child predator mid-scream. The priest's charred head was knocked backwards behind the chariot, bouncing off the ride and landing near the now incinerated kneeling body of the man who thought he was Lucifer incarnate. Both men had experienced the wrath of God.

Just as quickly as the thunder, lightning, hurricane-force wind, and torrential rains had arrived, the storm changed direction, moving back out to sea. One of the officers on the carousel found the storage room at the center of the ride, grabbed a fire extinguisher, and put out the fire that had consumed Father Fogarty. The driving rain had reduced the Satanic priest Bradford Natas to a smoldering heap of fused flesh, topped by a blackened metal staff with a pentagram. The month-long nightmare of the serial murders of respected clergy in Galveston was finally over.

Wade, Gates, and SWAT Commander Jeff Sedwick looked at the horrific carnage and then at the assembled officers. Brave men who often stare death in the face had been shaken; you could read it on their faces.

Wade, touched by the experience but still composed, made the sign of the cross and said, "In Revelation 12:9, it is written, *'The great dragon was hurled down – that ancient serpent called the devil, or Satan, who leads the whole world astray.'*"

"Gates, I don't know how you're going to write this one up, but in my opinion, what happened here tonight was nothing less than divine intervention," said Wade.

"Amen to that," replied Commander Sedwick.

"Well, that won't be in my report, but I certainly won't disagree with you, either," replied Gates.

"I'm just glad that Dakota wasn't here to witness this. If you can get a uniform to give me a ride to the hospital, I'd like to see her and bring her back to the RV. I think we've both had enough excitement for one night," said Wade.

"I'll do you one better. Pete, here is the OIC, and I think he can hold down the fort for an hour. I'll get Lenny and his CSI team over here for the crime scene. Then I'll personally drive you to the hospital, pick up your lady, get your dog, and drive you back to the Sandpiper," replied Gates.

"That's an offer I won't refuse," said Wade.

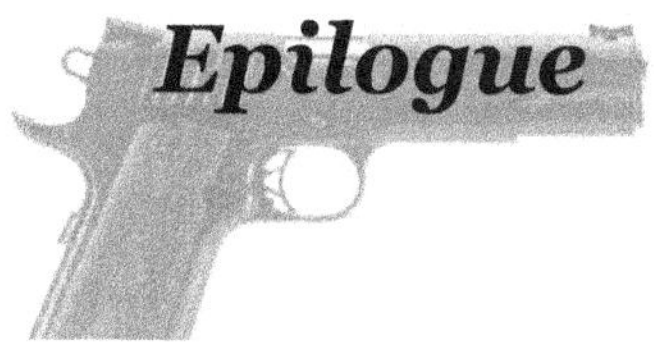

Epilogue

By the following morning, the storm had moved entirely out to sea and dissipated. The spring sun was back, and City of Galveston Public Works crews and citizens were busy cleaning up in the aftermath.

It had been a long night for Detective Sergeant Gates Sullivan and her partner, Detective Bill Hurd. In the middle of the night, Gates called the Chief of Police to inform him of the events from the previous evening. The Chief, in turn, scheduled a late morning press conference at the police department. Gates also called Wade and Dakota and invited them to attend.

"The Chief has asked that you, Dakota, and Professor Tzabar attend. I think you're going to like this. I'll be picking you up. I've also made reservations for several of us to have dinner at Gaido's Restaurant at 7:00 pm. It's on the Chief; his way of saying thanks for everything you all did to help us clear this case," explained Gates.

The press conference began promptly at 11:00 a.m. The department's PIO ensured that all the local press, including KWAV TV-4's obnoxious, self-serving reporter Johnny Costa, were in attendance. Gates, Bill Hurd, Lenny Spazzito with his CSI crew, SWAT Commander Jeff Sedwick, Wade, Dakota, and Professor Tzabar stood off to the side of the dais as the Chief took to the podium.

"Good morning, everyone. Glad to see that we've all survived the storm. I am pleased to report that the Clergy Killer serial murder case has been solved. Thanks to the efforts of our department's CID Homicide and CSI Units, along with special homicide consultants, retired Texas Ranger Wade Justus, Dr. Dakota Shannon, and Texas A&M Professor, Dr. Lyeb Tzabar, a suspect in the murders of our respected clergy was identified. I can also tell you that he is deceased and that no GPD personnel were involved in his sudden death.

"Last night, after several weeks of tireless investigation, our detectives were able to positively identify Bradford D'Ablo Natas, of Galveston, as the serial killer. Mr. Natas was a Satanic priest who led a small underground cult of local Satanists. Our investigation has been able to prove unequivocally that there was no racial motive for these killings. I'll repeat that, there was zero evidence of any racial or white supremacist motive by Mr. Natas to murder our clergy. Natas' singular motivation for his systematic, well-planned murders was his hatred for all religions and his own Satanic ideology.

"As I previously warned you, certain members of our local news media, for their own self-serving purposes, tried to promote the idea that these killings were the work of a racist, white supremacist. With the death of Mr. Natas and the evidence we recovered in two late-night search warrants yesterday, I can confidently say that the racism narrative was false.

"Unfortunately, I must inform you that before his own death, Mr. Natas was able to kidnap and murder a Catholic priest identified as Father Charles Fogarty of Our Lady of the Blessed Ascension Church in Midtown. GPD officers

valiantly attempted to save the priest. Still, they were unsuccessful. Also, during the execution of one of two search warrants, two GPD SWAT officers were critically injured by an explosive, incendiary device planted by Mr. Natas at a warehouse on Harborside Drive. We are praying for the complete recovery of these two brave officers. Our investigation is ongoing, and I will share more information in the coming week. Now I'll take questions," concluded the Chief.

Surprisingly, the usually aggressive reporter Johnny Costa was silent. During the Chief's briefing, he looked down at his cellphone, then tapped his cameraman, and the two of them slunk out of the room at the start of the Q&A session.

Police Information Officer Frank Fitzsimmons texted Gates while the group stood behind the podium, "Johnny Costa's just been fired by his network," accompanied by a smiley face. Gates bumped Wade and showed him her cellphone display. Wade smiled back.

That night at Gaito's Restaurant, Gates, Bill Hurd, Wade, Dakota, Lyeb Tzabar, Lenny Spazzito, and Pete Sedwick gathered for a seafood feast. It was not a celebration but a gesture of appreciation for everyone's hard work.

I made a few calls today to finalize everything. I've informed SFPD Captain Bob Mells and Father Michael about last night—Natas and Father Fogarty are both dead. I'm sure the San Francisco Archdiocese is glad the chapter on Fogarty is finally closed. That was a tough time for them," said Gates.

"Yeah, I noticed that the Chief was very concise about Fogarty's death, with no background or relationship between Natas and the priest mentioned," said Wade.

"What's done is done. Why create more mistrust? The Church already had enough problems to handle with Fogarty and Brother Chester. In the end, Natas did get his revenge, but like you told me last night, God had the final say on both of them," replied Gates.

"Amen to that," replied those seated at the table.

"Well, now you and Dakota can finally enjoy your vacation on the coast," remarked Bill Hurd. Wade and Dakota looked at each other and laughed.

"Don't anyone take this the wrong way, but Dakota and I have decided to head back to quiet Boerne in the morning. I don't think we'll see Galveston again for the foreseeable future. Dakota has her new job to prepare for, and I've got a ranch to run," said Wade.

The group shared their mutual thanks and appreciation for a job well done, enjoyed an excellent dinner, and appreciated the camaraderie of true professionals.

THE END

Trailer for Book 8 – Southern Justus

A criminal defense attorney and former police officer, representing a police officer in southern Georgia who faces political prosecution for homicide related to an officer-involved shooting, receives death threats. She seeks assistance from her former mentor, retired Texas Ranger Wade Justus, to serve as an expert witness in her case. Wade agrees to take the case and travels to the Deep South, where he quickly encounters a hostile, racially charged community. This community is driven by a revolutionary Black Power activist group committed to using lawfare to imprison the defendant officer for life.

As Wade investigates the circumstances of the shooting, he faces a biased investigation, deceit, missing evidence, reluctant witnesses, and threats to his own life.

The trial clock is ticking as Wade musters his own forensic team in a legal confrontation against unethical prosecutors to save the life of an innocent officer in a quest for Justice – *Southern Justus.*

About the Author

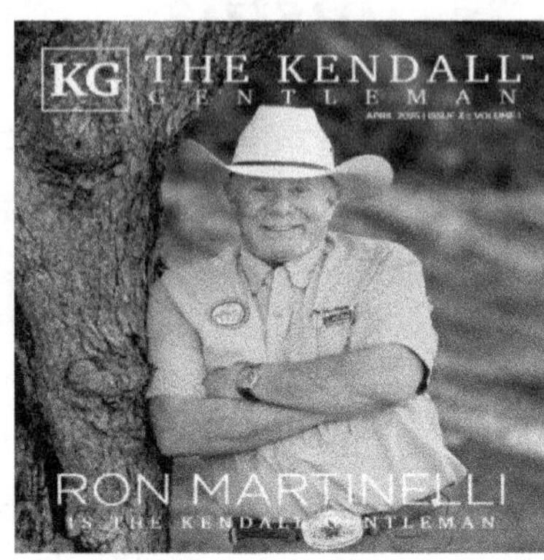

Dr. Ron Martinelli is a nationally recognized forensic criminologist, death investigator, and retired police detective. He is the Amazon bestselling author of the Wade Justus Texas Ranger mystery thriller and action-adventure series, praised for its realism and gripping storytelling. Recipient of the NY Four-Seasons Publisher's Award, his work is acclaimed for its accurate portrayal of law enforcement, forensic, and military detail. Ron and his wife Linda live on their ranch in the Texas Hill Country, where they raise PBR competition bucking bulls and draw inspiration from their travels worldwide.

www.ingramcontent.com/pod-product-compliance
Lightning Source LLC
LaVergne TN
LVHW010639110826
845149LV00014B/2893